YOUR
DEATH

BOOKS BY KIERNEY SCOTT

Forget Me Not
Cross Your Heart

CATCH YOUR DEATH

KIERNEY SCOTT

Bookouture

Published by Bookouture in 2019

An imprint of StoryFire Ltd.

Carmelite House
50 Victoria Embankment
London EC4Y 0DZ

www.bookouture.com

ISBN: 978-1-78681-541-5
eBook ISBN: 978-1-78681-540-8

For Alistair and G, my two favorite people in the world.

PROLOGUE

"Stop pushing!" a teacher with a clipboard shouted over the screech of metal grinding against metal as a train came into the station.

Not one of the students listened. They were too busy laughing and shrieking, enjoying the novelty and freedom of being out of the classroom and on the streets of DC. Such a great tradition, bringing classes across the country to see the capital; so much to learn.

He smiled, remembering his first trip here. He hadn't been much older, and he had immediately fallen in love with the history and architecture. He had known then this is where he wanted to spend his life.

"I said stop pushing!" the teacher screamed at two girls who thought it was a good idea to play tag at the edge of the platform.

She was right to yell. Someone was going to get hurt.

"You better listen to your teacher," he said to the schoolgirl next to him. "The city can be a dangerous place."

The girl's eyes widened, surprised that a stranger had spoken to her. Her face drained of color for a heartbeat and then went engine-red. She shrugged and turned away but not before rolling her eyes. She mumbled something under her breath that sounded suspiciously like "fuck off."

He sighed, more sad than annoyed. She was a perfect example of everything that was wrong with today's youth, petulant and ill-mannered.

Never mind, he had too much to do today to worry about a swearing adolescent.

He gazed over the sea of over-styled hair and pimpled faces.

He stood back as another train pulled into the station, watching, his gaze never faltering. He waited for the class to get on, because that was the polite thing to do. Not that he had much of a choice; they all pushed their way past him, even the teacher.

He patted his pocket before he reached his hand in, wrapping his fingers around the cool handle.

As the whistle sounded, he pulled it out, holding it by his side. He moved slowly through the carriage, brushing past people as he went.

"Excuse me," he apologized.

He gripped the handle harder. Light glistened off the metal blade as he brought it up.

Then he lunged forward, the blade cutting through muscle and sinew. The tender flesh offered no more resistance than a grisly cut of prime rib. Shame that everyone was wearing so many layers. He really would have liked to see all the blood.

Her eyes widened. Pain, or shock maybe. The girl should have heeded his warning: the city really was a dangerous place.

CHAPTER ONE

"Sorry, what did you say?" Special Agent Jess Bishop pulled up her pants and fastened the button. She stared down at the zip of her boot where snow had seeped in between the grooves of the metal teeth. A burning sensation throbbed in her toes from the biting cold as ice settled in the crevices. Only now did she notice she had been standing in snow for fifteen minutes. Funny the way sex could numb pain, emotional and physical. Nothing else worked.

Even her hand didn't hurt when she had sex. It was the only time the pain stopped. The mottled raised scars that crisscrossed her palm were a constant reminder of what had happened, of how she had fought back and escaped the clutches of a serial killer, and how the others hadn't. It was a map of her failure and frailties, and it wasn't going away anytime soon so neither was the anonymous sex.

She took out the bottle of ibuprofen and swallowed two to get ahead of the pain because the endorphins would soon wear off and the emotions would all come flooding back along with the guilt and shame and pain. She'd hoped it would last longer, but numbness was getting harder and harder to come by these days.

"I said that was fun. We should do it again sometime." He smiled. He had a nice smile, slightly crooked and not in the least bit threatening; that was why she had picked him. He looked nice, not that Jess trusted him. She trusted no one, which was why they'd had sex in an alley behind a bar rather than at her house or even in her car.

Jess buttoned the bottom toggles of her coat. She glanced down as he pulled the condom off and then looked past his bare thighs to the snow behind him. The streetlight cast a warm glow over the white mounds. In the daylight the snowdrifts were dirty, studded with gravel and the snapped twigs of branches, but at night they became pure again.

She didn't have a response so she remained quiet. She didn't know his name and she had not offered hers. He had served his purpose and given her a release and a few minutes of feeling numb. That was all she wanted but now came the awkward part where nice guys suddenly became worried about her feelings and pretended that they wanted to see her again. She could write a dissertation on the post-coital discourse of strangers. She certainly had a large enough sample to draw from.

"So, can I have your number?"

Jess sighed. She hoped for his sake the nice guy thing was just an act because she would feel like less of a shit for the next thing she was going to say: "No." She didn't follow up with an excuse because she thought women only looked weak by offering justifications and apologies, and she was many things but weak was not one of them.

His smile slipped, replaced by an open mouth.

She walked away, down the alley toward the Metro station. She glanced at her watch. If she hurried, she could catch the last train home. Her pocket vibrated when her phone rang. She snapped around to look at the man she had just been screwing against a wall; for a fraction of a second she thought it could be him on the other end of the line but he was still pulling up his jeans.

Her pulse spiked and then her heart squeezed to a painful stop when she saw the name of the person calling.

CHAPTER TWO

"Hello?" She didn't mean for it to sound like a question, but this was not a call she had been expecting. She had been on a forced sabbatical since the end of her last case, so a call from her boss at midnight on a Tuesday could only be described as unexpected. Officially she was on vacation because she had amassed too many days and the bureau insisted she take at least two weeks, but the truth was an FBI psychologist had ordered it.

She wasn't convinced by Dr. Cameron's logic. She very much doubted that she would be over the murder of her best friend after the requisite time out, or that she would have worked through the guilt of her own culpability in her death: the only reason Lindsay had become involved with the case in the first place was down to her. And she was certain that forcing her to take time off would not help her develop coping strategies that didn't involve screwing strangers.

"Jessica?" Jeanie Gilbert asked. Her boss's paper-thin voice was laced with concern.

She cleared her throat. "Yeah, it's me."

"Where are you? It sounds like you're outside."

Jess closed her eyes and sucked in a sharp breath. Jeanie could never know how she chose to deal with life. She wouldn't understand, and Jess admired her too much to deal with her judgment. "I was just stepping out for some air. My apartment is stuffy. Because I live on the top floor." She blurted out the meaningless bit of information at the end. If she were listening to this conversation, she would pounce on the unnecessary details, a telltale sign of lying, but Jeanie didn't seem to notice.

"Okay, that's nice. Do you have a minute? I realize this is an imposition but if I could ask you a favor—"

"Of course. Anything." Jess didn't hesitate. She had worked under Jeanie for over a decade, and there was no one she respected more. In most ways Jeanie was unassuming, easily overlooked, and underrated, but she was the most capable woman Jess had ever met. So much of her career was modeled after Jeanie's, watching how she commanded respect through competence rather than force. She was the embodiment of bridled strength. Even after ten years, Jess had never heard her swear and she could count on one hand the times she had raised her voice.

"It's my nephew, Levi. He is my sister Shona's youngest son. He's a senior at Gracemount Academy."

Jess nodded as she listened, wondering what this had to do with her. Was he in trouble? Did he need some sort of scared-straight intervention? She wasn't sure she would have picked herself to lead an impressionable youth back to the fold, but if Jeanie wanted her to, she would give it her best try. "Okay, what would you like me to do?"

"He's a really good boy. I know all aunts must say that, but he really is. He's an Eagle Scout. He is not the kind of boy that gets into trouble."

If he was a senior in high school, he must be near enough eighteen. That would make him a man so no number of scout badges was going to mitigate the situation if he had committed a crime. If it had been anyone else, Jess would have asked straight out what he had been charged with, but Jess respected Jeanie too much to be that brutal in her honesty. "What happened?" she asked instead. She bit into the sliver of nail left on her index finger as she braced herself for the response.

"There is something wrong. I can feel it. He's in trouble." Urgency clipped her words.

"What is it?" Jess pressed. Normally she wouldn't put credence into a feeling, but in all the years she'd known Jeanie, she'd never known her to overreact about anything, ever. If Jeanie thought there was a problem, then there was a damn good reason why.

"As you may know, I'm in Utah now visiting my family. Levi called me earlier tonight, but I didn't get it because I was getting my mom settled into her rest home. As soon as I heard his voicemail, I knew something was wrong."

"What did he say?"

"We're very close, especially since Shona died, and I could just tell. It's not what he said as much as what he didn't say. It was his voice. He was scared. I would go and check on him myself but the next flight out of Salt Lake isn't until tomorrow. I think there's something wrong. I'd really feel better if I could speak to him tonight."

This was the first time Jeanie had ever spoken about her family. She was intensely private and the separation between her personal and work life was complete. Jess had no idea she had family in Utah or a nephew and a deceased sister. Jess only knew she was married because she had met Jeanie's husband Paul at a Christmas party. Everything else she knew about her, she had pieced together through the years. "Have you tried calling him back?" she asked the obvious.

"Several times. No answer. I've texted and called him, but nothing, and I've called the school but it keeps going to voicemail. That's not like him either. He is so responsible."

"Do you want me to go check on him?" Jess glanced at her watch again. He was probably asleep but Jess would go wake him up and make him call Jeanie if that would make her feel better. There wasn't a lot she wouldn't do for her.

"Would you mind? I know this is terribly unprofessional of me to ask—"

"Of course, I'll go check on him. I don't mind at all. I'll text you as soon as I've spoken to him."

"Thank you, Jessica. I really appreciate it. I knew I could count on you. You were the only person I thought to call."

Heat spread over her skin at the small praise. Jeanie was never effusive. Compliments from her were few and far between. Her expectation was that everyone would work to a high standard so they did not need to be told when they were doing something well.

Jess said goodbye and then cut the call before she called a taxi. It was too late for the Metro now, and there was no stop at Gracemount Academy anyway.

Jess pulled up her hood and shoved her hands into her pockets to keep them warm as she waited for the driver to arrive.

Jess opened the door and slid into the backseat. According to the license stuck to the divider, his name was Tariq. "Can you please take me to Gracemount Academy?"

His dark eyes glanced back at her in the rearview mirror. "That's a fancy school. It is like fifty thousand dollars a year. It's the most expensive school in America."

Jess nodded as she buckled her seatbelt. "Is it?" She had seen the all-boys prep school advertised on the side of DC buses, but she had never looked into it further. Why would she? She didn't have kids and never planned to. The only reason the ad stuck in her mind was because the poster had five students gathered around a single Bunsen burner doing a chemistry experiment. There was one black student, one East Asian, one wearing a yarmulke, one Hispanic, and for good measure a white kid with bright-red hair. It felt like they were trying to make a point: look at us, we're inclusive. Every time she saw it she wondered if they had gathered up the only minorities in the entire school for a photo op.

"I think it is the oldest boarding school in America too. It was founded before the Revolutionary War. They have sent more kids to Ivy League colleges than any other school in America. And they have produced more CEOs of Fortune 500 companies than anyone else."

Jess met his gaze again in the mirror. "How do you know all this? Did you go to school there?"

"Ha! That would be a no. My parents didn't even make fifty thousand a year between them. And even if they did, they would not be throwing it away on something the government should be paying for anyway."

"So how do you know so much about it?"

He turned his blinker on before he merged into the next lane. "I drove one of the board of governors once. He bragged the whole time like everything that ever happened at the school was his own accomplishment. I mean, he was old but I doubt he was around back in 1744 so he can calm down about what visionaries the founders were."

She didn't have anything to add to the conversation but she wanted to acknowledge what he had said so she replied with, "Hmm."

"He was like one of those football fanatics that think they have bragging rights because they support the winning team."

Jess sat back and listened to Tariq talk, paraphrasing everything he had heard about the school. Jess was far from social so she normally preferred to drive in silence, but this saved her from looking up the school herself on her phone. It was like having her own private tour guide. By the time they reached the massive wrought-iron gates that marked the entrance to the school, she knew everything she could possibly want to know about Gracemount Academy.

"Should I drop you off here?"

Jess glanced out the window. The school was set back a good quarter mile from the gate and the snow had started again. Just looking at the flurries made her toes ache with frostbite. "Can you buzz in please? I'd rather not walk."

He turned around to face her. "Do you have a kid here?"

"No."

"If you don't have a kid here or work here, they're not going to let you drive in."

"Why don't you push the buzzer and let me worry about that."

Tariq shrugged and made an expression that said he thought she was wasting time, but he rolled down his window. He had to knock freshly fallen snow off the panel to reach the buzzer.

"*Alere flammam veritatis*," a woman's voice answered after five rings.

Jess silently translated the Latin motto: *Let the flame of truth shine.*

Jess leaned forward so the intercom would pick up her voice. "Good evening. I'm Special Agent Jessica Bishop. I'm here to speak with Levi Smith." If having an FBI agent turn up at his dorm to tell him to stop being an ass and making his aunt worry wasn't enough to make this kid toe the line, she wasn't sure what would be.

Tariq snapped his head back to face her. His eyes were wide. "FBI? You kept that one quiet. If I would've known, I would have had lots of questions. You could have starred in tomorrow's anecdotes. Now I'm just going to have to guess why you're here. I'll make something good up for my next customer."

For the first time in longer than she could remember, she smiled. "I'm fairly certain anything you come up with will be more exciting than the real reason I'm here anyway."

Jess paid him and shut the door. She looked up at the imposing red-brick building. Six Doric columns lined the front of the darkened structure. The only light came from the streetlamps, which cast an ethereal glow over the campus. It was picturesque, and quaint like a Thomas Kinkade painting.

She pulled out her badge. Before she had time to ring the doorbell, the lights turned on and a middle-aged woman came to the door. Her faded brown hair was cut into a sharp bob just below her pearl-studded ears. A navy-blue cardigan, buttoned halfway, showed the matching sweater below. Her eyes narrowed as she studied Jess and a spark of recognition flashed across her face.

Jess sucked in a sharp breath of air. Her trachea tightened in a painful spasm like someone had wrapped their hands around her neck and squeezed. *Shit, don't let her recognize me.* She couldn't deal with that tonight. Not here, not now. Usually when she was scared that someone had recognized her, she would call her best friend Lindsay to give her some perspective, but Lindsay was dead.

For a long moment they stood in silence while the woman scrutinized her. Jess squeezed her hands into tight fists at her side but she didn't flinch or turn away to hide her face. If the woman recognized her, Jess would deal with it. She had had a lifetime to prepare for moments like these but it never got easier. And it never would. She would never feel comfortable with people knowing who she was, or more to the point, who her father was.

Eventually Jess cleared her throat to indicate to the woman that if she wanted to say something, she needed to do it now because Jess wasn't prepared to leave that dagger hanging above her.

"I'm sorry. You just look familiar, but I can't seem to place you. Have we met before?"

Jess shook her head. "No, ma'am, we've never met. I just have one of those faces." Jess held up her badge for inspection. "Like I said before, I'm Special Agent Bishop."

"Sorry. Where are my manners? I'm Yvonne Crawford, the house mother for Levi Smith's dorm. I understand you would like to speak to him. May I ask what this is in connection to?"

Without fail, whenever Jess mentioned she was from the FBI, people asked questions. Normally she didn't respond, but in this instance, she didn't want to cause any alarm. "I'm a friend of Levi's aunt. I'm here on her behalf, strictly in that capacity."

Yvonne nodded. "He will be asleep now. We have a strict lights-out policy at ten. We don't even allow reading after lights out. And definitely no electronics. Can this not wait until tomorrow morning?"

"Unfortunately not." The request to return at a more sociable hour was perfectly reasonable, but Jess suspected Jeanie would not be able to relax until she had texted her to let her know everything was okay.

"All right, then. I will show you where his room is. He shares with another boy so if you could try not to disrupt him, that would be greatly appreciated."

"Of course." Jess followed Yvonne when she turned and walked down the hall to a wide stone staircase. Ornate scrolls were carved into the thick balustrade as well as the school motto Yvonne had used as a greeting. The treads of the stone stairs dipped from years of use. The entire building felt like it belonged in a period movie.

Yvonne led her down a darkened hall to a door at the very end. "This is Levi's room."

"Thanks." Jess knocked on the door. When there was no answer she opened the door. She was greeted by the sound of soft snoring. He and his roommate were obviously asleep but Jess needed to be able to say she had seen the whites of his eyes to confirm to Jeanie he was all right. She patted on the wall until she located the light switch.

She glanced from the boy sleeping open-mouthed to the empty, made bed on the other side of the room. "Is that Levi?" Jess asked, pointing to the drooling boy.

"No, that is his roommate, Tom." Yvonne's eyes widened at the sight of the empty bed.

"Where else would Levi be?"

Yvonne shook her head. "Nowhere. They aren't allowed out of their rooms until breakfast at seven."

It sounded more like a prison than a school. "What if they need to use the bathroom?"

"Every room now has an en-suite. It was part of the refurbishments done in the nineties." She pointed to the open door.

Just to be sure Levi wasn't merely taking a piss, she turned on the lights in the bathroom and had a look for herself. The toilet lid was up and it needed to be flushed but there was no sign of him. "There is no shower in here. Where are those?"

"On the ground floor. But they're not allowed to use them after nine."

"They're also not allowed out of their rooms. And we see how well that one is working out."

The tight slash of Yvonne's mouth turned down into a frown. Her expression told her that when they found Levi he was going to be in some serious trouble. God only knew what that meant in a place like this: demerit points, suspension, cold gruel for dinner? And then he would have to deal with the wrath of Jeanie on top of that. She hadn't even met the kid yet but she sincerely hoped whatever he had been doing was worth it because there was going to be some serious hell to pay.

Jess glanced at his roommate, still snoring away, completely oblivious. She turned off the lights and shut the door behind them. "Let's check the showers. If he's not there, where else could he be?" Her suspicions were that he was just trying to get some private time. He was a teenage boy after all, living in a very confined space. The poor kid probably just wanted to masturbate in peace.

"I suppose he could be in the library."

Because a midnight study session was much more likely than a seventeen-year-old boy needing alone time in the shower. Jess did her best not to roll her eyes. "Where's that?"

"It's on the other side of campus."

"Okay. We'll check there if he's not in the showers." She really hoped Levi was downstairs because she did not want to trek across the snow tonight. Her feet were still frozen and she really just wanted to get to sleep before she needed another dose of painkillers.

Jess followed Yvonne across the darkened hall and back down the stairs. She shivered when a draft of cold air hit her. "Did they not think of putting in central heating when they did the refurbishment? Or maybe upgrading the insulation? It's freezing in here."

"We have central heating. Children sleep better in cool environments."

Jess pushed her hands deeper into her pockets and hugged her arms closer to her body to conserve heat.

Yvonne stopped at the end of the hall. "Lavatory" was written above the door on a cracked sign with embossed black lettering. "These are the showers."

Jess gave a cursory knock to let anyone on the other side of the door know she was coming in before she opened it. The lights were off. The entire room was ensconced in complete darkness. "Hello?" She ran her hand along the wall until she found the switch. The lights flickered on and off a few times before finally committing to illuminate the room. Tiny black and white hexagons of tile fit together on the floor to create a weathered mosaic pattern. Partitions blocked off the row of shower heads to create individual stalls. The smell of fresh bleach burned her sinuses. "Hello," she said again, this time louder. "Levi, are you in here?"

A slow cadence of a drip tapped against the tiles, like the steady beat of a drum. Jess followed the sound around the corner. "Hello?" With each step, the tap of water bouncing off the hard floor grew louder until she reached the final stall.

And then she saw him.

CHAPTER THREE

Oh, shit. Jess's heart stopped mid-beat, squeezing the blood in her veins with a punishing force. Her mouth dropped open. She tried to speak but no air made it past the tightness in her throat. She felt like she was being strangled from the inside.

The lifeless body of a teenage boy hung from an overhead pipe. The metal cylinder strained under the weight, releasing a stream of water that ran down his bare chest and legs, soaking his black socks before engorged drops splatted against the drain. Bright-blue eyes gazed straight ahead, fixed in a permanent stare. The whites of his eyes were a mottled sea of red pinpricks from petechial hemorrhages. His mouth was slightly agape, his full lips brushed with purple edges.

She tried to suck in a breath, but nothing happened. She couldn't breathe or speak or even blink; all she could do was stare in horror. He was just a child. So young. *Not again.* Her mind flashed back to the first dead body she'd ever seen. He had been naked too. *No.* Her mind screamed at her. She couldn't let her mind be dragged back there but it was too late.

Her legs buckled under her as her vision went dark.

"Oh my God!" A scream tore through the room.

The echo bounced off the tiles, multiplying the intensity, breaking the macabre spell, bringing her back to the present. Jess's head shot up, suddenly remembering where she was.

"No!" Yvonne screeched again. She tried to push past Jess as she ran forward.

Jess turned to hold her back. She strained as she pushed against Yvonne to keep her in place. "You can't touch him." Despite the horror of the situation, the agent in her took hold and pushed out the gruesome reality of what they were seeing. "This is a crime scene." Though it was obviously a suicide, Jess didn't have the jurisdiction or power to make a definitive ruling. A coroner needed to examine his body and make that call.

"No," Yvonne whimpered. She shook as her body was racked with sobs.

"Is this Levi Smith?" Jess held her breath, praying to a god she didn't believe in that the answer would be no. *Please, for Jeanie, say no.*

Yvonne nodded. The small movement was like a stab to her heart, destroying any hope.

"I can't believe this happened to him too." She sobbed against Jess's shoulder.

"Too?" Jess's eyes narrowed. She pulled back to look at her. "What do you mean 'too'?"

"Not again." She sobbed.

"What do you mean 'too'?" Jess demanded. "Has this happened before? Has someone else committed suicide?"

Yvonne's eyes widened as her gaze darted around the room, not knowing where to settle. "I-uh-no," she stammered between frantic gulps.

The hairs on Jess's arms stood taut. Yvonne was lying, she could feel it in her gut. "This isn't the first suicide you've had at this school, is it?"

Yvonne didn't say anything, she just continued to sob, her face burning scarlet from the stream of hot tears.

"Tell me. Did someone else commit suicide here?"

"I knew we should've done more to stop it." She shook her head.

"Stop what?" Jess pressed. "What should you have stopped?"

"I-I don't know." She said something else, but it came out in an incomprehensible, garbled wail. She leaned heavy against Jess, no longer able to keep herself upright.

Jess turned her around, so she could look her directly in the eye. "Yvonne, I need you to tell me the truth. Was there another suicide at this school?"

"They were so young," she whimpered.

"They? So this isn't the first suicide? Who else? Who was the other boy? I need you to focus, Yvonne."

"Okay." Black trails of mascara ran down her face.

"Who was the other boy?"

"Ryan was the first."

A bolt of terror ran up Jess's spine. *First.* She pounced on the small utterance. The word implied that there were more than two. She would have said "other" if there had only been two. "There are more, aren't there? Not just Ryan and Levi," she asked, hoping for once that she was wrong.

"Yes," she sobbed. "After Ryan it was Eric, and then Sam, and Jason, and now Levi."

Jess sucked in a sharp breath as she silently tallied the numbers. *Five.* She squeezed the older woman's arms as she gave her a shake to focus her. "Five boys have committed suicide? At this school?"

Yvonne's mouth crumpled in on itself as she nodded.

"Five boys?" Jess asked again for clarification because she was unable to comprehend her words. "Since when? Since the school opened?"

Yvonne sniffed. "No, Ryan killed himself in August at the beginning of the school year."

Jess quickly did the math. "Five students have committed suicide at this school in the last five months?"

Yvonne's only answer was a pained cry.

"Yvonne." Jess held Yvonne's face between her hands to make sure she was listening. "Yvonne," Jess repeated and waited for her glassy eyes to focus on her before she continued. "You said you should have done more. What did you mean? What could the school have done to stop it?"

"They had a pact or something. We should have…" Her lip trembled as her words trailed off. "I don't know…" Her body vibrated as another sob tore through her.

Jess knew she wasn't going to get any coherent answers from her right now. "Is this the only entrance to the shower?"

Yvonne nodded.

"Good. Okay, I'm going to tell you what we're going to do. We are going to go back to the hall and we are going to call the police. We are going to make sure nobody goes in the bathroom because the coroner needs to come and take Levi away. Okay?" Jess spoke quietly so Yvonne would have to concentrate to listen. She made sure her voice sounded as calm and placid as she could because Yvonne would feed off any stress she exhibited. Jess physically turned Yvonne away, pulling her toward the door one step at a time.

Jess looked around the darkened hall. She turned on the flashlight feature on her phone, looking for a place for Yvonne to sit, but there were no seats, just the cold tiled floor. Jess kept one arm around her while she hit the first number on her speed dial.

After three rings a deep voice sounded on the other end of the line. "Jessie?" Agent Jamison Briggs answered. Sleep took his normal baritone to a raspy bass. It was obvious he had been asleep when she called. "You okay? What's going on?"

Jess squeezed the phone until her hand ached. "Jamison, I need your help." She wasn't even sure why she had called him. It was more muscle memory than choice. For over a decade, he had been the one she turned to. He had been her partner and her friend. But she no longer had any right to ask him for anything. Given their history, he was more than entitled to tell her to go to hell. She could have called Alex Chan; he was her partner now.

"What do you need?" he asked without missing a beat.

Her heart squeezed painfully at the response. He had always been there for her, no questions asked, and she had repaid his loyalty with suspicion and a point-blank range shot to his chest. "I'm at Gracemount Academy. There's been a suicide. I'm about to call the Metropolitan Police but I need you to come down here and help me secure the scene."

"What? Um…what are you doing at an all-boys boarding school? Were you… um shit, Jessie, I don't even know how to say this. Were you seeing one of the teachers… or students there? What am I walking into here?"

Her skin burned hot with mortification. The question slashed her to the core. Jamison was the only person other than her therapist that knew she used sex to deal with the realities of her life and numb the pain. Yes, she had sex with strangers, lots of them, but never with anyone not old enough to consent. Jamison should know her better than that. But then again, she should have known he wasn't a serial killer.

She bit her lip until she tasted the metallic zing of blood, hoping the pain would counteract the shame of the question. At first all she could do was shake her head but then she realized he couldn't see her. "No."

There was a loud exhale on the other end of the line. *Relief.* He honestly thought it was a possibility she'd have sex with a high-school student.

"This is the fifth suicide in less than six months. Apparently, there is some sort of suicide pact going on here. I want to get to the bottom of it and shut this down hard."

"Shit. Okay, give me a second to get dressed. I'll be right down."

Jess hung up and then called the police. The entire time she spoke to dispatch, she did not let go of Yvonne, who trembled against her. She held her awkwardly, allowing the woman to wipe her tears and snot on her jacket. Jess never hugged anyone. She hated physical contact other than for sex, but Yvonne needed someone to lean on and Jess was her only option, so she wasn't about to leave her to cry on her own. The poor woman was going to need a stiff drink after tonight.

Sometimes Jess forgot how distressing it was for people to see a dead body. Fortunately, or unfortunately, her father's crimes had hardened her. Few things shocked her since she had discovered the body of one his victims, naked and bloodied on their basement floor.

Nothing could ever hurt like that.

Jess gave Yvonne a soft squeeze. Her tears had slowed down and she hadn't made a whimpering sound in over a minute. Jess needed to interview her and now was as good a time as any, while everything was fresh in her mind. "When was the last time you saw Levi?"

"Tonight at dinner. We had chicken casserole. That's his favorite. He had seconds and he said how nice it was. He always compliments the kitchen staff no matter how bad the food is because he has such good manners. He is such a sweet boy."

Jess gave her a soft smile. Yvonne was still talking about Levi in the present tense. Lindsay had been dead over a month and Jess still caught herself talking about her in the present tense. Every time she picked up her phone she had the urge to call her. Sometimes she would bring up her number and pretend Lindsay was going to answer. She would imagine talking, and laughing, unloading her problems with the safest person she had ever known. Trust didn't come easily to Jess, but she had trusted Lindsay completely. She had never imagined a world without her but shit happens. Jess blinked to focus her thoughts. "Did Levi seem depressed or agitated? Anything out of the ordinary?"

"No." She wiped her eye with the back of her hand. "I mean, he was stressed but that is only because he was so conscientious.

He put a lot of pressure on himself to do his best. Is that why this happened? Was it the pressure?"

Jess didn't say anything because she didn't have an answer. Suicide was complicated. There was rarely one cause. Sometimes it was an impulsive act, spurred on by a single event, but more often than not it was brought on by a lingering insidious depression where the magnitude of the despair was so great that death offered the only hope for escape. "Did you notice a change in his behavior recently?"

"He's been agitated. Worried. I should have asked more questions." She gulped.

"It's okay. What was he agitated about?"

"I don't know." She shook her head.

"Was it his grades? How was he doing in school?"

"He has straight As. He has unconditional admission to Harvard, Yale, and MIT."

Jess looked up when she saw the pulsating light of a police car. The flashing lights weren't necessary but at least they hadn't turned on the sirens. The last thing they needed was to wake up every student on campus. That would be mayhem.

Jess and Yvonne walked to the entrance of the building, Yvonne still pressed to her side.

Five patrol cars and an ambulance had responded to the call. Admittedly Jess had never worked a suicide, but this was clearly overkill. They only really needed to send the one police officer to accompany the coroner.

"Hi, I'm Special Agent Bishop. This is the house mother, Yvonne Crawford. We found the body of the deceased, Levi Smith. He's in the shower area. We need to get that cordoned off before any of the other students wake up." Jess spoke to who she assumed was the most senior officer. He was wearing plain clothes so was most likely a detective. His silver hair was combed back, slick to his head, the severe ridges of gelled hair leaving grooves of exposed scalp.

"I'm Captain O'Rourke. Chief Hagan called me and asked me to come on down. These are my officers. They will handle it from here. Thank you for your help."

Jess's eyes widened. The chief of the Washington DC police department had sent someone to personally respond to a suicide?

Captain O'Rourke must have seen the surprise on her face because he added, "Hagan went to school here. So when he heard there had been an incident here, he called me and asked me to check it out. Again, thank you for your help."

Jess forced herself to smile. Thanking her was the polite way to say she was no longer welcome at the scene and they would not be requesting her help with any resulting investigation. "You're welcome. Neither of us have touched the body but you'll find my prints on the walls and light switch." Jess spotted Jamison walking up the snow-covered path. She held up her hand to him in a stagnant wave.

"Hey," he said when he reached the threshold. Jamison towered over everyone. At six foot four and two hundred and thirty pounds, he had the ability to make everyone feel small. His size was intimidating but not half as much as his sheer presence. Everything about Jamison demanded respect. He didn't even have to raise his voice to make grown men cower.

"Hey," Jess said. "This is my partner, Special Agent Briggs." He hadn't been her partner for a while but it was easier to introduce him like that than get started on their complicated history. "Yvonne, if it's okay with you, I'm going to leave you for a second with Agent Briggs. I think I dropped my wallet upstairs. I need to grab that and then we'll be on our way." She turned to address Captain O'Rourke again. "Before we go, I'll give you my direct line so you can call me with any follow-up questions."

Before he could respond, Jess was already making her way to the stairs. She stuck her hand in her pocket and absently stroked her wallet. She hadn't dropped it. That was an excuse to search Levi's room for a suicide note. Captain O'Rourke had shown his hand by telling her that the police chief was a Gracemount alumnus. O'Rourke was here for clean-up. This was all about disaster recovery. The school didn't want it to get out there had been another suicide here. Reputation was everything in these places.

Jess took the stairs two at a time. When she got to Levi's room, she glanced behind her to make sure no one was watching before she opened the door. She didn't bother knocking because she could hear Levi's roommate snoring. Jess turned on the flashlight on her phone. She was confident the roommate would sleep through the apocalypse, but just in case she didn't turn on the lights because she didn't need a witness to what she was about to do.

Jess did a cursory inspection of the room. Everything on Levi's side of the room was neat and orderly. His maroon blazer hung over the back of the chair. Under the school insignia were several badges: a winged foot that represented he was on the track team, a lacrosse stick that said captain, a treble clef, presumably because he was in a band. Another pin said honor society, another had weighted scales. If she remembered correctly, that represented the debate team. The final pin was a chalice with the Eye of Providence etched above lips with a finger pressed against them. Below were two arching wings that looked like they were cradling the goblet. Jess narrowed her eyes as she studied the pin. She had no idea what club it represented but it looked Masonic. She couldn't remember seeing anything like it when she was in high school, though to be fair she didn't remember most of high school. Her dad was arrested when she was eight and most of her childhood from that point on was a blur, punctuated by lengthy interviews with psychologists and law enforcement as they studied her to see how she was coping, and hoping to get some insight into her father's crimes through her. But Jess never told them anything of value. In the beginning, she was protecting her dad, but then she was protecting herself because no one could ever know that she had discovered her dad's macabre secret years before the FBI had, and that she had said nothing.

She scanned the small area, searching for anything that looked like a note or a journal. She picked up each of the binders she found and thumbed through them, studying each for anything that looked out of place before she sat her phone down on the desk that separated the two twin beds, but all she found were fastidious notes written in a small, neat script. The dark pencil strokes told her he pressed down forcefully as he wrote. There were comments in the margins from his teachers, all positive. So far, he looked conscientious, not suicidal.

She pulled the mattress away from the box springs. The faint light reflected off a laptop, which was wedged between the headboard and the wooden slats. Jess let the weight of the mattress rest on her back so she could use both hands to pull it out. But it was stuck. She tugged again, this time putting her foot on the bed for leverage. The sharp trill of metal scraping against metal sliced the silence of the room. When she pulled the laptop free, a fresh gouge marked the front. Jess reached in to find what the computer had been stuck under. She lifted a thick, leather-bound book and examined the tarnished metal clasp that the computer had caught on. Her heart picked up speed when she realized it could be a journal but her excitement was soon dashed when she saw the small typeset of scriptures. She thumbed through the pages. At the top were neon Post-it notes with comments related to the text. Levi had been hiding a bible under his bed. Jess shook her head. With most boys she would expect porn or stolen exams, not highlighted passages from Isaiah.

She unzipped her coat enough to hide the computer against her chest. If the chief of police had personally sent officers to respond, they were here to clean up and circle the wagons. They were here to cover this up. Five suicides in less than a year had the potential to destroy a school. She needed to find out exactly what had happened here that led to five boys taking their own lives.

Jess zipped up her coat and then put the bible back on the bed. She hesitated for a few seconds before she picked it up again and placed it under her coat with the laptop. The bible would probably be locked up in evidence if she left it, and the family might want it. If they did, they deserved to have it. Jess wasn't a believer but she respected other people's right to do whatever it took to get them through the day. She would make sure his family got it.

"Jeanie," Jess whispered into the silence. She shuddered as a chill ran the length of her spine. Jeanie was his family. She was who Jess would be giving Levi's bible to. Icy tendrils wound their way over her body. This wasn't a routine investigation, this was Jeanie's family. The realization hit her like a lead ball bearing fired directly at her chest, robbing her of breath. She had known all night this investigation was different, personal, but she had compartmentalized by letting herself observe and process at a cognitive level without letting the reality penetrate any deeper.

She closed her eyes for a second to give herself the distance she needed as the enormity of the situation hit her. All victims had families that loved and mourned them but Jess intentionally kept an emotional distance from victims' families because the pain was too much for her. But there was no getting away from it here. "Oh shit."

CHAPTER FOUR

Jess kept one hand pressed against her chest to keep the bible and laptop in place, and the other she wrapped around the banister as she ran down the stairs. She found Jamison and Yvonne at the entrance of the school. Yvonne was smiling and nodding. Her eyes were still red from crying but the color had returned to her cheeks. Jamison's hands reached wide as he told a story. He had managed to make Yvonne stop crying and smile, to temporarily forget herself. Jess was right to have called him. He could handle any person, any situation. Whatever life threw at him, whoever he came across, he adapted, taking everything in his stride. That was Jamison's gift.

His other gift was his ability to scare the living shit out of every person he met with a single glance. People feared and respected him in equal measure. There was a duality in him: terrifying and calming.

"We need to go," Jess said before she had reached them. Jess would have liked to stay to make sure Yvonne was okay but she had just interfered with an active investigation by stealing a deceased boy's laptop. It was not in her best interest to stay here and wait for the police to discover it was missing.

Jamison turned to look at her, his dark eyes narrowed in question, but then he clocked how she was awkwardly holding her arms against her chest and he nodded without commentary. Jamison was the best partner Jess had ever had. They just got each other. And she had ruined it all by believing a serial killer over him. Their relationship would never recover from that because neither of them could ever forget the betrayal, but Jamison was professional enough to pretend that everything was okay. He was the one person better than her at compartmentalizing. "Okay. I'll walk you back to your car. Where are you parked?"

Jess kept walking until they were past the line of police cars. The snow crunched underfoot. It was hard now, packed down and frozen like sheets of ice. "Can you take me home please?" She didn't have the right to ask him for anything, but here he was standing in the snow in the middle of the night.

"Where's your car?"

Jess looked down at the white ground and then past him to the school. She wasn't ashamed of how she coped and she would never apologize for it. "I got a taxi. I was out when I got the call."

The muscles along Jamison's jaw tightened under his dark skin but he didn't say anything; he just kept walking. They both knew what she meant when she said she was out. He knew the darkness that lived inside her and how she chose to quiet it. Once upon a time Jamison had been the one she trusted with all her secrets. Their past was long and complicated. They had gone from partners to friends to lovers and now here they were. There was not a word for the emotional stalemate they were locked in.

Jess had to increase her pace to keep up with Jamison. "Are you going to ask me why I called you?"

He didn't turn to look at her. "I don't think I want to know."

His words cut her. He still thought she was at the school to have sex. Bile rose in the back of her throat. "I came here tonight for Jeanie. She asked me to check on her nephew, Levi. When I got here, I found him dead. He's the kid who committed suicide."

Jamison's pace slowed. He turned back to face her. Fresh snow had begun to fall and two large flakes rested in his dark lashes. "What?"

"That's Jeanie's nephew they're carrying out right now in a body bag. She has no idea. I told her I would call her as soon as I found him. But how do I call her and tell her he is dead?" Her voice cracked under the strain of emotion she was trying not to let filter into her subconscious. Jess didn't do feelings, good or bad. Her preferred state could best be described as numb. Not for the first time, she wished she could call Lindsay and ask her what to do. She always knew how to respond.

"Shit." When Jamison exhaled, a long billowy puff of air trailed out.

"Yeah. Shit. And it gets worse. Levi is the fifth kid to commit suicide in that school in a year. And to make it even more complicated, Chief Hagan went to school at Gracemount Academy and he sent a captain to investigate. I need to find out why these kids did it. I need to find out for Jeanie." Jess wasn't like Lindsay: she didn't have the words to comfort people when they cried. She wasn't like Jamison: she couldn't make people feel better, but she could give people answers. That was her skill, the one thing she had to offer. She could investigate and give people truth. She would find out why Levi died because it was the only thing she could do for Jeanie. "I'm going to call Director Taylor. There is a reason the Metropolitan Police want jurisdiction here and we both know it will be so they can cover up anything that shows the school in a bad light." Jess glanced down at the time on her phone. It was just after two. She was not going to earn any points for waking up the FBI director in the middle of the night but she had to act fast. She didn't want to give the school time to concoct a cover story. She had to interview people now when they were raw. That was when she was going to get honest answers.

Jamison nodded. "You don't want to call her." It wasn't a question. They both knew Jess would rather do anything other than tell Jeanie someone she loved was now dead. She didn't want to hear Jeanie cry or feel the desperation in her voice, the unspoken pleas for answers. Dealing with the living was what haunted Jess, the people left behind to hurt. She could confidently walk into any prison in America and interview the most sadistic of killers but speaking to their victims destroyed her.

"I'll call her after I speak to Director Taylor. I need to get the go ahead to open an investigation."

"I'll call her." Jamison pulled out his phone. He sucked in an unsteady breath. The deep furrow that formed between his eyes told her that he did not relish the task either.

Relief washed over her. With three words, the knot between her shoulders loosened. "Thank you." She couldn't ask him to do it but she was grateful he offered, not for her but for Jeanie. She deserved someone better than Jess delivering the horrible news; he would be compassionate and empathic and strong—everything Jess could only pretend to be.

Jamison had been with her when she'd found Lindsay murdered. If he hadn't been, she would be in jail now awaiting trial for murder because he was the only person who could have stopped her from shooting the person who had killed her best friend.

CHAPTER FIVE

Jess took two ibuprofen before she knocked on the door and waited to be invited into the director's office. Not for the first time, she had already exceeded the daily recommended dose before lunch, but still the pain wouldn't shift. She had read the warnings, she was aware that it was bad for her liver and her heart, but the only other choice was to switch to a prescription painkiller and she wasn't prepared to do that. She wouldn't risk addiction. She needed to stay alert for her job. It was all she had.

She shifted from one foot to the other to control her nervous energy.

"Come in." His deep voice was muffled slightly by the door.

Jess went in and closed the door behind her. She glanced around the room. She had been in meetings with the director before but never in his office. It was larger than she expected but it was inviting despite its size. Solid wood panels gave the space warmth. Half of the room was the director's personal office space and the other was a conference table which comfortably seated sixteen. "I'm sorry for calling you so late last night."

"Under the circumstances, it was warranted, I would say." Director Taylor wrung his hands together. Dark spots covered his wrinkled skin, signaling his advanced years. He was nearing the end of his tenure as director, and once he had finished his decade in the position, he would most likely retire. "How is Jeanie holding up?" he asked.

Jess blinked. It was a simple question, one that she would know the answer to if she had had the courage and decency to call Jeanie herself, but she didn't. She couldn't bear to hear the inevitable distress in her voice and know there was nothing she could do to mitigate it, so she had left it to Jamison. "She's coming home tonight," was all she could say.

Director Taylor nodded, accepting her answer. "I can't even imagine." He pointed to the chair across from him, inviting her to sit. "And suicide no less. That is rough, always so many unanswered questions."

"Yes, sir." Leather squeaked as it stretched under her weight as she sat. "That's what I wanted to speak to you about. "Levi Smith wasn't the first suicide at Gracemount Academy this year. He wasn't even the second. His death was the fifth since August."

Jess paused, waited for him to react, but he didn't so much as nod. He just sat, his face impassive like he hadn't heard her.

"I've run the numbers and statistically it is highly improbable to have this many suicides in such a short space of time. It seems suspicious."

This time Director Taylor nodded though he still didn't say anything.

Jess sat, willing him to say anything but he just continued to stare at her. Her skin warmed under the scrutiny. She coughed to clear her throat. "Despite what a lot of people think, teenagers are not as likely to commit suicide as middle-aged or elderly people. The chances of five boys choosing to commit suicide without some connection or precipitating event seems very unlikely."

"Yes." He nodded.

Relief washed over her when he finally spoke but it was short-lived because he didn't follow it up with question or comment.

She sighed. "I think we should look into it, try to understand what's happening at that school to make five boys think suicide was the only option."

"I see."

Annoyance flashed in her. He was acting like she had just told him the trains were running five minutes behind schedule, not that five kids were dead. "I would like to personally look into it. With my team," she added. "If you give me two weeks, I think I could get to the bottom of what's going on." She only needed one, but she asked for two so she could barter. Suicide prevention was not in her team's remit, but they owed it to Jeanie to figure out why her nephew had killed himself. And if they could prevent another kid from dying, then it would be worth it. She just hoped he saw it the same way.

Director Taylor reached forward and pressed the intercom button at the front of his desk. "Emily, can you send in agents Scott and Smart, please?"

Her skin heated as annoyance bloomed to fully actualized anger. He was dismissing her without even giving her the courtesy of explaining why he was turning down her request; he was just calling in his next meeting.

Jess bit the side of her mouth to keep from saying something she would later regret. He was her boss, she reminded herself. She expected more of someone in his position but the truth was he didn't owe her anything but a safe work environment.

Twenty seconds later the door opened and two men walked in, both middle-aged and near enough six feet. Jess glanced up long enough to realize she didn't know either of them, but both were nondescript enough that even if she had met them before, she would have promptly forgotten their faces and names.

Jess's eyes narrowed when the thinner one pulled down the blinds on the small window to ensure privacy. He must have thought that Jess was going to be part of their meeting. She pushed herself off her seat to give it up to one of them.

"Agent Bishop, I'd like you to meet agents Calum Scott and Richard Smart. They are cyber agents investigating internet crime."

She forced herself to smile even though she could really do without a meet-and-greet right now. Jess raised her hand in a stagnant wave. Her social skills could never be described as stellar; usually she could at least fake it, but she didn't have the mental energy to make small talk.

"This is Agent Jessica Bishop. She is on Jeanie Gilbert's team," Director Taylor explained to them.

Jess glanced down, avoiding eye contact. It was a force of habit from years of fearing someone would recognize her and ask her about her father.

"Nice to meet you," they both said, almost in unison.

"Yeah," she nodded, "likewise."

"Let's all move to the conference table so everyone can have a seat," Taylor said.

Jess glanced at the two chairs in front of his desk. There was enough room for all three of the men. He must have expected Jess to stay. Curiosity prickled her skin.

Director Taylor waited for everyone to take a seat. Unlike the Formica table in her team's conference room, this one was black walnut with a stainless-steel inlay around the edge. Light reflected off its polished surface. This one was more decorative than functional.

"Could you please fill Agent Bishop in on your findings regarding The Last Supper? Agent Bishop is the one who discovered the body of the latest suicide victim. His name is—was—Levi Smith. His aunt is Special Agent Jeanie Gilbert."

Jess's eyes narrowed in confusion. What was he talking about? She looked around the table to see if she was the only one confused. She felt like she had walked in on a foreign film halfway through and someone had turned off the subtitles.

One of them, the one with glasses and a cleft chin, opened his briefcase and handed her a stack of papers. "Confidential" was written across the top in bold letters.

"For security purposes, I can only provide you with a hard copy of the report and it must remain in this room."

"Of course," Director Taylor answered on her behalf.

Unease crept along her skin and an ominous weight pushed down on her chest. "What is this?"

The thinner one rubbed the side of his sharp, beaklike nose. "We have discovered an online suicide game called The Last Supper, organized by an unknown curator. Levi Smith is the latest person to fall victim."

Jess's eyes widened. "Curator? What?" Questions fired in her from every direction but her thoughts would not slow enough to process the new information. That didn't make sense. "Are you sure? These things are usually hoaxes."

"We've been following it for several months."

"Months?" She could not keep the incredulity from her voice. "You've known about it for months and you haven't been able to shut it down?"

"The priority has been containing it and managing incidents as they arise," Director Taylor said.

"Manage? You mean covering it up?" Jess asked.

The corners of Director Taylor's mouth pulled down into a frown at the pointedness of her question. "I mean containment. If the media got hold of this, it would spread like wildfire. There would be copycats, and more people would be at risk. You know how these things can grow arms and legs. The aim is to manage this as effectively as possible while we find the person or persons behind the pact. This is an issue of public safety."

She bit into the side of her mouth and reminded herself that he was the director of the FBI, a position that commanded respect. She took a deep breath to try to push out the anger she felt. "With all due respect, five boys have died. This is not contained." She was not usually one for insubordination but she had just come from seeing a young kid's dead body hanging lifeless for anyone to find. He wasn't even in the ground yet and they were acting like he was just collateral damage sustained in the name of protecting the greater good. Levi was a person with a future and family that loved him. Jess wasn't prepared to just forget that.

A look flashed between the three men seated at the table, a knowing glance, pregnant with the fruit of collusion.

"What?" Jess demanded. She could read people's faces. Every micro-expression told the tales their mouths would not let them speak. "Is there something else? What am I missing?"

For a long moment, silence reigned, none of them willing to speak.

"Levi Smith wasn't the fifth victim," Director Taylor said at last. "He was the twelfth since the end of August. The problem isn't just at Gracemount Academy. It's nationwide. There have been cases in California, New York, and Texas, and then of course the cluster here at Gracemount."

Jess's mouth dropped open. "Twelve," she repeated in case she had misheard.

Director Taylor nodded. His mouth tightened into a white slash.

Every molecule in her body vibrated with frenetic energy, desperately pushing her to scream, but she didn't; instead, she tapped her fingers on the desk to the same frantic cadence of her heart. Twelve people were dead. By no sane person's definition was this situation in any way contained. Contained would have been shutting down the responsible parties after the first death.

She continued to pound her fingers and think until the jolt of the pounding numbed the bottom half of her hand. Several times she opened her mouth but snapped it shut again because she didn't trust herself to speak.

"All males?" She asked a question because any commentary from her right now wasn't going to be kind or helpful.

The one with the beak nose answered, "Nine males, three females. All between the ages of fifteen and nineteen."

She nodded. The gender breakdown was in keeping with national statistics on suicides: men committed suicide at a disproportionately higher rate than women, though women attempted it more often. "Is there a website they're all accessing?" What she wanted to ask was why they hadn't shut down any website associated with the pact, but that question would be too ripe with accusation.

"We haven't worked out all the details but it looks like the curator finds them through social media. Usually on Instagram. He seems to be looking for young people with pre-existing mental health issues to exploit," the one with the cleft chin answered.

"Sorry, I didn't catch your names," Jess said. The conversation was too serious not to know exactly who she was speaking with. She stopped short of asking them their exact qualifications but only because she could look those up later.

"I'm Richard Smart," the one with the bird nose answered. "And this is my partner Calum Scott."

"Thanks." She mentally noted that the one with the pointed nose was Smart and the one with glasses and a cleft chin was Scott. "What sort of mental health issues did they have?" she continued.

"Depression, anxiety, borderline personality disorder," Scott answered.

"How would the curator know this without access to their medical records? That doesn't make sense."

"Kids these days have no filter, no boundaries. They were advertising their personal issues on the internet." Taylor shook his head.

"Advertising? What do you mean 'advertising'?" Jess asked.

Agent Smart glanced at the director before he shot her a knowing look. "Hashtags. They all had posts on Instagram that told the curator they had mental health issues. All had #depression or #anxiety. One had #BPD. The curator reaches out to troubled teens via direct message and asks if they want to play a game."

"Wow. That's so calculated." A chill ran the length of her spine. She mentally added the new information to reasons she never wanted to have children.

"Not to mention the fact that no one should be advertising their deficits online. That will haunt them forever. Their future employers could just as easily have seen it. Kids these days just don't think," Director Taylor said.

Jess blinked. *Deficits.* He may as well have said "defects." Jess was more private than most and certainly would not post anything about herself online—hell, she rarely even confided in actual living people—so she could not disagree with the director's sentiment on that score, but she didn't see mental health issues as anything to be ashamed of. Brains, like any other organ in the human body, were subject to a whole host of ailments. There was no shame in that.

Before Jess could say anything, Smart added, "There was also one girl who sought out the game when she found out her friend was playing. She used #CuratorComeFindMe."

"So, it is spreading. Kids are finding out about it," Jess pointed out. Their efforts at containment were even less effective than they thought if kids had heard about the game and were actively seeking it out.

Smart shifted in his seat. "We're working with social media platforms. Any posts seeking out The Last Supper or asking for the curator are deleted."

"Well, at least there is that." Jess looked down at the packet she had been given. More than ever, she didn't want to read it, but she opened it and started skimming the screenshots. "Once the curator makes contact, what happens?"

"The curator gives them a chance to back out. He says—"

"Or she," Jess mumbled.

"What?" Smart said.

Jess glanced up, realizing that she had spoken the words aloud. "Sorry, I was just saying not all serial killers are men. Unless we have definitive proof this is a man, I think we should entertain the possibility it is a female assailant." The correction was more for herself, a reminder that men did not have the monopoly on evil.

Scott nodded. "Yeah, true. We don't really know much of anything about the curator other than it is one sick individual. Once he or she makes contact with the person, he or she then—"

"You can just say 'he.' As long as we all know it could be a woman, I'm comfortable with male pronouns."

"Thanks." Scott smiled. "It's much easier. So, like I was saying, the curator gives the kid a chance to back out by taunting and saying he doesn't think the kid can handle it because once you're in, you're in."

"He's baiting them," Jess said. "That's smart. It's like a dare. Kids will do the stupidest things if someone dares them. Plus, he's making it seem intriguing. Hell, I'd want to know what he was talking about."

"Exactly," Scott agreed. "But then once they've started, it turns sinister. That is when he tells them that he is watching them and will hurt or kill their family if they don't keep going on with the twelve steps."

"Twelve steps, The Last Supper. Those are some pretty overt religious references."

"And it has to be completed in forty days, which is also in keeping with Christian theology."

"Is there a religious component to it? Are we dealing with zealots here?"

"I don't know." Scott shrugged.

Jess glanced down at the packet again and then back up. She would read through it once she got a handle on what she needed to be looking for. "Take me through the steps. How does it go from a direct message to suicide? That's a massive leap even if we factor in depression."

"He uses classic mind control. It's a slow but relentless violation of their boundaries until they are broken. The first step is innocuous, waking up throughout the night, never sleeping more than two hours at a time. The person has to check in every two hours or their family will be killed. This is paired with self-harming. It starts with a single cut on each wrist. The next day they have to make a cut at a perpendicular angle to the first.

"To form a cross?" Jess guessed.

"Yeah. They have to do that every day, and if the cut isn't long enough or deep enough, they have to do it again. By the end of the forty days, their arms are covered in cuts."

"He also makes them confess their darkest secrets. He works them, keeps pushing by pretending he has secret dirt on them. It's really sad. The kids all buy into it and tell him all sorts of stuff," Smart said.

"Like confession," Jess said. This whole thing was reminding her way too much of her childhood in Catholic schools.

"Yeah," Smart said. "And the final step is sending a picture of their last meal and then live-streaming their suicide. The curator reminds them throughout the game that they are being watched and their family will be killed if they don't agree."

"Wow," she said again because she couldn't think of any words to encapsulate what she was thinking.

"I know." Taylor shook his head. "What sort of sick person would do this?"

Unfortunately, Jess had met far too many people who were capable of the darkest of depravities. Some looked out into the world and saw people going about their business but Jess saw monsters, trying to blend in as they stalked their prey. "What are you doing to find the person behind this?"

"We are currently monitoring social media and trying to trace the curator."

"And?" Jess pushed.

"He's using a proxy server. His IP bounces around the globe like a ping pong ball," Smart said.

"You haven't been able to track him in five months?" She tried but couldn't keep the incredulity from her tone.

The color in Agent Smart's cheeks rose to deep scarlet. The cyber agent on Jess's team, Tina Flowers, would have located the IP address by now, she had no doubt. Tina was that good, and just as importantly, she would not make excuses when she failed, she would just keep at it until she got there. "My analyst…" She paused for a second to consider how to phrase things without overtly offending anyone and getting their backs up. "Perhaps you could use some fresh eyes on this."

Smart and Scott exchanged an uneasy glance. She could see the cogs turning as they formulated their responses. It was only natural for them not to want to turn over their case. No one wanted to be sidelined, but the truth of the matter was that they had had the best part of six months to crack it, but they hadn't and now twelve kids were dead.

She cleared her throat. She hadn't been back at work since Lindsay was murdered. If it had been up to her, she would have come back straight after the funeral, but unfortunately the bureau thought she needed time to get her shit together—or in the words of her therapist Dr. Cameron, process and grieve. But the time had not helped her. She couldn't process what had happened because there was no way to make sense of any of it.

Jess wasn't scheduled to come back for another week but there was no way she was going to sit this investigation out. She needed to be here for Jeanie. And she needed to be back at work for herself, to give her days structure and her life meaning again. Catching monsters wasn't just what she did, it was who she was.

"My team should be on this case. We have skin in the game here. This is Jeanie Gilbert we're talking about. The last victim was her nephew. She deserves to know what happened to Levi, and to see the person behind the suicide game go to prison."

Scott's nostrils flared. "Aren't you on administrative leave?"

Jess forced herself to smile. "I'm not due back for another week but obviously the director can override that. Given the nature of this case and the fact you haven't had a break in six months, it seems prudent to get more people looking into this." She meant more competent people but she left it unsaid because everyone knew the score.

She glanced over at Taylor. His body language—his folded arms and the way he was angled slightly to face Scott—told her he wasn't convinced by her argument. She had to appeal to him on another level, something more personal. "We have been very lucky in keeping this out of the media. It would just take one reporter to cover this story and then you've really opened Pandora's box. You think we've had some bad press recently? Wait until America finds out we knew about a national suicide game and didn't use every resource at our disposal to shut that down." She paused for effect. "Ultimately, it's your decision. The buck stops with you, so it's your call… It's your reputation on the line."

"Stop. I've heard enough." Taylor held up his hand. "Gentlemen, if you'll excuse me. I need to have a word with Agent Bishop. In private." His words were directed at the two men in the room but his stare never left her.

CHAPTER SIX

Jess jumped when the door slammed shut. She tried to cover by rubbing her hands together and pretending she was cold. Loud noises had never bothered her before. She once had the unique ability to tune out almost everything, but recently the filter had malfunctioned and even small noises made her startle. It was nothing serious, probably just lack of sleep.

For an excruciating moment, Director Taylor didn't speak; he just looked at her. Her skin burned from the scrutiny. She wished he would just say what he needed to say and be done with it.

"You've had a distinguished career. No one can deny you've been an asset to your team."

She bit into the side of her mouth while she waited for the *but*. People liked to soften criticisms with banal compliments, sandwiching them between platitudes to make it more palatable. She hated that. She would take the truth straight every day of the week. She didn't need it prettied up.

Director Taylor let out a dramatic sigh. "But I wouldn't have approved your recruitment."

She did her best to conceal her shock, but she could not control the way her lungs constricted like a vice was squeezing out the air. She tried to speak but she couldn't. He couldn't have said something more hurtful if he'd tried. Her job was her life. It was the only thing she was good at, and now it was the only thing she had.

"But I wasn't the director then, so you were allowed into Quantico. And obviously you did fine there."

Jess's head snapped up. "With all due respect, I didn't just do fine. I excelled." Now was not the time for false modesty—he was openly questioning her fitness for her job. That was the one area of her life she had no doubt about. She was good at her job and deserved to be here.

"You didn't ask me why I don't think you were an appropriate candidate for the FBI."

She shrugged. "Does it really matter? It seems a moot point now." An uncomfortable heat prickled her skin. She knew where he was steering the conversation and it was not a place she wanted to go. Ever. That part of her life was dead and buried.

"You're very smart. Probably one of the brightest agents I've known."

She didn't thank him or even acknowledge he had spoken because she knew this was the sugar that came before the sting.

Director Taylor leaned forward. "It's that intelligence that got you here. When I took over and became aware of your particular situation, one question kept coming back to me." He paused like he wanted her to ask him what it was, but she didn't. She didn't want to know his thoughts on this particular subject. When she didn't speak he said, "I've been trying to think of how to phrase this delicately."

"Don't. Just say it. I care about the content not your delivery." The only reason he wanted to think about his phrasing was so he could feel good about himself. He didn't get to say something offensive and then congratulate himself for saying it well.

"Okay then, I'll just ask. How did you pass the psych evaluation?"

Jess blinked, unsure of the question.

"Given your childhood…"

The desire to run away overwhelmed her. Her muscles coiled tight, ready to bolt, go anywhere but here. But she wouldn't. Not today. "Obviously I have more fortitude than you give me credit for."

"Fortitude? Or was it your intelligence? Was it simply you knew how to answer the questions?"

She forced the muscles in her face to be completely impassive so she wouldn't give anything away. He was merely guessing. There was no way he knew anything. She had never told anyone that she had gamed the system by studying every psychometric measurement known. It wasn't difficult. She'd spent her entire childhood in the company of mental health professionals. She knew what they wanted to hear. "I have no idea what you're talking about."

"One of our psychologists did raise questions about you though, didn't he?"

Her back straightened. "My appointments with Dr. Cameron are confidential."

"But the results of the assessment aren't."

She had no response. Dr. Cameron was the first therapist to see through her shit, or at least the first to call her on it.

"Can I be frank with you?" he asked.

"Was that you holding back before?"

His mouth twitched into a quick smile. "Jeanie Gilbert speaks very highly of you. She's why you have a career. She championed your appointment. She saw something in you."

Jess's chest tightened. She didn't know that Jeanie had been the one who went to bat for her in the beginning. Maybe on some level she'd known because her entire career she'd looked up to Jeanie, emulated her, did her best to make her proud.

"I trust her implicitly and she trusts you. Despite my reservations, I'm going to put you in charge of this investigation. I'll have the current stipulations for your return waived. I hope you don't let her down."

CHAPTER SEVEN

Jess took the lid off the bottle of ibuprofen and swallowed the last two tablets without water. Luckily, she had a pharmacy's worth of the small white pills in her bottom drawer because she wouldn't make it through the day if she missed a dose. She glanced up to see Special Agent Alex Chan enter the conference room, a brown paper bag in one hand and a Styrofoam cup from the Coffee Kiosk in the other. "I heard you convinced the boss you weren't really crazy after all. Kudos on faking sanity," he said as he handed her the cup.

She accepted the coffee and took off the lid to let it cool down. "Good to see you too," she admitted. The insult was probably the most heartfelt thing he would say all day. Chan was a jerk and a womanizer but she had missed him, because familiarity made him her jerk. She got him, that the jibe was his way of saying he was sorry about what had happened with Lindsay and he wanted everything to be okay again. Normal people would use those words but she preferred Chan's way because she didn't do normal-people emotion either.

"Here, I got you this too." He handed her the bag. "It's lemon-poppyseed. Tart like you."

She smiled. Coffee and a muffin—he must have really missed her.

"So, I heard you really pissed off a couple of cyber agents this morning," he said.

She shrugged. "Pissing people off is kind of my specialty." She would ask how he had heard but she knew Chan was a gossip magnet; he always had his ear to the ground for bitch intel. She might have stepped on some toes but she wasn't about to apologize for it because the suicide game deserved an entire team devoted to it, not just two cyber agents running around trying to clean up the mess afterwards. This wasn't a game of whack-a-mole. These were kids' lives.

She glanced up when her analyst Tina Flowers walked in. David Milligan and Jamison Briggs followed a few steps behind. Other than Jamison, she had not seen any of them since Lindsay's funeral. Her breath caught in her throat as a tsunami of grief hit her when she realized again that Lindsay was really gone. She could almost ignore it before, pretend she was just away on vacation somewhere, but seeing the rest of her team here and not having Lindsay just down the hall ready to chat and support her made it all too real.

Tina had texted and called, but Jess had always had an excuse not to go out. She didn't want to be around people or try to feel better, and she really didn't want to have to make believe that things were returning to normal for her because they weren't. They never would.

Tina crossed the room and threw her arms around Jess. "Welcome back."

Jess froze. She didn't like to hug; she hated it, in fact. She hated all physical contact outside of sex. That is what she had always said, and Lindsay had respected that boundary. But she regretted it now, not hugging Lindsay when she had the chance, so she stood perfectly still and allowed Tina to embrace her even though having someone touch her made her skin burn with anxious heat.

"I'm so glad you're back," Tina whispered as she pulled back. Unshed tears made her green eyes sparkle like polished marbles.

"Thanks," Jess said. "Me too."

Jess waited for everyone to take their seats before she started. "Thank you all for clearing your schedules. I know you have been working a strangler case while I was away but we have been reassigned and I want to get you briefed as soon as possible so we can get ahead of this."

"Aren't we going to wait for Jeanie?" Milligan asked. His mousy-brown hair had been cut recently. The short cut looked tidy but unfortunately his wardrobe kept him from ever looking entirely put together. He was wearing his blue silk tie with the marinara sauce stain on it. All of his clothes had a hole or stain on them somewhere, all small blemishes dotted around the fabric. She would die of shock if he ever turned up without pizza or sauce or baby formula somewhere on his person.

"Unfortunately, Jeanie is not able to work with us on this case because there is a conflict of interest."

"What?" Milligan's face contorted in confusion.

Jess stood up and handed out copies of the packet she had been given by Agent Smart. She had been allowed to make copies for her team only after she had sworn that they would not leave the building. "This is a copy of the report on our new case. As you can see it is classified and you are not allowed to take the report out of this room. It must be given back to me at the end of every meeting. I will keep them locked in my office if you need to reference them at any point. And it should go without saying, but you are not to discuss the case with the media or online—not with anyone, for that matter. This is strictly confidential."

"Why so cloak and dagger?" Chan asked as he flipped open the first page.

"Just read it." It was easier than trying to encapsulate everything she had learned in the last twelve hours. She glanced around the room, watching as the expressions on her colleagues' faces changed from confusion to horror as they read. She looked down and studied the scar on her hand, every mottled shade of purple, every jagged turn, as she waited for everyone to finish reading the report.

Chan's head snapped up. "Is this for real?"

"Yeah." Jess nodded. "Twelve kids have died so far. We don't know how many more are playing."

"Oh my goodness." Tina shivered. "I need to call my brother and warn him to keep his kids off the internet. This is scary stuff."

"No, you can't tell anyone about this. We need to keep this under wraps. We don't want copycats. And we don't want to draw attention to this. There are a lot of vulnerable kids out there who could be sucked in. We just need to find the curator and shut this down before anyone else dies."

"I don't get it." Milligan shook his head. "Why do the kids keep playing? I get why they interacted with the curator at the beginning—kids are dumb and curious and it seems innocuous to chat with people online—but why did they keep interacting after it started to get weird? I would have bailed the second someone asked me to cut myself."

"Would you really have?" Jamison asked. His tone was neutral but the question was pointed.

"Yes. I'm not going to self-mutilate because some creep on the internet says to, even if he does threaten me or my family. That's a crock."

Jamison closed the report. "People do all sorts of messed-up things when people in a position of power tell them to. History is littered with examples of decent folk just doing what they were told."

"But those people were being given orders by real-life people, and there were actual consequences for not following orders," Milligan said.

"There were consequences for these kids, at least perceived ones. They thought their families were at risk. The psychology of power dynamics is complicated. People are programmed to follow directions from authority figures. We tell children from birth to do what they're told. Society would break down if we didn't. Following rules is a good thing but people in power can exploit it. Did you ever read the experiment where people administered electric shocks to other people because they had been instructed to do it by a professor? Most of the participants in the experiment showed clear distress and didn't want to keep administering shocks, especially after they heard the screams of the ones being tortured, but they kept going because they didn't know they could stop. People listen to authority."

"That's just messed-up," Milligan said.

"Yeah, it is, but we are all susceptible to it," Jamison said.

"I still don't see how you could force anyone into committing suicide who didn't want to do it."

Jess stepped in. "These kids were predisposed to mental health issues. Most demonstrated suicidal ideation, but even if they hadn't, the curator still had a fighting chance of getting them to commit suicide based solely on the mind-control techniques he employed. This is calculated and very well-thought-out." She hated that she sounded like she was praising the monster behind this, but there was no denying the game was expertly thought-out. The mind behind this was as brilliant as it was evil.

Milligan shook his head, clearly not convinced. "But how is this a murder investigation? They are killing themselves. No one is actually forcing them."

"Do you remember the Stanford Prison Experiment? I've never seen a study that more aptly demonstrates the power of situations and authority. It showed that we all have the propensity for evil and insanity. It's all about the situations we are put in along the way. Going into the experiment, the participants knew it was not real and they could leave at any time. They were not really arrested and held against their will. Hell, they were even paid to participate, but people still got caught up in it and forgot they had the choice to leave. It affected both the subjects playing wardens and the ones playing inmates. It stopped being make-believe for them within hours. Almost immediately the wardens began to abuse their power and the inmates took it because they thought they had to. The first mental breakdown happened at the thirty-six-hour mark. The poor guy forgot he had the agency to leave. In less than two days, he was a broken man. Now put that dynamic on a vulnerable teenager and add in mind control and threats to their families. Perceived threats are real threats. There is no longer choice; that's why it's murder."

Milligan gave a single nod.

"You said Jeanie has a conflict of interest," Chan reminded her. "I don't see that in here. Why can't she work this case?"

Jess took a deep breath. "Another victim was discovered last night. There hasn't been time to update the report. His name is Levi Smith. He was a seventeen-year-old senior at Gracemount Academy and he was Jeanie's nephew. That is why she is not allowed to investigate the case."

Milligan's eyes widened. "Shit."

"Yeah, shit is right," Jess agreed. "Director Taylor has authorized me to lead the team on this, and we are going to put the fact that we know a member of the victim's family to the side and investigate this the way we would any other crime. Jeanie will be kept in the loop in the same capacity as any other family member, but she will not be involved in the investigation and we are not to share information with her that could threaten the case once it goes to trial. Remember there is no use catching bad guys if we can't put them away." The mantra had been drilled into her at Quantico and it was always in the forefront of her mind. Doing things by the book was paramount to an investigation if they wanted to ensure a successful prosecution.

Jess glanced around the room. "Our primary objective is containment. Director Taylor was very specific about that. If nothing else, we keep any more kids from dying and we keep it out of the press. We need to find out as much as we can about this game if we're going to get ahead of it. I have Levi's laptop. Hopefully you can pull something off this." She slid the computer across to Tina. "I don't have the password but I can try to find out. Two cyber agents have been working this case for nearly six months trying to clamp down. Chan and Milligan, I have scheduled you and Tina to meet with them to get you all up to speed."

It wasn't until Jamison's eyes locked on hers that she realized what she had said. She had partnered Chan and Milligan, leaving her to work with Jamison. Everyone's stares trained hard on her. Even Tina looked shocked. Heat spread over her chest and up her cheeks. She had not been partnered with Jamison since before she shot him. They had barely even spoken.

Her pulse spiked as mortification roiled through her. She had no business pairing herself with Jamison. She could not ask him to work with her when her actions had nearly killed him. She opened her mouth to correct herself but slammed it shut before she could speak. Changing her mind would only make her look weak and indecisive. For this case, she was the team leader. She needed to act like it. If Jamison objected to the pairing, she would assign him to work with Milligan, but if he was prepared to ignore their history, so was she.

Jamison stared at her, studying her, his eyes narrowed in confusion. The hairs on her neck stood on end. She willed him to say something and give her an out but he didn't. She couldn't read him at all. In an instant, his face was impassive again, impossible to read. He was a consummate professional. Any ill will or misgiving he had would be pushed down. Nothing got in the way of a case for him. She had always admired that.

Jess cleared her throat when she realized Jamison wasn't going to say anything. She turned her attention to Tina. "The agents who were leading this, Smart and Scott, have had no luck in locating the curator. Frankly I think they have been useless. I told Taylor that you could sort that out. So, you're now in charge of tracking the curator. Smart and Scott will take orders from you."

Tina bit the corner of her lip as she flipped through the packet. Her brows knitted together as she read.

"What?" Jess asked. "You can trace him, can't you?"

"Um… I mean, yeah, no, I can. It's just not as straightforward as that. From this it looks like this guy is good. He's covered his tracks really well."

"But you're better," Jess said. She wasn't blowing sunshine up her ass. Tina was the best analyst she had ever worked with. She had specifically asked for her to be added to their team because they needed her skills. Tina could find things in seconds that would take Jess days. She was smart and she was methodical.

Tina smiled at the praise, making her eyes sparkle like they were lit up from behind. "Thank you. We can find him but it's not going to be easy. He's using a proxy server and onion routing. The IP is bouncing all over the place."

"Onion routing, I've never even heard of that," Chan said.

Jess's heart sank to the pit of her stomach. She had heard of it and she knew it meant that their guy was hidden under layer upon layer of the dark net. "How are you going to trace him?"

Tina blew out a stream of air and the small gust pushed her bangs up from her forehead. "From what I'm seeing here, it looks like the investigation to this point has been mostly traffic analysis to try to cut out the proxy server. That's slow work and not always reliable. A good defense attorney could shred this." She tapped her pen on the table as she thought. "We could try to get a warrant for more records but my gut says that even the friendliest judge is going to think it's a fishing expedition and not grant it."

"So, what do we do?" Jess pressed. She could only discuss a problem long enough to understand it before she switched her focus to finding the solution.

"I think we should keep monitoring it and wait for him to make a mistake. I know it sounds lame but most of the time that is how these people are caught. It only takes one time where they're lazy or tired or in a hurry, and they log in without covering their tracks and we get them. It's as simple as that. We wait for them to make a mistake while we continue with traffic analysis. I know you want a simple answer, but the simple answer is we might just have to play the long game on this one."

"Might. You said might." Jess pounced on the seemingly meaningless utterance. All words had meaning, every careless phrase or throwaway comment betrayed the thought process of the speaker in some small way. Tina was holding something back. "What are you thinking? What's the other option?"

Tina's throat bobbed up and down as she swallowed hard. The edges of her lips blanched where she had clamped her mouth shut to keep from saying anything else.

"What?"

Tina sighed. "There is another option. I'm not sure I would recommend it—"

"What is it?" Jess pressed again.

Tina's seat squeaked as she shifted uncomfortably, crossing and then uncrossing her legs. She looked like she would rather pour acid in her own eyes than contribute any more to the conversation. "We could try to set a trap. It would be risky. Obviously if we are caught, it will push him underground even further, we could lose him forever, or we might put more people at risk."

Jess rubbed the knotted scars of her palm as she thought. Tina wanted to take the conservative option and follow Smart and Scott's lead of observation and incident management. She could hardly blame her. Since Tina had joined the team, the cases she had worked had resulted in Jamison getting shot and Lindsay being murdered. Tina was understandably gun-shy at this point.

"What would the trap look like?" Jamison asked.

"Well…" Tina flipped through the pages. "This girl Kayli Lewis sought out the curator. Other kids were targeted but she invited him to contact her. We could use the same hashtag as her. We could create a profile, maybe even link it to someone who has already died playing the game, and then invite the curator to make contact."

Jess glanced around the room to gauge people's reactions to the idea.

"That sounds risky. It could tip him off," Milligan said.

Chan shrugged. "Maybe, or it could bait him, make him cocky and more likely to make a mistake. Hackers and hubris go hand in hand. Keyboard warriors want to be noticed. Maybe we should let him know we're on his track and see if he wants to engage."

"I don't think that's a good idea," Tina said, mortification flashing across her face.

"Well, we can't just do nothing," Chan said. "There are twelve dead kids. How many more bodies do we let pile up while we sit here doing nothing?"

"She isn't suggesting we do nothing, she's suggesting we be cautious. That's not a bad idea after—" Milligan stopped mid-sentence. He looked over at Jess, his cheeks flushed. "Never mind."

A heavy silence fell on the room. Jess tapped her fingers on the desk as she thought. Milligan was right: if the last two cases had taught them anything, it was that if something could go wrong, it would go wrong. Maybe they should be more circumspect, but then again there was a fine line between caution and cowardice, and she never wanted to be on the wrong side, especially when there were kids involved.

She waited for someone to say something but no one did. She blinked with surprise when she realized they were waiting for her to tell them what to do.

She was in charge.

Her head spun with the realization. She closed her eyes for a second to give herself the emotional distance to focus.

She looked to Jeanie's empty seat. Jeanie was the one who made the decisions. That's how it worked. As her agents, they made their case and fought their corners, but it always came down to Jeanie.

Not this time.

Jess took a deep breath. "Let's try to lure him out. Tina, I need you to lay the groundwork, set up some fake profiles, and see if he bites. We need it to look legit. Make them active across several social media platforms. Give them an internet presence that will pass the sniff test. If he doesn't bite, we can use one of the profiles to actively seek him out. You're right: the last thing we want to do is scare this guy off."

Tina nodded. "Okay, I'm on it."

Jess stood up to collect the reports so she could lock them safely in her office. "Great. If any of you need me for anything, I'm on my cell. There's something I need to take care of."

CHAPTER EIGHT

Jess zipped up her coat and then pushed her hands deep into her pockets. The tips of her fingers burned from the cold, even on her good hand. She had dropped one of her gloves somewhere earlier in the week but she didn't want to retrace her steps to find it because she wasn't particularly proud of any of the places she had been or any of the men she had spent time with. "You didn't need to come with me."

"You're welcome." Jamison's breath came out in white, billowy puffs.

"Thank you." She didn't want to do this and he knew it, which was why he'd insisted on coming with her. She could handle death or decomposition but dealing with families was excruciating at the best of times.

She glanced up the drive, behind the black iron gate, to the red-brick colonial house. Her boot sunk into the fresh snow. It was dry and loose, perfect for skiing or making a snowman.

"I've never been here. I couldn't even tell you her address before today," Jess admitted.

"Me either. She's always been private."

Jess stopped and turned to Jamison. She had to crane her neck to look up at him. Most people were terrified of him but she was glad he was here. She couldn't say those words, but she was.

"How was she? When you told her?" Jess asked.

Jamison shrugged. "I wasn't sure she'd heard me. She was shocked. That's not a call anyone expects."

fact, but she needed to treat this like any other interview. Jeanie had called her for a reason, because she knew she could depend on her to be professional and get to the bottom of what was happening. Jess couldn't let her down. She cleared her throat. "Last night you said Levi called you. Can you tell me exactly what he said?"

Jeanie reached into the pocket of her sweater. "It's not as much what he said but his tone. I knew something was wrong. I wish I would have picked up the phone." A tear slid down her cheek and settled into the deep crevice of a smile line.

"It's not your fault," Jess said.

Jeanie didn't answer. Instead she typed in her password and played the saved message. A chill ran down the length of Jess's spine when a young man's voice filled the room. Hearing the voice of the dead boy was like listening to a message from a different dimension.

Auntie Jeanie... it's me. Um... it's late here but I really need to talk to you. Um... there is something I really need to tell you. Please call me. I-I-uh love you and I'm sorry. I'm so, so sorry...

His voice cracked as he trailed off. He sounded so scared. And so young. He was terrified. Grief squeezed at Jess's lungs. What must he have been thinking when he decided to end his life? Clearly, he was having second thoughts. He didn't want to die but he thought he had to because he had gone so far. If only Jeanie had answered the phone. She pushed the thought away with a shake of her head. She could never tell her that.

"What time did you get the call?" Jess asked.

Jeanie glanced down at her phone. "It was at 6:48 MST. It must have been just after he had dinner."

His Last Supper.

Jess shivered. "I know this is very difficult, but did Levi seem depressed at all before he died?"

"No, I don't think so." Jeanie shook her head. "Maybe... goodness I don't know anymore. He was stressed. I thought it was just normal adolescent angst. But it wasn't and I missed it."

Paul reached over and wrapped his fingers around hers. "It's all right, love," he whispered to her. "It's not your fault."

Jess didn't want to push but she had to. Four other boys at the school had also committed suicide that year. She needed to know if there was a reason that the pupils at Gracemount were more susceptible to suicidal ideation. "Did he ever say what was stressing him out in particular? Was there any problem with his classmates or his teachers?"

Jeanie thought for a second. "I don't know. I've played conversations over and over in my mind but nothing stands out. Did I push him too hard?"

"No, honey. He pushed himself. He always did since he was little," Paul explained. "He was always conscientious, since he was a kid. He always pushed himself to do his best but he wasn't over the top. There was balance. He knew how to unwind and cut loose."

Jess's ears perked at the turn of phrase. "Cut loose? As in alcohol or recreational drugs?"

Paul and Jeanie shook their heads in perfect synchronization. "Never. He would never violate the honor code of the school or the Word of Wisdom," Jeanie said.

"Word of Wisdom as in Mormon?" Jamison asked.

"Yes," Paul answered.

Jess looked away, over at a framed picture of a temple. "Is that the temple in Maryland?" She already knew the answer but she wanted time to formulate the delicate question she needed to ask.

"No, that is the Salt Lake Temple. We were married there," Paul said.

Jess didn't know how to ask the question in a tactful manner so she was just going to say it. "Was Levi struggling at all with his sexual orientation?"

Jeanie blinked. "No, why would you ask that?"

"LGBT youth have an increased risk of suicide." Jess left out the part that it was particularly difficult for teens from fundamentalist communities who risked being ostracized for their sexual orientation.

"No," Jeanie said softly. "He wasn't gay."

Jess pulled out her notebook. "We know there have been four other suicides at the school this year. Did Levi mention them?"

Jeanie's eyes widened. "What? How is that possible? No, Levi didn't mention it and he would have."

"Kids can be non-communicative," Jess said.

Jeanie shook her head. "He wasn't a withdrawn, moody kid. We talked. We saw him every Monday for family-home evening and of course on Sunday for church, and he called during the week to talk. He would have told us. It would have come up." More tears welled in her eyes, threatening to spill over.

Paul's brow knitted together in concern. "Are you sure there have been five suicides? This year? That doesn't make sense."

"Yes, sir," Jamison said.

"Why didn't the school tell us?"

Jess had asked herself the same question. Parents and guardians needed to know what was going on so they could speak to their children. She took a deep breath and reminded herself that she couldn't share everything with Jeanie. It felt like a betrayal to hold anything back from her but they had to keep the delineations of roles clear for the sanctity of the investigation. "Jamison and I are speaking to the principal tomorrow." She glanced down at her notes. "Mr. Sturgeon, I believe his name is."

"There is no way we would have kept him there if we knew that four boys had committed suicide. We should have been told." Jeanie's voice broke.

"So, he never mentioned any boys committing suicide at all?" Jamison clarified.

"No." Paul shook his head. "But it is a big school. He probably didn't know them."

"Yeah, probably," Jess said because she didn't want to press the point any further.

"What were their names?" Jeanie asked. She wiped her eyes and pulled her glasses back down. Her voice had changed, the fragility gone. The boss that Jess knew came back into focus. "Paul, can you hand me that pad and pen?" She pointed to the closed lid of a grand piano.

Jeanie wanted to investigate this herself. The agent in her demanded answers.

Jess paused for a beat to consider if she should tell her. Would she tell any other grieving family member? Probably not, but most family members didn't have the resources to look it up on their own. She flipped to the page in her notebook with the names. "The first boy to commit suicide was Ryan Hastings in August. Eric Beauchamp in September, Sam Peterson in October, Jason Davenport in December."

Jeanie's face drained of color. Her pen fell through her fingers, bounced off the oak floorboards, and landed under the couch. "What?" she whispered.

Jess's eyes narrowed in confusion. She glanced over at Jamison but he looked just as confused. "Have you heard of those boys?"

"Yes," Paul answered for her. "Those are, were, Levi's best friends. Are you sure they're dead? He would have told us."

An anxious heat spread over Jess's body. For a flash of a second she wondered if she'd written the names down wrong but that was impossible. She had copied them down from death certificates; besides, the probability that she would have randomly picked the same names as Levi Smith's friends was infinitesimally small.

"Why didn't he tell us?" Jeanie shook her head.

"Why didn't the school tell us?" Paul demanded. "They should have told us so we could have supported him."

Jess couldn't disagree. When she was a freshman in high school, a senior had committed suicide. The school had hired grief counselors and had an assembly about recognizing depression. Every single kid in the school had been given a pamphlet with suicide prevention hotlines. At the time, she thought it was over the top, but perhaps they had done the right thing because there wasn't another suicide for the rest of her time there.

"Why did none of the parents tell us? Why? Why did no one tell us?" Paul asked, obviously grasping to make sense of what was happening.

"The same reason we're not invited to family day: because we're not parents." The weight of Jeanie's despair hung heavy in her voice. "Why would they tell us? We're just the pathetic childless couple who made believe that they had the chance to be a real family." Her lips blanched white as she fought to hold back more.

"No, love, that's not it," Paul assured her.

Jess's chest tightened. Grief radiated from them, ugly and raw. Being here, asking them questions, was only deepening a gaping wound. She felt like a cruel interloper, feasting on their pain. She couldn't watch people grieve and not think of her father, all the things he had done, the pain he had caused so many people. "I'm sorry. We just have a few more questions. Does Levi have any social media accounts? Facebook, Twitter, Instagram? Anything like that?"

Jeanie shook her head. "No, he has email for keeping in contact with his friends in Utah, that's it. We don't allow him any other social media."

Jamison caught her eye and gave her a knowing look. Levi had to have social media to play the suicide game. Her real question was whether they knew he had social media, and they didn't, which also meant they would not be able to help her with his passwords. That was okay: she could get a warrant for the information, it would just take a bit longer.

"I found his computer at the school but it's password-protected. Would you happen to know what that is?" It was a long shot given that they didn't even know he had social media accounts, but she had to ask.

"Choose the right. Capital C, no spaces. It has been his password for everything since he was a little boy," Jeanie said.

Jess wrote down the information to give to Tina so she could analyze his computer. "Okay, thank you. I might have some questions later but I think we're okay to stop here." Jess stood up. She looked over at Jamison to see if he had anything to add but he didn't. "Oh, one more thing." She stopped and reached into her bag. "I don't know how long it will take for the police to release Levi's things but I wanted you to have this. I found it in his room." She handed Jeanie the leather-bound scriptures she had taken from under Levi's bed.

Jeanie's lip trembled. "Thank you," she murmured, the words almost swallowed by tears.

CHAPTER NINE

The metal legs of the chair scraped along the concrete floor when Jess shifted in her seat. Her butt had gone numb from sitting in the same position for so long. "Have you ever had to wait this long at the morgue?" she asked Jamison, who was sitting beside her reading an old copy of *People*. The issue was at least a year old and she knew Jamison didn't give two shits about any of the people in the magazine, but he sat and pretended to read it just the same, like he didn't have a care in the world.

The snow from his jacket had melted and dripped on her shoulder, soaking her, but she didn't move because there was nowhere else to sit and she liked Jamison's calm energy. She always hoped that some of it would rub off on her.

"They know we're coming, right?" Jamison asked.

"Yeah, I called this morning. I spoke to the chief medical examiner and said we would be in by five at the latest. She said that wasn't a problem and just to give her a call if we were running late."

"So why the hold-up?"

Jess shrugged. "I have no idea but it's been over an hour." She stood up and pushed the buzzer. She had never been left in a waiting area for this long.

After thirty seconds, she pushed the buzzer again. Finally, a middle-aged brunette woman in green scrubs answered. She held the door open just enough to speak to them. "Can I help you?" Her words were clipped and her tone exasperated.

She held up her badge for inspection. "Yes, I'm Special Agent Jessica Bishop. This is my partner Special Agent Jamison Briggs. We are here to see the body of Levi Smith and to get the preliminary autopsy report. I called Dr. Leicester this morning and she said it wouldn't be a problem. We could come in any time before five."

The woman made a show of looking at the clock before looking back and rolling her eyes.

"I know it's almost six now but we've been waiting for almost an hour," Jess said. "I'm sure you're busy but this won't take long. We really just need five minutes to examine the body."

"Did you say Levi Smith?" A deep furrow formed between her dark brows. "His body was released for burial half an hour ago. Someone from the funeral home was literally just here."

Jess shook her head in confusion. "What? How could you release the body before the autopsy report was filed? Bodies are never released this quickly."

"I don't know. I didn't do the autopsy myself. Dr. Massif did."

Annoyance niggled at her. Jess had specifically called to make sure they could see the body. Something had been bothering her since she learned about the steps in the suicide game. All of the victims were covered in cuts from the weeks of self-harming, but there were no cuts on Levi's arms that Jess could remember. Admittedly it had been a shock, and her primary concern had been trying to keep the house mother from screaming down the house and waking up every child on campus, but surely she would have remembered if Levi had cut chunks out of his arms in the shape of a cross. That would have stood out. "Did he take photos of his arms? What about a toxicology report?"

The woman shrugged and agitation flashed in her eyes. "I don't know. Like I said, it wasn't my autopsy."

Jamison stood up and walked over to them. "Can we speak to Dr. Massif?"

"He's gone home. He will be back at nine tomorrow. Now, if you'll excuse me, I have work to do."

Jess opened her mouth to speak but Jamison cut her off. "Can you please have him email the preliminary report as soon as he gets in?"

"Yeah, sure." She didn't wait for a response before she let go of the door and let it slam shut.

Jess spun on her heel to face him. "What was that? I need to know if Levi Smith has the same cuts as the victims and she was totally blowing us off!"

Jamison pulled out his phone. "I know she was. She was also wasting time we don't have."

"What are you doing? Who are you calling?"

"Tina. There are more than a dozen funeral homes in DC. That's a lot of places to call. She will be able to find him faster than we can."

CHAPTER TEN

Ernest Edwards Funeral Home was located in Centreville, Virginia. On a good day, it would have been a forty-five-minute drive; however, rush-hour traffic and an eight-car pile-up on George Washington Memorial Parkway meant the journey took over three hours.

"Finally, we're here," Jamison said when he spotted the Welcome to Centreville sign on the side of the freeway.

"Why would Jeanie choose a funeral home this far away?" Jess wondered aloud.

"I don't know. Maybe she has family out here."

"No." She shook her head. "I checked this morning. All of her family is in Utah. Paul has a sister in Idaho and two brothers in Wyoming; nobody out here." She realized she sounded like a stalker for knowing that level of detail about her boss, but she knew that much about everyone involved in an investigation.

Jamison shrugged. "Maybe it was the first place she found. I doubt she wants to be looking through Yelp reviews at a time like this. She probably just called the first place that came up in the search."

"Yeah," Jess agreed. She looked out on the sea of white. Flakes had started swirling again, adding a fresh layer to the already icy roads. The snow was even higher here than in DC because the roads and buildings of the capital soaked up solar radiation to create an urban heat island and kept the city warmer than surrounding areas. "The morgue shouldn't have released the body. Why can't people just do their jobs properly? I hate incompetence."

"I know you do." He turned on his blinker and pulled into the exit lane.

"I'm sorry we had to drive all the way out here. I know we could have just waited for the report to come through."

"That's okay. It's my job."

Jess rubbed the knotted scar tissue of her palm. "I might be wrong…" She may as well tell him then rather than later, and admit that most of last night had been a blur. "There could have been cuts and I missed them or something. I don't know. I saw him and I… um, I…" She couldn't bring herself to finish the sentence, admit that seeing Levi had brought back memories of the night she had spent most of her life trying to forget.

"It's okay, I get it. It's not a big deal if you made a mistake. I've certainly made my fair share." He parked beside a Mercedes C-Class and turned off the engine.

The building was completely dark except the illuminated letters of the sign and a single light at the entrance.

Jess zipped up her coat and pulled up her hood. Gravel crunched under her feet where they had just gritted the path for the fresh onslaught of snow. A middle-aged woman with tight curly hair opened the door before they even made it up the path. "You must be Agent Bishop and Agent Briggs. I'm Geraldine Edwards. Your colleague called to let me know you were on your way. Come on in. It's cold out there."

"Thank you." Jess extended her hand to shake Geraldine's. "I'm sorry it's so late. We got held up in traffic. I'm Jess Bishop and this is my partner Jamison Briggs."

"That's all right." Geraldine opened up the door further to let them in. The entryway was decorated in cream and ivory. Oil paintings of tranquil scenes lined the walls. Gold light fixtures cast a glow over everything. It was warm and calming, almost serene.

"Is Levi's body being prepared for burial?"

"No, ma'am. He is scheduled for cremation in the morning. We were going to do it tonight but Gus needed to get home. He lives out of town and didn't want to get snowed in."

"Can we see the body, please?" Jamison asked.

"Of course. He's in the crematorium."

They followed her down the hall, past a chapel, and through to a smaller room. It was similarly proportioned and decorated as the foyer with its cream and gold fixtures but there was a cremator at the front. Bouquets lined the front of what looked like a conveyor belt, and the sickly-sweet smell of lilies tickled the back of her throat.

Jess looked around for a casket. "Where is he?" she asked.

"He's in the back. Follow me." Geraldine kept walking. She opened the door to a smaller, windowless room. Unlike the other rooms, there were no cream carpets or paintings in gilded frames. It was an industrial room with concrete floors and cinderblock walls. Light came from a single-filament bulb.

In the corner was a gurney with a cardboard coffin. "Is that him?" Jess asked. She expected something grander than a lidded box. Suddenly her mind went back to her childhood, to the first dead body she'd seen, naked and bloodied. Did that boy have a cardboard coffin too?

Her heart raced; a frantic buzz hummed through her body. She fought to take a breath but the air wouldn't make it past the painful constriction in her throat. The room tilted on its axis. She was going to fall. She reached out to brace herself but the solid grip of Jamison's arms kept her from falling. He pulled her against him to right her.

Concern flashed in his eyes but then just as quickly as he'd grabbed her, he let her go and turned away.

"Are you okay?" Geraldine's brow knitted together in concern.

Jess opened her mouth to speak but nothing came out. It took her a few seconds to shake off the visceral hold of the memory. "Sorry I-uh…" She could not think of an excuse.

"That's all right, honey. It can be hard seeing people this way."

Jess nodded like that was what the problem was. She had seen hundreds of dead bodies. She had seen and smelled every state of decomposition; it had never affected her. And it wouldn't now. She wouldn't let something that happened nearly thirty years ago affect her now.

"You okay?" Jamison's low voice was laced with genuine concern.

She took a fortifying breath. "Yeah, I'm good. Let's get this done so we can get home." Jess reached into her bag and pulled out two pairs of surgical gloves and some evidence bags.

"They will have collected evidence at the morgue," Jamison reminded her.

"They were also supposed to wait to let us examine the body before the autopsy and that didn't happen, so better to collect our own, just in case."

Jamison snapped on a pair of gloves and helped her remove the cardboard lid. Levi's body was wrapped in sheets of plastic held together with duct tape. She had been expecting a body bag with a zip, not for his body to be wrapped up like trash you didn't want to drip everywhere while it rotted. She also would have expected there to be a proper casket but she didn't have the right to judge. People were as different in grief as they were in anything else. There was no one-size-fits-all to bereavement. If Jeanie had decided not to do a traditional funeral, for whatever reason, she had no right to question it.

She turned to look at Geraldine. "Do you have any scissors?"

"In my office, give me two minutes," she said as she left the room.

Jess peered down at the body while she waited for Geraldine to return. He looked so thin, bound up like this, long and lanky.

"Here we go," Geraldine said when she returned. She handed the scissors to Jess.

Her fingers tried to close around the cold metal but her hand froze in a painful spasm. She winced. She reached across with her other hand before either of them noticed that her grip was not working, but Jamison took them instead. "I got it," he said softly.

Jess gave a faint smile of thanks.

Layers of plastic peeled away as Jamison sliced through the wrapping. He started at the head and worked down until he reached the feet, and then stripped back the clear sheet to expose Levi's naked body.

Jess stared down at the corpse. She looked at his abdomen, searching for the post-mortem incisions, but there were none, nor were there any under his sternum or on his skull. Her head snapped up to look at Jamison. "They didn't do an autopsy. They sent him for cremation without doing a post-mortem. Unbelievable." An angry heat spread over her. Shoddy work in any capacity annoyed her, but this was straight-up incompetence.

The body needed to be taken back to the medical examiners for a post-mortem. She silently began to format the pointed letters of complaint she would be writing that night.

"Look at his arms, Jessie. You were right: there are no cuts."

She wasn't crazy. Part of her had worried that she was losing it, that Lindsay's death was the final push she needed into the dark abyss of insanity. Relief washed over her but it was short-lived, too soon replaced by confusion. "That doesn't make sense."

Jamison glanced at Geraldine and then back at Jess, to remind her they shouldn't have this conversation in front of her.

Jess nodded to say she understood. "Look at his knuckles. There are fresh bruises and scratches. Those are defensive wounds. They haven't even had time to start to scab over. And look under his fingernails. That's blood. He was in a fight recently."

CHAPTER ELEVEN

Jamison pulled in through the front gates of Gracemount Academy. It looked different in daylight: older and grander. In the distance, students in maroon blazers looked like splotches of blood against the white snow. The school grounds seemed to go on forever. The campus and surrounding area occupied over 300 acres.

"I got the impression he really didn't want to see us this morning," Jamison said as he put the car into park.

Jess glanced up from her phone, on which she was reading her notes on the principal, Greg Sturgeon. Normally she would have started preparing for an interview the night before but she had got home so late she just had time to take her dog out for a pee before she went to bed. She had been so tired, she actually slept through the night, which was no small feat for her. "I don't think he wants to talk to anyone. He will be like a dog chasing his tail right now. Five kids are dead. It happened on his watch. I don't see how he could keep his job after this. He is probably trying to figure out who will employ him after such a colossal fuck-up."

"True." Jamison opened the car door and got out. "He probably also wants to speak to a lawyer before he makes a statement because this has lawsuit written all over it. These parents trusted the school to take care of their kids."

"Yeah, I don't see this being a good day for the school's public relations department."

The snow had been shoveled to clear the path, but a fresh layer had fallen to give the street a white sheen.

They followed the signs past a courtyard to a red-brick building. "This place is swanky. Remind me again how much it costs a year?" Jamison asked.

"Fifty thousand."

"Dang." Jamison pressed the button on the intercom. "Like my grandma Patty used to say, some people have more money than sense."

Jess couldn't help but smile. Jamison didn't often speak about his family. He was almost as private as her when it came to protecting his secrets, but he had confided in her because they had been friends once.

More than friends.

Jess closed her hand into a fist. The tender flesh of her palm screamed out at the small movement but she needed the pain to focus her, remind her that she had lost the right to call him a friend that same night she had mangled her hand.

"*Alere flammam veritatis,*" a woman's voice answered.

Jamison introduced them and then the woman buzzed them in.

"I wonder what their motto means."

"Let the flame of truth shine." Jess pushed the door open.

"I knew you would know."

Jess's skin warmed. He used to call her the trivia queen, back when they talked.

Jess looked around the room. Unlike the dormitory which maintained most of its original features, the office had been completely modernized. The décor was all done in shades of pale gray and white.

A receptionist sat behind a horseshoe-shaped desk. Her wiry gray hair was cut into a sharp bob that fell just below her ears. "Hello, I'm Ms. Stewart. Mr. Sturgeon is running behind schedule this morning. He asked me to tell you that he will call you to reschedule."

Jess looked up at Jamison. He shot her a dubious glance that told her they both knew the principal was avoiding them. He wasn't compelled to speak to them but she was fairly certain she could force his hand. "Oh, that's no problem. We wanted to speak to some students anyway. We will just head to the main campus and start asking around and see what everyone has to say about what happened two nights ago."

"Yeah, good idea." Jamison turned to head for the door.

The wheels of the receptionist's chair squealed and it was propelled backward as she bolted up. "No, actually… you've come all this way. Let me see if I can juggle some things around." She sat down and picked up her phone. She spun her seat around so she was facing away from them.

She spoke in hushed tones. The only word Jess could make out was "prudent."

Ms. Stewart turned to face them, her expression now an impenetrable, placid mask. "Mr. Sturgeon has ten minutes before his next meeting. He would be happy to fit you in just now."

Jamison smiled, exposing two rows of straight white teeth. "Thank you." He leaned down and whispered to Jess, "I just love it when people suddenly find it in themselves to be amenable."

They followed Ms. Stewart to Mr. Sturgeon's office. The space could easily have belonged to the CEO of a Fortune 500 company: everything was high-end, state-of-the-art. No expense had been spared in kitting out the room. Jess glanced at the stainless-steel frames on the wall. Mixed in with Mr. Sturgeon's many credentials were pictures with former alumni. The photos were like a who's who of the American political elite.

Jess glanced at a picture of Mr. Sturgeon with Chief Hagan at some black-tie event. She squinted at the silver pin on Chief Hagan's lapel: a chalice with the Eye of Providence etched above lips with a finger pressed against them. She had seen that somewhere before: on Levi's blazer.

She opened her mouth to ask what the pin represented, but before she could speak Mr. Sturgeon came from behind the desk, his hand outreached to shake hands, first with Jamison and then her.

"Thank you so much for coming out to see us today. I know how busy you must be. And, of course, thank you so much for helping us two nights ago until the police could come and deal with the situation. You were a tremendous help to Miss Crawford. I don't think she could have dealt with the events, had you not been here. It's such a tragedy—he was so young, had so much going for him." He let out a dramatic sigh. "Again, thank you for coming in."

Jess noted the way he had shaped the narrative to make it seem like he was grateful, even eager, to meet with them. Smart. He obviously had some people skills to be in the position he was. He would know that by being gracious, most people would be inclined to match his tone and intensity, but Jess wasn't most people. Social engineering didn't work on her because she knew the game and didn't want to play.

"Can I get you something to drink: coffee, tea?"

"No, we're fine, thank you," Jess answered for both of them. She sat down before he had the opportunity to ask her to be seated.

She sat down, folded her hands, and crossed her legs to look as closed off as possible.

When Mr. Sturgeon realized Jess wasn't going to say anything, he looked to Jamison, but he didn't speak either. Mr. Sturgeon wanted them to speak first and show their hand—and she might have if he hadn't been disingenuous.

Jamison got comfortable in his seat. He was a master at smoking people out. He had taught Jess most of what she knew. He knew that in novel social situations, people hated silence. The lack of communication was invalidating and off-putting. Jamison knew that and used it to his advantage. He could make people confess all manner of things without saying a word. It also didn't hurt that he looked like he could snap someone's femur with his bare hands.

Jess watched as the color in Mr. Sturgeon's cheeks deepened ever so slightly. He cleared his throat. "So, I believe you're here to discuss Levi Smith's suicide."

Jess nodded. "Among other things."

His mouth pulled down into a pronounced frown. "It was such a shock."

"Really?" Jamison shot him a dubious look. "After five kids? The first one would be a shock but number five I'm thinking more mild surprise."

Mr. Sturgeon's Adam's apple bobbed up and down when he swallowed. "Yes… we have had an unfortunate start to the school year."

"That's certainly one way to put it," Jamison said.

"When I spoke to Levi's aunt, she was completely unaware of the other suicides. Is there a reason she wasn't informed?"

"She is not his legal guardian."

Annoyance prickled her skin. "Was Levi's father informed?"

"I'm sure you appreciate that with minors there is an issue of confidentiality. It's a—"

Jess held up her hand. She didn't have the patience to listen to him talk in circles. "Were any of the parents informed, or did you rely on their kids filtering back the information?"

Mr. Sturgeon's mouth tightened to a puckered white slash.

"What?" Jamison asked. His eyes widened in surprise as he realized the reason Mr. Sturgeon didn't answer. "Did you not tell the students either?" Incredulity dripped from his deep voice.

Mr. Sturgeon cleared his throat again but he didn't answer.

"Seriously? You didn't tell them?" Jess demanded. "How could you keep that a secret? It would seem rather obvious that their friends were dying off. Where did they think they were going? What did you tell them had happened?"

Mr. Sturgeon took a deep breath. "This has been a huge learning experience for all of us. I'm sure you'll appreciate that this is not something that any of us were prepared for. We have taken advice from professionals."

"What professionals?" Jess asked.

"After Ryan Hastings' death, the school board, along with our school psychologist, decided that we didn't want to glamorize or fetishize suicide in any way. He was a very popular student and we didn't want people copying him, so we decided to not tell the student body what had happened."

"We see how well that worked out for you." Jess's head spun at the admission. Questions fired out of her from every direction. "So, none of the parents have been informed about what's going on? You haven't told the families affected that there have been other suicides?"

He shook his head. "This is a learning curve for all of us. We've taken the lead from our psychologist—"

"Who is that? I need a name."

"Jim Iverson."

Jess flipped open the pad and wrote down the name. "Well, Jim Iverson gave you some pretty shitty advice." It was unprofessional of her to swear but she could not contain her anger. Kids had died. "Honestly, where did he do his training? Suicide is not contagious. Talking about it does not make it more likely."

"This has been a learning experience for all of us," Mr. Sturgeon repeated.

"Five kids have died under your watch. From where I'm sitting, you still have a whole lot to learn," Jamison said.

"Kids aren't stupid. They would have seen that their friends were missing. What exactly did you say happened to them?" Jess asked.

"You have to understand, we have three thousand students at this school. They come from every state in the union and every corner of the world. Kids come and go. There is a certain transient nature to a school of this caliber. For example, a sheikh has two sons here and they're going back to Saudi Arabia at the end of the term. We also have an ambassador's children here. When his term is over, they will return to Nigeria."

"You didn't answer my question," Jess pressed.

"It is a very delicate situation and we had to respect the wishes of the families. The truth is, we took their lead. Whatever explanation they wanted, we went with that. Perhaps not surprisingly, the families didn't want the circumstances surrounding the death of their children advertised."

"Are you saying the parents wanted you to cover up their children's suicides?"

Mr. Sturgeon gave a small nod. "It surprised me too. I try not to judge but… yes, I'm surprised and a little disappointed, I suppose, in the reactions from the families." He shrugged. "I don't know. I've never been in this position. I don't know what I would do if the roles were reversed."

Sadness pulled at Jess as she wondered if it was grief or shame that compelled the families to cover up the deaths of their sons.

"So now you see why our psychologist made the difficult decision not to tell the students. It would be too confusing to tell them half-truths, and it would invite questions we couldn't answer without betraying the wishes of the families."

Jess glanced down at her disfigured hand. With every heartbeat, pain pulsed in her palm. She knew all too well that shame and guilt twisted people, made them illogical, and colored every decision they made. She wanted to judge the families and the school, say that they had done the wrong thing, but she couldn't. Even now, knowing the consequences of concealing her past, she knew she would do it over again because some things were so ugly they had to be hidden if you were going to survive. Maybe that was what the suicides had been for the families left behind.

"Obviously there is something happening at this school that is making these young men more susceptible to suicide. What is it?" Jess asked.

Mr. Sturgeon's shoulders slumped. "I don't know. I wish I did. They were all such good kids." Sadness flashed across his tan features and his blue eyes glossed over with tears. For the first time, Jess did not question the genuineness of his response.

"Have you put them under undue pressure for academic achievement?" Jamison asked.

"Probably," he admitted. "I've asked myself that so many times since Ryan died. Why? Why did it happen? What could we have done differently? I have always told them that these are the most important years of their life. But they're not. It's everything that comes after that matters. There are very few things that you can't get over, get past. But not if you're dead. Maybe that's what I should have told them: don't worry about being perfect, just make sure you don't make any mistakes you can't come back from."

The weight of his words pressed down on Jess. She had needed that advice before.

"What are you doing to prevent this from happening again?" Jamison asked.

Mr. Sturgeon wrung his hands together. "This morning I had an emergency meeting with the school board. Obviously, I'd prefer that what I'm about to tell you go no further." He took a deep breath like he was trying to fortify himself for what he was about to disclose. "We've mishandled this up until now. We did the best we could with the advice we were given at the time but clearly it was wrong. We realize that now and we are doing our best to rectify the situation. Crisis counselors are coming in today. We are going to sit down and come up with a plan of action and decide how we are going to explain the situation to our students. We need to have a hard look at our school and find out why these boys felt they couldn't reach out to anyone. If there is any advice you could give us, I'm all ears. This is not what I thought I would be dealing with when I chose to become an educator."

Jamison looked over at Jess, waiting for her to answer. She blinked. For a second she didn't remember that she was in charge of the investigation. She rubbed the scar on her palm while she thought. Her instinct was to tell Mr. Sturgeon to monitor or even cut off the students' access to social media but that would mean telling him about the suicide game, and she had been explicitly instructed by the director not to tell anyone. "I'm sure the therapists you've hired will have the best advice for this situation."

She could only hope that was true.

CHAPTER TWELVE

"Hang on, Stan. I know you're hungry, buddy. Just give me a minute to get my keys." She bent down to scratch her dog behind his ears before she reached into her pocket.

It was selfish for her to have a dog. She worked too many hours to give him the attention he needed. She felt guilty that he spent more time in Doggy Daycare than he did with her. She tried to make it up to him by taking him on her morning run but it wasn't enough. He needed more. He deserved someone who could give him more attention but she couldn't bring herself to rehome him. He was the only tenuous connection she had to Lindsay. Stan had been her dog.

"Okay, I'll feed you. I always do. Please stop acting like you've never seen food. Someone is going to report me for animal cruelty." As soon as she opened her apartment door, Stan pushed her out of the way, bounded inside, and ran straight to the kitchen.

Jess turned to put her keys down on the bookshelf but stopped when she saw the open lid of her fish tank and one of the fish lying dead beside it. She shook her head in confusion. She never left the lid to the tank open. She only opened the tank to clean it and give the fish their food pellet. Then she always immediately closed it. Always.

Before she could figure out how it had happened, a loud bang of her bedroom door slamming shut snatched her from her thoughts.

Her heart stopped with a thud. "Who's there?" she demanded. She drew her gun from her running holster and slammed her back against the wall so no one could sneak up behind her. "I'm armed and I'll shoot to kill."

Her heart vibrated against her ribs, pumping so fast the beats merged. Stan whined in distress. "Show yourself!" she screamed, edging closer to her bedroom.

She opened the door with enough force to bang it hard against the wall. The door frame bit into her back as she rounded the corner. Her eyes darted around the room, taking in information, looking for the intruder, but she didn't immediately see anyone. She threw open her closet door. "Identify yourself now or I will shoot," she warned. Frantically, she pulled clothes off the hooks so no one could hide behind them.

She turned and looked under her bed. There was nothing there except a dusty suitcase.

Blood whooshed in her ears as her pulse pushed dangerously high. She swung open the door to the bathroom but there was no one there. She tugged at the shower curtain. Metal pinged on the tiles as the rings went flying as she ripped the curtain from the hooks. With the final tug, the rail collapsed.

"Where are you?" she screamed.

The curtains billowed as a gust of wind blew through the window. She stood for a moment, dazed as she stared at the raised pane of glass. Someone had been in her apartment and killed her fish. But why? To send a message? Was it someone from this case or revenge for someone she had put away before? Dozens of names sprang to mind. She would check the status of all of them.

She pulled out her phone to call the police and her hand cramped in a painful spasm as she squeezed it. What would she tell them? That someone broke through her fifteen-point deadbolt to kill one of her fish? Or maybe they climbed up the drainpipe to the sixth floor and opened her locked window.

Oh God, she was insane.

Her back hit the tiles as she slid down the wall. She pulled her knees to her chest. She couldn't be crazy. She wouldn't let herself be. She was stronger than that.

Stan's paws tapped against the hardwood floor as he ran through to the bathroom. He whined as he pushed up on her chin with his snout.

She looked down into his pleading eyes. He needed her to get her shit together and feed him. "It's okay, buddy. We're okay."

CHAPTER THIRTEEN

Jess took two ibuprofens and swallowed them with black coffee. That would have to count as breakfast because she had been too spaced out that morning to eat. But she was okay now. It was a blip. Nothing to do with bereavement or trauma, just a shitty start to the day. It happened to a lot of people. She just needed to stuff it all away in the deepest recess of her mind and just get on with it like she always did.

She looked up when Tina entered the room.

"Good morning," she said from the doorway, her laptop tucked under her arm so she could hold her coffee and open the door at the same time. Her hair was tied in a loose bun secured with a pen through the middle. She came in, put her laptop down on the Formica table, and plugged it in to charge. "Before you ask: none of the autopsy reports have come in from any of the kids at Gracemount, but the out-of-state ones have and I'll keep working on the ones for the local boys."

"What's the hold-up on the Gracemount cases?"

"They're still looking for them." Tina rolled her eyes.

"What? How can you lose autopsy reports?"

"Apparently they are having a problem with their network and files have been corrupted or something. I don't know." She threw up her hands in exasperation. "I don't buy it. I think someone messed up and forgot to enter reports and now they're blaming technology. When in doubt, say the computer did it."

Jess frowned. "What about the warrants for computer and phone records for the victims?"

Tina sighed. "I have warrants for all the out-of-state ones. Those went through like *that*." She snapped her fingers to demonstrate her point. "But the District of Columbia is being a pain in my neck. None of those warrants have been granted."

"None of them? Hmm." Unease spread throughout her body, settling in the pit of her stomach. Something felt off. "No autopsy reports and the warrants haven't been granted. That's quite a coincidence. It sounds like we're being stonewalled." It sounded paranoid even to her, but she couldn't think of any other explanation.

At that moment Chan walked in with Milligan and Jamison behind him. "Ooh, a conspiracy. You know I love those." Chan handed her a Styrofoam cup from the Coffee Kiosk.

"I didn't say there was a conspiracy." She thought it but she wouldn't say it because she didn't need anyone else questioning her mental health; she had that one covered. "Thanks for the coffee." She already had a coffee but she would never turn down another.

"So, what's going on?" Chan asked.

Tina briefly summarized what they had been discussing.

"Interesting. I'd say that sounds like some grade-A obstruction." Chan took the lid off his own coffee and added three packets of sugar to the beige-colored concoction. He put in so much cream and sugar that it was coffee in name only.

"Or incompetence with a side of bureaucracy. Judges want to be on the right side of the law. The last thing they want is to have a warrant challenged and have the case collapse because everything that is found is fruit of the poisoned tree," Jamison said.

Chan's nostrils flared but he didn't say anything to challenge Jamison. The antipathy between the two of them simmered just below the surface, ready to explode. When it did, it would be Chan losing it, because Jamison was too in control. Chan would be like a raging toddler swinging at his father's knees.

"I do have some promising news though," Tina said. She stopped when the door opened and Agents Scott and Smart walked in.

They weren't supposed to be here. "Can I help you?" Jess asked.

Scott spoke for them. "Director Taylor has asked for an update."

"And he forgot my number?" she asked before she managed to stop herself. She didn't have the right to take out her shit day on anyone else, but if Taylor had any regrets about assigning the case to her, he could take it up with her himself, not send people to keep tabs.

"I guess he thinks it should be all hands on deck." Again, it was Scott who spoke for them, indicating he was the dominant personality. "Sorry, I didn't mean to interrupt. Please keep going."

Tina looked over at Jess for approval before she continued. "I was just saying that despite the lack of cooperation from anyone in DC, we have a very interesting lead thanks to Jess's quick thinking by securing Levi Smith's laptop."

A look of surprise flashed across Scott's face but it was gone almost as quickly as it appeared, replaced by a faint if not forced smile. "Excellent."

"Jeanie was right about Levi's password. We found an Instagram account connected to his email address. That is where he connected with the curator."

Jess tried to shrug off the sudden onslaught of sadness but she couldn't. Her mind flashed to Jeanie, her insistence about Levi, how she really knew him. But she hadn't, not the demons he'd failed to tame. Maybe no one knew anyone. "Jeanie was sure he didn't have social media," Jess said.

"Well, he did. He wasn't all that active but he did have an account and he used it to play the suicide game. I have gone through all the correspondence between him and the curator." The keys clicked as she typed and the screen at the end of the conference room lit up. "As you can see, he completed all the steps of the game." She clicked to enlarge a picture. "Here we have a picture of the first time he was asked to self-harm."

A graphic photo filled the screen. The deep cut ran from his wrist to his elbow, intersected by a shorter slash to form a cross. Blood was smeared over his wrist from the torrent of blood. *What the hell?* In an instant, her sadness turned to disbelief. Her mind raced, searching for an explanation. Those marks weren't present on Levi's body when she viewed it at the crematorium. Jess's neck snapped up to look at Jamison.

"Who is that?" Jamison pointed at the screen.

"What?" Tina looked up from her computer. "It's Levi Smith. It's from his account. He sent it to the curator."

"I can see that, but it's not him," Jamison said.

"Who else would it be?" Tina's eyebrows knitted together in question.

"That's not Levi. He didn't have any cut marks anywhere on his body," Jess said.

Scott held up his hand. "With all due respect, you saw the body for what, thirty seconds? How can you say with any certainty it's not him?"

Jess's back straightened at the challenge. She didn't mind being questioned, it was vital to the iterative process, but she objected to the incredulity that dripped from his tone. She was many things, but incompetent was not one of them. "First of all, I would have to be the least observant agent in the history of the FBI to not notice a ten-inch gash carved into the flesh of a dead child. Second of all, Agent Briggs and I re-examined his body and there were no injuries, recent or healed, anywhere on him." She stood up and walked over to the screen to make her final point. "Third, that arm is the wrong color. Levi was pale and blond. The hair on his arms was almost white. This kid has tan skin. Look at this black hair."

For a long moment, no one spoke as they examined the picture for themselves.

"Yeah, it's not him," Chan said. For the first time in the history of their working relationship, he agreed with Jamison.

"But if it's not him, who is it?" Milligan asked.

"I don't know," Jess admitted. The unease she felt earlier amplified, spreading through her, insidiously pushing out all reason in its path. She couldn't think rationally. It didn't make sense. None of this did.

"He obviously faked it," Scott said with complete certainty.

Jess's head snapped up to look at him. She was open to all suggestions, even stupid ones, but there was no room for hubris. Over the course of any investigation, they got things wrong far more than they got them right. She needed people around her that had the maturity to understand that and park their egos at the door. "Have you ever seen a dead body? I'm not talking about a great-aunt laid out in her casket."

Scott shifted in his seat, obviously uncomfortable with the question—or, more precisely, the answer.

"The color and the viscosity are consistent with real blood: see the way it has coagulated here and here?" She pointed to the screen. "Obviously I can't say with any certainty if it is indeed blood but what I can say is that we can't rule it out." She turned to Tina. "Can you please run an image search and find out if Levi downloaded the image from somewhere else?"

"Yeah, I'm on it."

"Great, thank you."

"Why would he fake the self-harm but still commit suicide? That doesn't make sense to me." Milligan shook his head.

"Me either." For once she appreciated Milligan's propensity for being their very own doubting Thomas.

"Clearly, he was dubious of what was going on, at least at the start," Jamison said.

"He definitely was." Tina looked up from the keyboard. "That was what I wanted to say I found on his computer. There were emails to Eric Beauchamp, Sam Peterson, and Jason Davenport where he tells them he is really scared, I'm guessing about the game. The weird part is that he sent the messages to them after they had already committed suicide."

"What?" Milligan's voice rose high in question. "That's insane."

"Shit! No, it's not." Jess held her hand up. "Gracemount Academy didn't tell the students about the suicides, so Levi wouldn't have known. Sorry, I was going to send a memo to tell you all about our conversation with the principal."

Chan pulled out his phone and pointed it at her. "Don't mind me. I just want to document this occasion, the day Jess Bishop forgot to update us on something. It took ten years but I knew it would happen."

"Ha ha, very funny. Sorry, it just slipped my mind." A rush of panic flooded her. She tried to smile but the muscles would not comply. Chan was right. It was not like her to forget anything. She sent several updates a day with even the most mundane development, just so she could be sure they were all on the same page.

"Okay, that makes so much more sense." Tina clicked on another box and opened another page. "I thought he had gone crazy or had some sort of existential crisis and was pretending his friends weren't really dead to cope. Their emails make so much more sense now in light of that. This is the first one he sent to Eric Beauchamp after he died."

Hey Eric, where are you? I'm worried. I'm really scared and I need to talk about it. I'm really freaking out over here. I don't know what to do. I'm scared. Please call me, even if it is to say you don't want to talk. I just need to know you're okay.

"What was he scared about?" Milligan asked. "Is he talking about the suicide game? Did he ever say?"

Tina shook her head. "He never specifically mentions the game but he talks about being scared a lot. He sent more or less the same email to Sam and Jason too after they died."

"What about Ryan?" Jamison asked. "He was the first one to die and we know from Jeanie he was one of Levi's best friends."

"Um... no. I don't think so. I don't think I found any emails to Ryan. But he did mention him in an email to someone, I think. Let me see if I can find it." The keys clicked as Tina typed. "Where are you? Nope, not there." She closed the folder on her computer and then opened another. "Sorry, I don't know where I put it."

"That's okay. You can find it later. It's probably not relevant anyway," Scott said.

Jess's eyes widened in surprise. She turned to look at him. He had been with the team less than five minutes and he was already trying to call the shots. She was about to say something when Tina said, "Oh, there you are. Sometimes my organizational systems are a bit too complicated for me. It's like when you hide something away in a really great place and then you promptly forget about it. Never mind, here it is." She clicked on a tab and another email appeared.

Hey Jason, I'm really scared. I want someone to talk to. I wish you would write me back. I'm really worried. I can't sleep or eat. I just want to run away from everything. I can't do this anymore. I just want it to stop. I saw Ryan's mom yesterday. I just froze. I couldn't move or talk. It was like someone pushed pause. I was stuck. Luckily, she didn't see me. Please write back and let me know you're okay. Please. I'm begging you, man. I can't do this anymore. I just want this to all be over. Is there an over? I don't even know anymore.

"Shit, that looks a lot like a suicide note," Chan said.

Jess nodded. A now familiar pressure built behind her eyes but she ignored it and the ache in her chest. Desperation radiated from his words. His pain stabbed at her. She understood it, that inescapable darkness. It was a place she had been fleeing from with varying degrees of success since she was a child. Her mind traveled back to the first time she had felt the bleakness: his small body naked and bleeding on the floor of her basement, her father standing above him, the blades of the circular saw spinning so fast they blurred into a haze of motion.

"Jess," Jamison's deep voice called.

She blinked, realizing that she had been a million miles away. "Sorry, did you say something?"

Concern was written on his dark features. "I asked if you think the writing is consistent with a suicide note."

"Um…" She looked at the screen. She should know this. She did know this but her mind wouldn't work. It was a simple question. She had almost finished a PhD program in psychology. She had studied the lexical choices of suicide notes. She knew this… but she couldn't remember anything. "Yeah," she said because she needed everyone to stop looking at her, and they did—everyone except Jamison. His dark brow knitted together in concern.

Heat spread through her from the scrutiny.

"What does the part about Ryan's mom mean? Why was he scared of her?" Milligan asked. Again, the question was directed at her. All questions were now directed at her. The pressure of it was like a weight around her neck, slowly dragging her down. She was made to take orders not give them. She was a foot soldier not a general.

She took a deep breath to clear her thoughts and then silently reread the email, searching for an answer in the context clues. "I don't know," she admitted. "We need to speak to her. We need to find out what he meant by that. Jamison and I will do that.

Chan and Milligan, I need you to speak to the parents of the other boys. They're all out of state so you're going to need to pack up. Tina, can you please get the flights organized?" She paused for a second, trying to remember what else she needed to get done. Jeanie usually took care of everything behind the scenes, all the tedious administration and bureaucracy so they could focus on catching killers.

Tina gave her a gentle smile. "I'm on it."

"We'll help Tina with the traffic analysis," Scott said.

Jess gave him a hard stare. She had to bite the side of her mouth to keep from snapping at his presumptuousness. She took another deep breath and reminded herself that she didn't need to like her co-workers, they just needed to work together to find the person responsible for the suicide game.

CHAPTER FOURTEEN

Jess turned down the car radio and looked over at Jamison. She had spent the best part of twenty minutes thinking about what she wanted to say, how to phrase it so she didn't sound like someone who thought the Soviets were sending her messages through a little man in a transistor radio. "Lynette Hastings really doesn't want to speak to us. She couldn't put down the phone fast enough. Are you sensing a theme?"

"Does anyone ever really want to speak to us? We're federal agents."

"True." Her shoulders slouched as she turned back to look out the window at the evergreen trees that lined Skyline Drive. She wished she could go back to the way things used to be with them before he had gone undercover, before he had married someone else... before she had shot him. Because that was a time she could tell him anything, but the reality was she wouldn't have told him about what happened this morning. Maybe some things were just too upsetting to say aloud.

"What do you think Levi meant when he said he was upset about seeing Mrs. Hastings?" Jamison asked.

"I don't know." She couldn't think properly. She tried to clear her mind and focus on the case but all she could think about were the inconsistencies and coincidences that marred it. It all felt staged, which was crazy.

"What are you thinking about?"

"What?"

"I've known you a long time, Jessie. What's going on?"

Before she could answer, her phone vibrated in her pocket. It was Tina. She slid her finger along the screen to answer. "Hey. You're on speaker. We're about an hour away from Lynette Hastings' work."

"You might want to make a detour."

"Why?" Jamison asked.

"I think we found the curator. He made a mistake. He accidently logged on via an unsecure server and we've traced the IP address to a hunting lodge in West Virginia. Property records show it was purchased two years ago by Jim Iverson."

Jess's pulse spiked. "The psychologist at Gracemount Academy?"

"Yeah, that's him."

Her gut clenched in a painful spasm. It made sense: the bad advice he gave the school, covering up the suicides.

"Chan and Milligan are at Dulles about to get on a flight to San Francisco. Should I tell them to meet you at the hunting lodge?"

Jess thought for a second. "No, they're already on their way. I think we have enough to get a warrant for Iverson's house but we've had shit luck with judges on this case so I won't count our chickens. Call the field office and get SWAT to meet us. Hopefully Mr. Iverson will play nice, but if not, I want backup to take him in."

"Okay. I'm on it."

"Good job tracing it, Tina. That's really great work."

"Actually, it wasn't me who spotted it. It was Scott."

Jess rolled her eyes. "Of course it was."

CHAPTER FIFTEEN

The drive through the Blue Ridge Mountains belonged in a scene in a snow globe. Everything was covered in white. The branches of the eastern hemlocks bowed under the weight of the snow. Several had already snapped but the thick blanket made it look bright even though the sky was dark.

They had chains for their tires ready to go but luckily the main roads had been plowed and gritted that morning; a new snow was falling and the roads would soon need to be plowed again.

"When this guy gets away from it all, he really gets away. This is the back of beyond," Jamison said.

"Yeah, he doesn't want people bothering him, that's for sure," she agreed. "The nearest supermarket is forty miles away. State police are meeting us there to serve the warrant."

Jim Iverson's log cabin was nestled against the side of the mountain. Fortunately, he had recently cleared the road up, or they might not have been able to make it. They pulled over at the bottom of the hill and waited for the state police to arrive. Once upon a time she would have chosen to take the lead on everything, but now she appreciated just how quickly everything could turn to shit, and she'd rather not be in the direct line of fire if she didn't need to be.

"I really hope this will be painless."

She didn't realize she'd said anything until Jamison let out a heavy sigh. "Yeah, me too. We haven't had the best of luck with our last cases, have we?"

Her breath caught in her throat. She turned to look at him. They didn't talk about what had happened. After months of avoiding him, she had tried to broach the subject, to apologize for what she'd done, and to say she was sorry for the part she had played in his wife's death, but he had shut her down hard. He didn't want to talk to her about anything other than the case at hand. She carried the apology ready to go, just in case, but looking at him now she realized she could never really make amends. Maybe that was part of her punishment.

There was nothing more to say so they sat in silence until the headlights of a police cruiser pulled up behind them.

She got out to greet them and flinched when a cold gust of air caught her cheeks.

Both of the officers looked like they were nearing retirement. The heavier one took off his glove to shake her hand. "Evening, folks. You're a long way from home."

"Yeah it was a bit of a trek. Thanks for meeting us. I'm Special Agent Jess Bishop and this is Special Agent Jamison Briggs."

"I'm First Lieutenant Martin Wilson and this is Sergeant Paul Lewis. Just call me Martin. And you can call him Paul." He pointed to his partner, who was pulling on the hood of his parka.

"Thanks, Martin." Jamison reached across Jess to shake his hand. "Do you have the warrant?"

Martin patted the breast pocket of his thick winter coat. "Right here. But something tells me he won't be asking to see it."

Jess crossed her arms tight against her middle to try to conserve body heat. "What makes you say that?"

Martin pointed to the log cabin. "The fire's not on. It's too cold for him to be out here in this weather without the fire on."

Jess's shoulders slouched when she looked up at the chimney. They had driven for five hours across state lines and Iverson wasn't even there.

As if he could read her mind, Jamison said, "We still have a search warrant for his house. It's worth the trip for that."

She nodded. "Yeah, true."

She watched as the three men made their way up the hill to the cabin. She glanced down at the fresh layer of snow. In the pristine white was a set of fresh tracks. She squinted as she noted the overlay of wheel impressions. Someone, probably Iverson, had recently driven up the hill and back down again. She took out her phone and snapped a picture of the tracks because soon they would fill with fresh snow.

"The lights are on." Jamison pointed at the window. "And it sounds like a TV or radio. Maybe he just went into town for a while and he'll be back soon."

Jess walked up the steps to the covered porch and peered in the window at the kitchen. One of the shaker-style doors had been left open and there were dirty dishes stacked in the sink.

"He must have left in a hurry," Paul said. "Do you want to search the cabin before he gets back?"

"If he comes back," Jess said. Anyone who could orchestrate such elaborate mind control and evade detection for this long was not stupid. Iverson probably realized he'd messed up for logging on from an unsecure server and took off. If he was smart, he would have a contingency plan worked out for this eventuality. They wouldn't see him here again.

She took in a sharp breath when her palm connected with the icy handle. The metal was so cold it felt like it was burning her hand. To her surprise, the handle turned. "It's not locked," she said as she pushed the door open. "There's something blocking it." She held her breath as she gave a push.

"Jessie, look down."

She glanced down at the knotty pine floorboards. A reddish-brown liquid welled between the deep grooves. "Oh shit. That's blood."

CHAPTER SIXTEEN

With one hard push, Jamison opened the door.

For a moment, everyone was too stunned to speak. Jess stared down at the blood-soaked rag rug and the lifeless body of Jim Iverson, his jaw slack and his tongue protruding. The left side of his face was unrecognizable: the exposed blood and muscle had been pulverized by a gunshot to the head.

"Oh my God. Is that his brain?" one of the police officers asked, but Jess didn't answer because she was too busy examining the Beretta in Iverson's hand. His hand was wrapped around the grip, his index finger pressed against the magazine release, not on the trigger.

The hairs on the back of her neck stood taut. It was possible for muscles to freeze into spontaneous rigor mortis at the time of death. If that was the case, Iverson's finger would be on the trigger. If not, the gun would have fallen. And the shot was to the left side of his face. Only ten percent of the population was left-handed. She would have to check if he was, but it seemed far more likely that a right-handed assailant was facing him and shot him on the left side of his head. Anxious heat crept down her spine.

The suicide had been staged.

Everything from the position of the body to the placement of the gun felt off. She needed a medical examiner to officially confirm it, but she was certain. It just didn't feel right. She was about to say something when Martin said, "Here's the suicide note. He says everything is explained on his laptop." He held up a sheet of lined paper.

Jess's eyes narrowed on the paper. "Where did you find that?" she demanded. Her pulse spiked as unease spread through her. She tried to beat back the now familiar flood of paranoia but there was no holding it back. She was naturally suspicious of everyone and everything, but it was amplified now, her reactions more acute. It had to be because Jeanie was involved. She would not entertain the possibility that it was anything else.

"It was right here." Martin pointed at the leather couch.

"You didn't think to put on gloves? Now it has your prints all over it. Convenient."

"Jessie." Jamison's dark brow raised in question.

Martin's nostrils flared. "What does that mean?" he demanded.

Jess shook her head, surprised at her own rudeness. Admittedly, she wasn't the best with interpersonal skills, but it wasn't like her to be rude. And it really wasn't like her to go about implying that fellow law enforcement officers were shady. "I'm sorry."

Martin's back remained rod-stiff, his face contorted in rage. "What exactly did you mean by that?"

Before she could answer, Jamison spoke, his voice low. "This is her first case back. We lost an agent on the last case, her best friend."

Jess's cheeks burned hot with mortification. Anger roiled in her stomach. He had no right to say anything or make excuses for her.

"I'm sorry," Martin said. His face changed, the anger replaced with compassion. "I understand. Years ago, I lost my partner in a traffic stop gone wrong. I wasn't the same for a long time after that."

Jess didn't know what to say so she looked away. She would rather he think she was rude and unprofessional than feel sorry for her. She knew what to do with the antipathy that came her direction, but compassion was something else entirely.

"We need to get crime scene investigators in and get the body to the morgue." Jamison took over, organizing and giving orders, which gave Jess the opportunity to wander around the cabin and piece together what had been happening just before Jim Iverson died. She refused to think he had committed suicide but she conceded that Martin and Paul had nothing to do with it. Implying that they had was unprofessional. But something was off: she could not shake the feeling that something bigger was at play. There were too many coincidences, and Jim Iverson's death too convenient, but she couldn't say it out loud, not in those words, unless she wanted people to think she had gone insane.

She glanced around the room. The embers of the fire still glowed red; it had only recently been put out. There was a used towel on the bathroom floor and the bed hadn't been made. She took in every aspect of the cabin, taking pictures and making mental notes. Slowly her anger at Jamison dissipated. He had diffused a situation she had created. She couldn't blame him for the way he had chosen to do it.

"Jessie," Jamison called from behind her. "They're here to take the body."

She spun around to face him. "That was quick."

"Not really. It's been over an hour."

She blinked. It had only felt like a few minutes. She had been so lost in her thoughts. "Did you get photos of his body? Of his hands?" The crime scene investigators would take pictures but she wanted her own.

"Of course. I've met you."

"Thanks."

They walked back into the main room. A technician stood bent over a white body bag. He zipped it and then stood up. Jess watched as they carried Iverson's body to the stretcher and then down the hill.

Martin turned to them once the body was loaded. "Are you coming?"

She needed five minutes alone in the house but there was no way to ask for it without raising suspicion. "I just need a few minutes to… breathe… It's hard, you know… seeing that… after, you know…" She let her voice trail off. She dabbed at her eyes with the back of her hand as she pretended to be on the verge of tears. It was a stab in the heart to realize she wasn't above using Lindsay as an excuse. If she were a better person, she would have come up with another excuse, but somewhere between shooting Jamison and getting Lindsay killed, she had given up on being a good person. Now she settled for being a good agent.

The sheriff reached out and patted her shoulder. "That's all right, darlin', you take your time. We'll just finish up here. You take all the time you need."

She gave him a faint smile and then looked away. She waited until Iverson's body was loaded up and taken away. Slowly the flurry of activity died down until it was just her and Jamison standing on the front porch. When she was sure everyone had left, she snapped on a pair of gloves and went back inside the lodge.

Jamison was two steps behind her. "What are you doing?"

She stood at the edge of the room and examined the bloodstains that had soaked into the rag rug. "He chose to come almost to his front door to commit suicide."

"You're not buying that."

"No. Not at all. Look around. We are surrounded by woods. I could see him going outside to be with nature to do it. I could see him sitting in a chair or lying in his bed. I could see him doing it in the bathtub to make clean-up easier for whoever had the misfortune of finding him. We've seen all those scenarios. We've never seen someone lay out evidence, go to the front door, and then blow their brains out. Never."

Jamison rubbed his jaw with his knuckles as he thought. "There's a first for everything, Jessie. We've seen a lot of crazy stuff. This doesn't begin to touch the sides."

She thought he would say that. That was his job, to challenge her, make her think. That's why they were a good team. "What about this?" She pointed to a small splotch on the door frame. That's blood and it's fresh. It could be transfer that happened when the killer staged the crime scene. You saw the way he was holding the gun. His finger wasn't on the trigger."

He gave it a long, hard look. "You can't say that's blood without testing it."

She opened her bag, took out a swab, and rubbed it against the mark before she stuck it in an evidence bag.

"What are you doing? If you wanted that swabbed, you could have asked one of the technicians."

"It's not my fault they missed it." She put the evidence bag back in her case.

"What's going on with you, Jessie? Is this about Lindsay? What is it?"

Her back stiffened at the mention of her best friend's name. They both had things they didn't want to talk about, and Lindsay was on that list. "I'm just covering all my bases."

He gave her a look that told her he wasn't convinced but he didn't press the issue any further.

"I need to check one more thing before we go and I need your help."

He rolled his eyes in exasperation. "What do you need?"

"I took a picture of the tread marks on the drive before everyone got here."

"Of course you did."

"It had just snowed so they were fresh tracks. I couldn't not take a picture of them, could I? I want to check if they're a match to Iverson's car, but the garage is locked. I could pick it myself but you're a lot faster, and I'm pretty sure you want to get home before dawn."

"You can't play me, Jessie. I've known you too long. We both know you know your way around a lock better than anyone."

"Well, in that case, it's only right you use the skills you acquired in your misspent youth. Consider it penance."

His full lips hitched into a lazy smile. "Fine, but not because you tried to play me, because I want to get to sleep tonight."

Jess felt herself smile, a genuine smile. For a flash of a second it felt like old times, the way they used to be. She looked away and reminded herself it could never really be the way it was. "Come on. Let's get this done."

She walked out to the porch and then down the steps. She had to lift her knees high in awkward, pronounced movements to wade through the fresh snow on the footpath that led to the garage. Iverson must have cleared the drive recently and piled the snow high on the sides.

Jamison followed a few steps behind her. An automatic light turned on when they reached the garage. She stood to the side to give Jamison room to work.

He knelt down in the snow. A second later, he looked up and smiled. "You didn't need to sweet-talk me—it's not even locked." The wheels of the door screeched against the metal tracks as the door opened.

Inside there was a black Bronco parked beside a workbench full of woodworking tools and a piece of oak.

She knelt down to examine the tires. Her pulse crept higher as she examined the tread. "The tracks aren't from this car." She took out her phone to show him the pictures she'd taken. "Look: the car that left these tracks has a feathered tread. Now look at these. They're like interlocking bricks."

Jamison looked from the phone to the car and then back again. "Dang it, Jessie."

"So, you see it?"

"That our case just got a hell of a lot more complicated? Yeah, I see it."

CHAPTER SEVENTEEN

Jess glanced out her office window. Frozen rain pelted against the glass. She picked up her phone to look at the pictures she'd taken at Jim Iverson's cabin. A message flashed up to alert her she had two missed calls from Jeanie. She sighed. It was too early to return the call but she didn't know what to tell her anyway. More than anything she didn't want to let her down. With every case came a pressure to do what was right by the victims and their families, but she felt it more acutely now. The memory of Jeanie crying flashed in her mind. She closed her eyes and pushed the thought away. She couldn't think about that now; she had to focus on the case.

She opened up the picture of the tread marks she'd found. She squinted as she examined the pattern. Snow and dim lighting made the impressions more difficult to see but they were definitely there, and the more she looked at them, the less she could deny they looked like the winter tires of a Ford SUV, the same as the cars her team used. And the same car that many agents within the bureau drove.

It wasn't definitive proof of anything, but it did raise more uncomfortable questions. She rubbed her sore eyes and let out a pathetic noise that sounded like a whimper. Was she actually contemplating the possibility the real curator was an FBI agent? Oh God, she was insane, or quickly headed that direction. She had been down this rabbit hole of suspecting her colleague and it had ended with Jamison bleeding out on a serial killer's floor.

She wouldn't let her paranoia destroy her again. "Lots of people drive SUVs. This is America for God's sake," she said aloud to her empty office.

She was startled when someone knocked on her door. "Come in."

Jamison opened the door. He frowned when he saw her hunched over her desk. "Have you been crying?" Concern laced his deep voice.

"No, I just didn't sleep last night."

In an instant the concern was gone, replaced by annoyance. The muscles along his jaw twitched as he ground his teeth together. He thought she meant she had gone out to screw a stranger. She didn't blame him for the assumption. That was who she was, the woman who quieted the voices in her head with random men. She couldn't even remember the last time she knew the name of the person she was having sex with. But that's not what she'd done last night. She had asked her dog-sitter to keep Stan all night so she could come into the office and work, but she would rather Jamison think she was out. Best that neither of them forget who she really was.

"Director Taylor wants to see us."

"Why?"

He shrugged. His casual demeanor had changed, replaced with an impenetrable wall of ice.

She smoothed her hair back into a ponytail and put on some of the deodorant she kept in her top drawer. She hoped her breath didn't smell as bad as her mouth tasted because she'd run out of toothpaste, so there was nothing she could do about it now.

As she stood up she remembered her last interaction with the director. "I need a coffee."

"You don't have time."

When they got to the director's office, Smart and Scott were already seated. Tina was standing near Taylor's desk, looking at the pictures that lined the wall.

"Great, I'm glad you're all here. Please sit down. Chan and Milligan won't be joining us because they're on a flight back from San Francisco." Taylor paused for a moment to give everyone the opportunity to take a seat. "First, let me say thank you to Agent Bishop for leading the team."

The muscles along Jess's spine tightened. She'd heard this speech before when someone was being removed from an investigation. It was always important to thank someone before you fired them, as if being polite would soften the blow. She clenched her hands until her palm screamed out, using the pain to focus. She wouldn't show she was upset.

"Also, thank you to Agent Scott for working throughout the night, accessing Jim Iverson's files. They've made for some interesting if uncomfortable viewing."

Jess glanced over at Scott. He was typing on a laptop. With a click, the screen filled with a picture of Ryan Hastings, Eric Beauchamp, Sam Peterson, Jason Davenport, and Levi Smith. It was a candid shot taken in a cabin of some description. There were metal dormitory-style bunk beds. She didn't recognize the room. It wasn't Iverson's cabin or Levi's dormitory at Gracemount. Based on the angle, the photo was taken from above, possibly ceiling height.

"That looks like it was taken with a hidden camera," Jamison said. "Look at the angle and the way they're all just going about their business, getting dressed. They don't know they're being photographed."

"Filmed actually," Scott said. "It appears Iverson put cameras in the boys' dormitory so he could film them."

Jess was about to tell them that it was not Levi's dorm when Scott said, "In addition to the videos, we recovered over fifty thousand pornographic images from his computer, mostly featuring pubescent boys. It's clear he was a pedophile."

"Hebephile," Jess corrected.

"What?" Scott looked over at her, clearly unimpressed with the interruption.

"You said all the images were of pubescent boys; that would make Iverson a hebephile. Pedophiles are attracted to prepubescents. The Last Supper victims were all mid-to-late teens. If you're suggesting Iverson was sexually attracted to them, that would make him a hebephile, again not a pedophile."

Scott's nostrils flared. "Whatever. He was into child porn. You can call it what you want, he was into kids."

"I'm not being pedantic. If you're suggesting there is a sexual motivation for the suicide game, we have to be very clear about the parameters of Iverson's proclivities. Also, if the porn only featured boys, that means he is a preferential offender, and we shouldn't have seen any female victims. But there were three."

"Well, we did, so maybe he didn't get the memo about how to be a textbook sex offender." Scott smiled at his own joke.

"Sex offender? He has no convictions or charges. But even if he was, there is no evidence of any sexual component to the suicide game at all. The curator never once asked for a sexual picture or engaged in sexually explicit chat. He had complete control of these kids. If he'd wanted, he could have gotten them to send pictures or videos. It doesn't make any sense to think there is a sexual component to this."

"Well, I'm sorry this case doesn't conform to your preconceived ideas."

Jess shook her head. She was the first person to look for a sex offender angle, but it felt contrived. She may very well be going crazy but she couldn't shake the feeling that Jim Iverson had been scapegoated by the real curator, and whoever he was didn't do a great job of laying the ground work. This just wasn't well-thought-through. "Go to Finder and show me the dates he downloaded the porn."

"What? Why?"

"If you can't find it, Tina can," Jess challenged when he didn't reach for the mouse, hoping he would find the threat emasculating enough to acquiesce and do what she asked. He seemed the type who would get bent out of shape to be showed up by a woman.

"No. I got it." The keys clicked as Scott banged on the keyboard and brought up the list of dates.

Her pulse spiked when she saw the dates on the screen. A surge of adrenaline mixed with vindication shot through her. Every image had been downloaded on the same day in December. She wasn't crazy, at least not about this. Jim Iverson had been set up—but by who? "Did you find anything illegal downloaded before December third?"

"No," Scott admitted. His normal confidence had slipped along with his grin.

"So, you're proposing that last month Jim Iverson developed deviant sexual attractions that caused him to set up a national suicide game five months before that. Talk me through your thought processes."

"There might be more pornography I haven't found yet," Scott said.

"Or it might be a new computer?" Smart offered. "He bought the computer and then he transferred over his stash."

Jess nodded. That was the first thing from the pair that made sense.

"Tina, can you check his debit and credit cards and see if he recently purchased a new laptop?"

"Yeah, I'm on it."

Scott held up his hand. "It's academic at this point. He admitted it all in a suicide note."

"About the suicide note. It doesn't read right." Jess had read and reread the note over and over, trying to make sense of it, but she couldn't.

"Read right?" Scott held up his hands in exasperation. "What does that even mean?"

"Can you bring up the note, please?" Director Taylor asked. A photo of the note filled the screen.

I'm sorry for what I have done. I didn't mean for things to get out of hand. I didn't think anyone would really take part in the game. Once it started, I didn't feel like I could stop. I apologize to the families. I hope they can find peace.

"That's not a suicide note. It's barely a note. Real suicide notes aren't explanations. They focus on hopelessness. Death is their only option to end the pain. Where is the desperation here? There is no emotion to speak of. That's not typical. Also, where are the mundane practical instructions for the people left behind? There is no mention of a will. Genuine suicide notes tend to say things like, 'Tell mom I love her,' and, 'Don't forget to clean out the lint trap in the dryer.' People want to make sure things are going to be okay after they die so they include instructions."

"Well, this one didn't, and yet he shot himself in the head, so there you go," Scott shot back.

"Has it been tested for prints?" Jamison asked, trying to diffuse the tension.

No one immediately answered.

"Well, has it?" Taylor asked.

Scott pursed his lips together. "No, sir, I don't believe it has."

"It needs to be tested," Jamison said.

Director Taylor nodded. "Yes, it should have been. Get that done and we'll add it to the report so we can close the case and put it behind us."

Jess's eyes widened. "Closed? We're not even certain Jim Iverson committed suicide. Why did he start the game? How did he pick his victims? What made the boys at Gracemount so susceptible to suicide? There are too many questions."

Taylor frowned. "Perhaps we'll never know. I suppose that's the nature of the beast."

"That's not enough for Jeanie. She deserves answers." Jess bit into the side of her mouth until she tasted the metallic zing of blood. There was so much more she wanted to say but she wouldn't challenge Taylor in front of everyone because she wasn't ready to add insubordination to her extensive list of character flaws.

"Sadly, it's going to have to be enough because Iverson took all his secrets with him," Taylor said.

He kept talking, offering platitudes, but his words were lost on her. She couldn't stop thinking of Jeanie's red-rimmed eyes, hearing her cry. Every time she heard a victim cry, she thought of her father, all the people he made cry, the lives he ruined. In an instant, she was transported back.

"Agent Bishop."

She was startled. Her head snapped up to find everyone in the room staring at her. "Sorry, what did you say?"

"I was just saying that I spoke to Jeanie this morning and she isn't yet ready to return to work. Agent Bishop, you've done such an excellent job leading this investigation. We've both agreed that we'd like you to stay on as team leader until Jeanie is ready to come back."

"What?" Her mind froze, like a gearbox stuck in neutral. She looked from Taylor to Scott. She wanted to bring up the staging of Iverson's body, the SUV tracks, and the transfer blood on the door, but Scott would just shoot her down and Taylor would nod his head like a placid puppy because he wanted this case behind him. The investigation was closed and nothing she would say could change their minds. "I mean, thank you, but-I-uh-I can't. I mean I can't right now. This case has brought up—" she closed her eyes so she could get out the rest of the words "—too many memories. I'd like to take the time Dr. Cameron suggested."

Jamison's stare was heavy on her. They both knew she would rather pour acid in her eyes than be off work.

CHAPTER EIGHTEEN

"Jessie, wait up."

Jess kept walking, pretending she couldn't hear Jamison. She didn't want to add insult to injury by lying to him. But she couldn't tell him the truth because the truth was she was probably batshit crazy and he didn't deserve to be sucked into it. She'd hurt him before; she wouldn't do it again.

"Jessie." In two steps, he caught up with her. His hand wrapped around hers, stopping her. An electric burst of pain shot through her hand when his calloused fingers brushed against the tender flesh of her scarred palm but she didn't let on it hurt. "What's going on?"

She didn't turn around. "I just need two weeks."

"For what?"

She squeezed her lids together. "I've never taken my vacation time. I just need some time off."

"Can you at least look at me when you lie to me?"

She spun on her heel to face him. She had to crane her neck to look him in the eye. His hand was still on hers. Part of her didn't want him to pull away—she'd always hated to be touched but it felt good to have someone who at least pretended to care. She'd felt so alone since Lindsay died. "I just need some time. Now can you please leave me alone?"

"Fine." He dropped her hand and walked away.

CHAPTER NINETEEN

Jess waited until everyone from her team had left the building so no one would see her head for the lab in the basement. She didn't personally know anyone there. It was the place she sent stuff, and results magically appeared on her computer a few days later.

She glanced around, taking in everything, searching for her target, eventually focusing in on a twenty-something bent over a microscope. His tight curly hair was tied back in a low ponytail.

"Hey," she said when she got closer.

He was startled when she approached. "Sorry. You scared me." When he spoke, he didn't look at her; instead, he fixed on a spot in the distance. Toothpaste was crusted in the corner of his mouth.

"No, I'm sorry, I didn't mean to startle you. I'm Jess Bishop. My office is literally just above here." She pointed upward at the paneled ceiling. Her office was actually on the other side of the building but she was trying to build a rapport, remind him they were on the same team.

"Okay."

She waited for him to introduce himself but he didn't; luckily his ID badge was clipped on the pocket of his lab coat: Jason Neilson.

Jess pulled out the swab she'd taken from Jim Iverson's door frame.

"Jason, I have a swab I need tested. I need blood type and DNA." She didn't ask him to do a phenolphthalein test to make sure it was blood because she knew it was, and that it belonged to Jim Iverson, and that the killer had transferred it when he repositioned the body.

Jason walked to the front of the lab, opened a metal file cabinet, and pulled out a sheet of paper. He attached it to a clipboard and handed it to her. "Fill this out."

Jess didn't bother looking down at the work order because she wasn't going to fill it out. This needed to be off the record. "This isn't an official investigation."

Jason scowled, clearly uncomfortable with the idea.

Jess rubbed the knotted scar of her palm as she considered the best way to come at it. She hadn't figured out how she was going to play this before she came to the lab because she needed to know who she was dealing with. She wasn't above flirting or coercion to get the job done but she needed to know which would work, and she wasn't getting a clear read off this guy so she went in blind with a generic spiel and hoped for the best. "It's for my neighbor. She's going through a bad divorce. We think her husband broke into her apartment and—" usually she thought quicker on her feet but she was too tired to lie with the required fluency "—killed her fish," she offered lamely. It sounded even more pathetic out loud than when she was having a breakdown in her apartment.

One of his brows rose in question. "What kind?"

"Of fish?"

"Yeah, were they saltwater or fresh?"

"Fresh. They were Bubble Eye goldfish."

"Ah *Carassius auratus auratus*. Beautiful fish also known as Prussian carp. They originated from a wild species in Siberia but were developed into the modern species we know in China in the fifteen hundreds."

"Cool." Jess nodded, smiling to herself that she had managed to get him on side already.

"Their only downfall is those air-filled sacks around their eyes can prove too tempting, and other fish end up eating them."

"Exactly. That's what happened to mine—I mean my neighbor's."

He glanced down at the evidence bag. "That's awful that he killed her fish."

"Yeah, he's awful. Anyway, I just want to make sure it's him that broke in. If it is, I'll tell her to press charges."

He took the bag from her. "You really should. I'll run this after work and get you the results. What kind of monster would kill an innocent creature?" His eyes turned down in genuine sadness.

"Thank you." Jess smiled, wishing she inhabited a world where the murder of a fish was the worst thing she saw in a day. "While I'm here, can you check on something for me?"

Jason bit into his bottom lip. "I'm really not supposed to do anything without the correct paperwork. I could get in a lot of trouble."

"It's okay," she assured him. "I've filled everything out. I'm just waiting on the results."

The furrow between his eyes flattened. "Oh okay. I can do that. What are you waiting on?"

"I put in some fingernail scrapings for Levi Smith and I haven't gotten anything back." She pulled out her phone to give him the ID number.

"Let me check."

Jess followed him to the computer terminal and waited as he typed in the relevant information. "Are you sure that's the right case number?"

Jess checked it again, making sure he entered it into the computer correctly.

"Nope, it's not here. Nothing was logged in that investigation."

"Can you check by the victim's name or date of birth?"

"Yeah, let me check." Jason kept typing. "Hmm."

"Hmm what?" Jess asked.

"There's nothing here."

"Are you sure."

He nodded. "Here, look for yourself. That's your name and number." He pointed to the screen. "According to this, you haven't submitted anything to the lab for testing since before Christmas."

Jess's heart stopped with a painful thud and then started again with frantic beats, trying to make up for the lost time. Her head spun with questions, internal voices coming at her from every direction.

She wasn't crazy. Someone was intentionally trying to thwart her investigation from inside the FBI.

CHAPTER TWENTY

Jess jammed her finger into the buzzer on the intercom. When he answered, she realized she'd never been to his apartment. She had spent the entire drive over looking in her rear-view mirror to see if she was being followed. No matter how many times she told herself to stop, she couldn't.

She turned around one last time to make sure no one had followed her before she pushed the door open.

When Chan opened the door, the smell of his aftershave wafted into the hall, tickling her throat. Like always he was perfectly presented, not a hair out of place.

"Hey." She glanced around his apartment. It was exactly how she expected: white walls, black leather couches, and a flat-screen TV that took up a quarter of the wall. Everything was pristine, not a single thing out of place. It was so clean it didn't actually look like anyone lived there. "Do you have it?"

"No small talk? No how was the flight?"

"Do you want to talk about your flight?"

He shrugged. "Not really but it's nice to be asked. Do you want a drink?"

"No thanks. I just want the file. Are you going out?" She pointed to his leather jacket.

"Yeah, I have a date."

"Well, in that case, my condolences to the woman involved."

Chan's face split into a broad smile. "You're just bitter because it's not you. The offer's still on the table."

"No, I'm good. Thanks." They both knew that asking her out was just part of his shtick. He had no actual desire to sleep with her, he just hit on her because that was what he did with all women. She doubted he would know what to do with himself if she actually green-lighted him, but she was never going to find out.

"Suit yourself. Sure I can't get you a drink? You seem like you're wound even tighter than usual."

"No, thanks. Just the file, please."

Chan shook his head. "Geez, you're like a broken record. Give me a second. It's in my briefcase. Why did you want a hard copy? Why couldn't I just email it to you?"

Jess took a deep breath, trying to decide how much to tell him. She trusted Chan, as much as she trusted anyone, which was not a whole hell of a lot. He would never go out of his way to screw her over but he'd proven time and time again he wasn't reliable either. He was too selfish to consider anything past his own needs. "Because the case is closed. Iverson is dead and that's all Taylor needs to shut down the investigation. You're back on the strangler case."

"What about you?" he asked over his shoulder as he bent down to look for the papers.

"I'm going to finish my vacation time. Jamison's in charge until I come back."

Chan groaned. "Jamison, seriously? I hate that guy."

Jess didn't need to tell him that the feeling was mutual. There had never been any love lost between them. They were just fundamentally different people. Civility was the most they could hope for.

"Here you go." He handed her a file. "It's on the fourth page, I think."

Jess flipped to the fourth page. An electric current shot up the length of her spine. "Oh, shit. You're right. This is the same picture." Just to be sure she took out the file on the Last Supper game and opened it to the section with the contents of Levi Smith's computer. After the meeting with Taylor, Scott had come to her office to collect all the copies so they could be destroyed, but she'd kept one.

She laid the pictures side by side on the coffee table so she could examine them and make sure she wasn't seeing something that wasn't there. The pictures were black and white, which made it more difficult to assess skin tone, but there was no denying the photos were identical. Levi had sent the autopsy photos of another Last Supper player to the curator as proof he had carved a cross into his arm. "Whose autopsy is this?"

"That one is Rick Rivas, seventeen, from Oakland. Died October thirtieth."

"How did Levi get access to his autopsy photos?"

"I have no idea. There's no connection between the two boys that I can see, no mutual friends. They've never lived in the same time zone, let alone the same city. There is no way Levi should have had access to this picture."

"And it's not posted anywhere online," Jess thought out loud. "Which means he didn't download it. So where did it come from?"

"He could have uploaded it from somewhere."

"Or someone uploaded it for him. The same someone who killed him."

"You don't think he committed suicide?"

She didn't know what she thought anymore or who she should tell. She sounded crazy, but she wasn't. There were too many coincidences to be explained away. "He had no self-harming scars but he did have fresh defensive wounds on his hands and blood under his fingernails. He fought with someone right before he died. I think that person is the real curator."

CHAPTER TWENTY-ONE

Jess leaned forward and wiped the condensation off the inside of the windshield. She turned the key in the ignition to turn the heater back on. It was a miserable, cold day. Slushy rain had begun to fall, melting the snow drifts. She'd been sitting in her car for over an hour, waiting for Lynette Hastings to come out of work. She picked a spot facing the entrance of the hospital so she wouldn't miss her. So far all she'd seen were nurses and patients coming out to smoke.

Jess had called her four times but Lynette refused to talk. She tried going to her house but Lynette had pulled the curtains closed, turned off the lights, and pretended she wasn't home.

Jess looked up at the movement of the sliding doors opening. A blond woman came out wearing a black parka over surgical scrubs, her hair pulled back into a tight French braid. Jess glanced down at the photo on her phone and then back up at the woman. She looked older now, probably from the stress of losing a child, but it was Lynette Hastings.

"Lynette," Jess called as she got out of the car. She slammed the door and then ran through the hospital bay to the entrance.

The woman looked over at her, a flash of panic in her blue eyes. "What do you want?"

"I'm Special Agent Jessica Bishop. I just need to ask you a few questions." Jess held up her badge to be inspected.

"I don't have anything to say to you." She pulled her hood up and started walking.

Jess's eyes stung as frozen rain pelted her face. She used the back of her hand to mop off the drops but more fell as quickly as she wiped them away. "Aren't you going to ask me what I want to talk to you about?"

"Please just leave me alone."

Jess broke into a jog to keep up with her. "I will when you tell me why Levi Smith was scared to see you."

Lynette spun around. "Please just leave me alone. I don't want to be seen with you. Just go."

"I'm afraid I can't do that. One of the last things a dead boy wrote is that he was upset to see you, so I need to know what you did."

Lynette spun around to face her. "Levi's dead?" Her face drained of color. "No."

Jess's eyes narrowed as she studied her reaction: the dilation of her eyes, the shock on her face all seemed genuine. "You didn't know he died?"

"No." Lynette shook her head. Unshed tears welled in her eyes. "How?"

"It appears he committed suicide."

"Oh God, no. Not Levi." A mascara-laced tear traced a path down the side of her face, settling in a groove of a laugh line.

"A few days ago."

"Have they had the funeral?"

"They're going to have a service in Utah."

Her lips trembled. "He was a good kid, so kind. He always looked out for my Ryan. He was my favorite of all Ryan's friends."

"Why do you think Levi was upset to see you?"

She shook her head emphatically. "He wasn't. That doesn't make sense. Levi couldn't have been scared of seeing me because I haven't even seen any of the boys from the school since the day Ryan left for Pine Ridge."

"Pine Ridge? What's that?"

Her eyes widened as she clamped her hand over her mouth.

"What's Pine Ridge?" Jess asked again.

"Please," Lynette begged. "I didn't say anything. I don't want to be seen with you. They can't know I've spoken to you. I have two other sons I need to support. I can't deal with this now. Just leave me alone."

She turned to walk away but Jess reached out and held onto her arm. Pain radiated through her palm and up her wrist into her arm as she forced her hand to clench together to keep Lynette from getting away. "Who are 'they'? Who don't you want to know that I've spoken to you? Did someone threaten you? Are you scared of someone? I can protect you."

"Please. Just leave me alone." With a final tug, she pulled away and ran to her car.

CHAPTER TWENTY-TWO

Jess wrapped her hands around the mug and took a sip of the coffee. It tasted burnt but it was hot and strong and that was all she needed. "Thank you." She smiled.

"Can I get you anything else?" The waitress picked up the empty plate and then took a rag out of her yellow apron and wiped down the ring left by the coffee mug.

"No, thanks. That was great. Just the check please."

Jess looked out at the banks of fresh snow. The small diner was the last stop before chain checks further up the highway, so she had decided to stop and think before she drove the rest of the way to Pine Ridge Lodge.

A simple internet search told her Pine Ridge was an environmental living camp just outside Shenandoah National Park. It originally opened thanks to a grant from the Gracemount Academy trust but now it was open to the public. It was mostly used by schools but corporate groups also brought their staff there for camping and team-building exercises.

Jess paid the check and went back to her car. She'd rented an SUV for the trip because her own car would not have made it in the snow, plus she felt more anonymous in a rental.

Fortunately, the drive to Pine Ridge wasn't too bad. Although the lodge was closed for the winter, park rangers had kept the roads clear for maintenance trucks to get in and out.

She parked at the entrance to the main building and did a cursory inspection, looking for CCTV cameras or any other signs of a security system. When she didn't find any, she silently prayed that meant there were no alarms at the camp because breaking in was one thing but setting off a blaring alarm was another, not that there was anyone around to hear it.

She took the duffel bag she'd packed from the passenger seat and threw it over her shoulder. She glanced behind her again to make sure no one had followed her, which was probably unnecessary as she hadn't seen a single car on the road since she'd left the diner.

A snow-covered path snaked its way down the steep embankment. Her boots sank into the powder. She took a few cautious steps before her foot slipped when she misjudged the edge of the cobbles. She tried to right herself but she couldn't. "Shit," she muttered as she landed on her ass. The impact radiated up her spine. She swore again as she stood up and dusted the ice off her backside. Her fingers throbbed from the cold, reminding her again that she was an idiot for losing her gloves.

Finally, she made it to the dormitory. She looked around at the pine trees that surrounded the building. At the moment, it was hard to imagine them without snow, but she was fairly certain they were the trees in the picture of the dead Gracemount boys that was found on Jim Iverson's computer. She could look around at the landscape all she wanted, but there was only one way to find out if this was the place the photo had been taken.

She laid the duffel bag down in the snow but stopped before she unzipped it. All she had in life was her career. It was who she was, not just what she did. A boulder formed in the pit of her stomach. She felt like she was going to be sick. Shame settled heavy on her, pulling her down from the inside.

Was she really going to do this?

She had always prided herself on being law-abiding, a rule-follower, everything her father wasn't, but somewhere along the way she'd lost that. She barely recognized the person she'd become.

She always excused her shortcomings, all her rough edges, the lack of interpersonal skills, and the penchant for anonymous sex by telling herself she was still a decent person because at least she followed the rules.

If she did this, she wouldn't be able to say that anymore.

She could leave now and go home; she hadn't yet broken any laws. She stood frozen and shivering, unsure if it was the cold or something else that made her shake, but she couldn't stop.

She pulled out her phone.

"Hello," Jeanie answered, her voice weak.

For a second Jess couldn't speak. A lump formed in the back of her throat and no matter how hard she tried to swallow, the tightness would not leave her.

"Jessica, is that you? Are you there?" Jeanie asked.

She nodded. "Yeah, it's me. I just wanted to… see how you are doing." Her words sounded stupid, even to her. They both knew how she was doing. She'd just lost her nephew: she wasn't doing well.

There was a long pause on the other end of the phone before Jeanie sniffed. "I'm… I'm going to be all right."

Jess didn't know what to say. She'd never been good with people and emotion but now she couldn't even form a basic sentence. She should tell her that she was right, that she would be okay, but she wasn't sure she would be. Jess was still waiting to feel okay again after Lindsay's death.

"Thank you for calling. I know you've been busy with your investigation but now that's over I wanted to tell you that you were the only person I thought to call about Levi. And if it had—" Her voice broke off in a hushed sob. "I'm sorry. If it had to be anyone to find him, and to investigate, I'm grateful that it was you. There is no one else I would have trusted more. Thank you for helping my family."

Jess winced. The words stung. The knowledge that she had failed Jeanie was too bitter to allow herself to think about now.

"Taylor called yesterday to tell me about Jim Iverson, about the suicide game he started at the school. Just evil. To do to children… But they're confident that the game has died with him."

Jess squeezed her hand together until her palm ached. "Yes, they are," was all she could say because she couldn't bring herself to lie to Jeanie.

"Thank you," Jeanie said again before her voice was lost entirely to sobs.

After she hung up, Jess held the phone against the ache deep in her chest.

Jeanie deserved the truth.

Jess might not be the moral person she had hoped to be but maybe she could give Jeanie some closure. She had become an FBI agent because she wanted to be a good guy, but now she realized that doing the right thing and following the law weren't always the same thing.

She let out a heavy sigh, unzipped the bag, and took out a pair of latex gloves. She snapped them on before she reached for the crowbar and hammer. She stood up, walked to the window, and examined the frame.

She breathed a sigh of relief when she saw the cheap aluminum frame. She tossed the hammer down next to her, grateful she would not be needing it. She might be prepared to break and enter private property, but she preferred not to vandalize anything while she did it. At least this way there would not be any broken glass for some poor schmuck to clean up.

She anchored her foot against the wall to brace herself before she wedged the claw behind the metal frame. With a single push the window popped out in one piece. She tried to throw down the crowbar in time to catch the window but she wasn't fast enough and it landed on the ground with a thump. A flurry of snow puffed around it like smoke, breaking the fall, leaving the glass un-shattered.

Jess smiled down at her handiwork. When she was done, it would slot right back into place and hopefully no one would even know it had been tampered with.

Only after she was in the room did she realize she had left the flashlight in the duffel bag. She patted the wall until she found the switch and the light flickered on. Three sets of bunk beds lined the olive-colored walls. She looked around the room trying to visualize the picture. This wasn't the bedroom. The window was in the wrong place.

She walked down the hallway, looking into every room before she found the one that matched the layout of the picture. She went in, closed her eyes, and pictured the photo, where everyone was standing. Levi had been by the bunk bed nearest the window, Ryan in a chair next to him. Whoever took the picture must have been standing at the door.

She looked up at the red flashing light of a smoke detector on the ceiling. That was the exact angle. Her eyes narrowed as she examined it. She wasn't tall enough to reach it. She needed a ladder or table. Or a chair would do.

Before she could pull the chair out, heavy footsteps sounded in the hall.

She wasn't alone.

CHAPTER TWENTY-THREE

Jess sucked in a frantic breath, taking in air until her lungs burned. She pulled her gun from its holster. Her fingers refused to close around the polymer frame so she clasped her other hand on top and forced her grip to close.

The door swung open and a man's tall shadow came into focus.

"Fuck!" she screamed. "What are you doing here?"

Jamison's large form filled the door frame. His full lips pulled down into a frown. "Put your gun away. I'm making sure you don't do something you'll regret."

Her body vibrated with the surge in adrenaline. "Dammit, Jamison. I could have shot you."

"You already have," he said, pointing to his chest. "But I don't think that gun would be much use to you now. Your hands are shaking too much to get a clean shot. Could you even hit a target?" His deep voice was laced with annoyance.

"I'm fine."

He gave her a dubious look. "You're holding your gun in the wrong hand. On what planet is that fine? You're obviously still hurt. There's no way you could defend yourself: you can't even hold your gun properly. How were you even cleared to come back to work?"

"I'm fine," she repeated like a mantra.

"Keep saying it all you want. It doesn't make it true."

She wished he wouldn't pretend to care. At some point, she would forget that it wasn't true and the sting would be worse for it. She needed to remember she was alone in this, the way she was alone in everything now. "You shouldn't have followed me here." She shoved her gun back into its holster.

"What are you even doing here?"

"This is where the picture from Iverson's computer of the boys in the suicide game was taken. That's where Levi was standing." She pointed to one of the bunk beds. "And Ryan was sitting over there." She pointed to the window. "That tree is in the shot."

He nodded "How did you figure all this out?"

"I spoke to Ryan Hastings' mom. I wanted to know why Levi was upset when he saw her."

"Did she tell you?"

"No. She couldn't get away from me fast enough. She was scared of something or someone and she really didn't want to be seen with me. But she did let it slip that the last time she saw Levi Smith was before the boys came here to Pine Ridge. The trip couldn't have been any later than August because that's when Ryan died."

"So, Jim Iverson had the last known picture of Ryan Hastings on his computer?"

"Yeah, and based on the angle of the picture and the fact the boys seemed oblivious that they were being photographed, I think it was taken with a hidden camera."

Jamison looked up at the smoke detector on the ceiling just above him. "Is this what you're looking for?" He reached up, pulled it down, and handed it to her.

"Yes, thank you. I had forgotten about the perks of being partnered with a giant. Maybe that's why Jeanie put us together all those years ago. You're tall enough to reach things and I'm small enough to squeeze through windows." That reminded her. "How did you get in?"

"I picked the lock on the front door."

"Of course you did."

"There was no way I could have fit through that window. I would have had to dislocate things to fit through that opening. Even then it would be touch and go."

She placed the smoke detector down on the table, pausing, scared that she would open it and find nothing but batteries. They had both separately broken the law to break into the building based on her hunch. She would feel like a real asshole if there wasn't anything to be found.

"What are you waiting for?" Jamison asked.

"I just want to make sure your prints aren't all over it." She pulled her coat over her hand and used it like a makeshift rag to wipe down the plastic.

"Who knew you'd be the better criminal?" A hint of a smile played on his full lips.

The alarm whined a high-pitched squeak before the lid snapped off. A bit of plastic went flying through the air as it opened. "Shit. I've broken it." She turned to search for the missing piece so she could put it back together.

"Jessie, look."

She glanced down. Her pulse spiked. Validation coursed through her. She wasn't crazy, not about this. "That's a camera with an SD card. Someone was videoing those boys without their knowledge."

She fished out the card and put it in a fresh evidence bag, ready to send to the lab. She froze when she remembered what the lab tech had told her, that according to the official records she hadn't logged anything for testing since her last case. She couldn't afford to have these results go missing too.

"Jessie, what's wrong? You were right."

She pinched the bridge of her nose between her thumb and index finger while she thought about what to tell him, how far she should involve him. She felt trapped in a stalemate, unable to go forward or make any move. "You shouldn't have followed me here. You don't need to be part of all this shit. It's not just someone setting up Jim Iverson to take the fall. I think this is bigger than just a suicide game. I think these boys could have been murdered, and the suicide game was to cover it up, and I think it involves someone in our office."

His face remained impassive, not registering even the smallest shadow of emotion, but that wasn't surprising. He was a master of control, nothing fazed him. Maybe that's the real reason Jeanie had put them together, because she knew Jess needed the constancy and stability he offered.

"Please, Jamison. Go home. Pretend you didn't see this."

"So, let me get this straight: you tell me you think there is someone within the FBI killing kids, including Jeanie's nephew, and you want me to walk away and pretend I didn't hear that? What kind of man do you think I am? Jesus, Jessie. I'm not Chan or Milligan. Give me some credit." The smallest sliver of emotion crept through but instead of looking angry, he looked hurt.

"Jamison."

"No. Are you the only one who gets to give a shit about Jeanie and doing the right thing?"

"Stop. That's not what this is about. And you know it."

"What's it about, then? Tell me."

She shook her head. She didn't know what to say. If there were words, she couldn't find them. "I don't want anyone else getting hurt." By that, she meant him. She'd hurt him more than anyone should have to endure. He'd lost his wife and unborn child because of her.

"I think I can handle myself."

She thought for a second, searching for a way to push him away, far enough to keep him safe. "Okay. You want to know what we're dealing with? The faked self-harm pictures Levi Smith supposedly sent the curator were actually photos from a victim in California. I think the out-of-state victims were targeted just to muddy the water and cover up the murders of the five Gracemount boys. Last night I went to check on the scrapings I took from under Levi's fingers, and I was told that there was no record of me submitting any evidence for testing since before Lindsay died. Add to that the botched autopsy on Levi, my failure to secure any warrants, and the fact the Metropolitan Police sent a captain to investigate an apparent suicide. I could go on. There are too may coincidences. At some point, we have to call bullshit."

"So, your plan is to jeopardize your entire career, the only thing you have in your life, to investigate on your own?"

The words should have stung but they were the truth. They both knew she had nothing else going for her; this job was all she had. There was no point in trying to pretend. "Yes, that's my plan."

"Or we could take it directly to Taylor."

"At this point he would just shut me down. I don't have enough evidence and I don't know who is involved with this, and let's just say his confidence in me isn't high."

"So, what are you going to do? Do you have a plan? Or are you winging it and breaking laws along the way. I want to make sure we're on the same page."

"I'm going to see where the evidence takes me. Once I know what I'm dealing with, I will tell Taylor. Right now, it's just my gut feeling and loose ends. That's not enough to reopen an investigation. We both know that. Taylor wants this gone."

He rubbed his chin with his knuckles as he thought. "We'll see what's on the card and then decide what to do next."

"Fine," she agreed. "Do you have your computer?"

"Yeah. It's in my car."

"Okay. I'll meet you out front. I need to put the window back."

Half of his mouth pulled up in a lopsided grin.

"What?" she asked. "It's still snowing. It will cause water damage if I don't board it back up."

"I'll give you your due, you're a considerate felon."

"First of all—" she gestured around the room "—misdemeanor at most, and it would be pled down because I'm otherwise law-abiding and it's my first offense."

"Yeah, you're a model citizen."

Jess traced her footsteps back and climbed out through the window she'd removed. Lifting the glass was more difficult than taking it out, but after three failed attempts she managed to hoist it into the frame. It would need to be properly bolted back into place but at least it would keep the elements and wild animals out.

She tucked an escaped curl behind her ear and hiked back up the hill to the parking lot. In the summer, the trek would take thirty seconds, but the snow slowed her pace because she kept losing her footing.

The windscreen of Jamison's car was steamed over and wispy white puffs of smoke billowed out the tailpipe.

"I was wondering if I needed to send out a search and rescue party."

"I'm starting to hate the snow," she muttered as she slid into the passenger seat and shut the door. Her fingertips throbbed with every beat of her heart, burning from the cold. She put her hands in front of the hot air of the heater and winced when the blood began to circulate and full feeling returned.

"You should have gloves." Jamison pulled off his scarf and handed it to her to wrap her hands in.

"Thanks."

"Do you have the memory card?"

"Yeah." She reached into her pocket for the evidence bag. "Here you go."

Jamison inserted the card into the computer. Anticipation niggled her as they waited for the video to load.

"What if it's a virus?" she asked.

"It's too late to worry about that now."

"True." She brought her index finger to her mouth to bite but there was nothing left of her nail so she moved to the next finger and then the next before she finally found a sliver. A metallic zing of blood filled her mouth as she misjudged the length of her nail and bit into the quick. She winced at the pain but didn't pull her hand away because the pain took some of the edge off.

Finally, the file was ready and the video opened to a shot of the empty dorm room. A few minutes passed without anything happening; no one entered or left the room. It felt like the monotony of a stakeout in a digital format. Most likely there were hours of footage of an empty room. "Can you fast-forward?"

Jamison pressed a key and the image zoomed to the next frame, still of an empty room, so he fast-forwarded again, moving the video forward in short bursts so they didn't accidently miss anything.

Jess tapped him on the arm. "Wait, what's that? Go back."

Jamison clicked the keys and a new image came into focus. "What the hell?"

"What is he wearing? Is that a monk robe?"

"Dear God, he looks satanic. Seriously, he looks like he's preparing for an animal sacrifice."

Jess squinted at the screen. A man in a hooded robe had entered the room, his back to the camera so they could not make out his age or ethnicity. His height plus the broad shoulders and relatively narrow hips indicated that it was a man, but there was no way to determine anything else about him.

The man came in, put a case on the bed, got on his hands and knees, searched for something under the bed, then put what he found in his bag and left. The entire sequence took less than thirty seconds.

"What's in his hand?" Jess asked. "Can you rewind it and zoom in?"

"We really could use Tina for this."

"No!" She didn't mean to shout but the idea of involving anyone else in this made her stomach clench. If she'd kept Lindsay out of her last investigation, she would still be alive. If there were any risks involved with this investigation, they were hers to take. There was no way Jess was going to endanger anyone else.

Jamison nodded. She didn't have to explain her reservations. After a few attempts, he was able to stop the video at the right moment, and the contents of the bag came into focus. "Are those disposable cameras?"

Jess nodded. "Yeah. But why? Did he leave cameras in every room for the kids to use? Oh, shit. I think I know what the cameras were for." Her stomach clenched in a painful spasm. She was going to be sick. She held her hand over her mouth.

Jamison didn't say anything. He knew how her mind worked. He knew that it was impossible for her to look at a man and not see a predator, or at least the potential to become one. The relentless suspicion was the gift her childhood had given her. Other people could see a dad playing with his kids in the park, or a man coaching a soccer team, and think it was an idyllic scene but Jess would only ever see a hunter stalking his prey.

"We need to find those cameras."

Jess closed her eyes. She didn't want to see the images. She already had her own that she could not escape. Visions from her past fired at her from every direction.

"Jessie, you okay?"

She took a deep, fortifying breath before she opened her eyes. "Yeah. I'm fine. Play it again." She would watch the video again and again until she had synthesized every bit of information it had to offer.

Jamison started the sequence from the beginning.

"There." She pointed at the screen. The man turned to the camera just before he left the room. "Zoom in on that."

"You can't see his face."

"No, not his face. His lapel on the left-hand side, just above his heart. There is something embroidered on his robe. What is that?"

The keys clicked as Jamison zoomed in.

"There. That's it." Her heart hammered against her ribs. "That emblem." She pointed to the outline of a chalice and the Eye of Providence. "I've seen it before. Once on Levi's school blazer and then in Sturgeon's office, in the picture with Chief Hagan. He was wearing that same pin. I've never seen it anywhere else. I was going to ask Sturgeon what it meant but something tells me he wouldn't have told us anyway."

CHAPTER TWENTY-FOUR

For the first time since she moved into her apartment, Jess considered taking the elevator. Her legs were like lead wading through quicksand. She was bone-tired and ready for a shower and bed. She might even be able to sleep, and she wouldn't need some random man to help her get numb first.

"Hold on, Stan. That's cheating. You can't start before me." Jess shoved her keys into her pocket and started up the stairs, desperate to get home and sleep. Tomorrow she would keep researching the emblem they had found, but first she needed her bed.

Every time she brought the dog inside, they raced up the stairs to her apartment on the sixth floor. He always won but tonight she wasn't even a contender. The combination of the long day and the freezing temperature had left her exhausted. "At least give me a chance, buddy," she called up the stairs after him.

"Why are you growling?" She stopped on the stairs to listen. Stan gave an annoyed bark.

"There better not be a mouse," she muttered as she started on the final flight.

"Hey, buddy, what's wrong?" she asked as she rounded the corner.

"What the hell?" Her eyes narrowed at the open door to her apartment. A sliver of golden light shined between the frame and the metal door. The hairs on the back of her neck stood taut. She never left the apartment without bolting the deadlock.

"Shh, Stan. Come here." She leaned down and pulled her dog close against her to comfort him. "Shh, you're okay, buddy," she whispered against his fur as he whined.

There was music coming from her living room. She stood silently and listened to the lyrics of Hall and Oates' "Private Eyes".

A bolt of terror shot down her spine. Tendrils of fear, electric and constricting, crept over her skin, singeing a path as they went.

She pulled the gun from her holster. A mocking voice in her head reminded her she could barely grip her gun let alone shoot a moving target. Her hand was supposed to be getting better but it wasn't.

The day her fish died, someone had broken into her apartment. She wasn't crazy. Anger pounded through her with each staccato beat of her heart, pushing out the fear. She hated that someone was fucking with her but she hated it even more that she was no longer confident in her ability to protect herself.

She shoved her gun back in its holster and pulled out her phone. "Pathetic," she muttered to herself before she dialed.

"Nine-one-one, what's your emergency?"

She was law enforcement, she shouldn't have to call the police. "Hi, this is Special Agent Jessica Bishop. My apartment has been broken into. I need a forensic team to dust for prints and uniformed officers to speak to my neighbors and pull security footage from local CCTV." She started running through the checklist of things that needed doing before she realized she was micromanaging. This wasn't her case, she didn't get to call the shots.

"Ma'am, are you safe? Is the assailant still in the apartment?"

"I don't know. I'm standing outside in the hall."

The dispatcher asked her to confirm her address and then said, "Okay, stay on the phone. We have a patrol car in your area."

"I can't stay on the phone. I need to call my partner." She didn't want to end the call because she felt safer with someone listening, but the truth was she was alone. A voice on the end of the line couldn't protect her anyway. She closed her eyes just for a second, long enough to get some emotional distance from the situation.

She hung up and called Jamison, who answered on the first ring. "Hey, what's up?" he asked.

"I'm sorry to call you but I need some help. Do you have any connections from your time undercover with the police in Alabama? Anyone you trust?" Jess asked.

"Yeah, I might, but I think I need some context."

She took a deep breath to try to slow the frantic beat of her heart, but it refused to cooperate. "My apartment was broken into again tonight. The police are on their way but what's the point of collecting evidence if we can't trust the lab to process it?"

"Again? Jesus, Jessie. Your place was broken into? Twice? Why didn't you tell me before?"

Jess ignored the concern in his voice, reminding herself that it didn't mean anything. "I'm telling you now. I wasn't sure when it happened the other day but now I'm sure."

"I'm on my way."

Jess knelt down and cuddled Stan again while she waited for the police. It was as much to keep her calm as him.

Finally, sirens blared outside. She ran down the stairs to let them in. Water splashed onto the sidewalk as a police car drove through a puddle of melted snow. A few seconds later another car pulled up.

She held onto Stan's collar so he would not bolt when she opened the door. When she saw the first police officer come toward her, her initial instinct was to look down and let her hair obscure her face so she wouldn't be recognized. Cognitively she knew it was ridiculous, and the odds of someone guessing her identity now almost thirty years later was infinitesimally small, but the knee-jerk reaction to meeting someone new was always the same. That would never go away. She forced herself to look the police officer in the eye. "I'm Jess Bishop. I called in the break-in. My apartment is at the very top. It's number 36. The door is open and music's playing so it's hard to miss." She pulled Stan to the side to let in the four uniformed officers.

"Did you see anyone inside?" the first officer asked her.

She relaxed when she didn't see any sort of recognition on his face. "No. I'm not sure anyone is in there."

"Okay, stay here with Officer Tibor. We'll go check it out." He nodded to the man coming in to indicate who he was talking about before he and his two colleagues headed for the elevator.

Stan growled, unimpressed by the commotion and the fact he hadn't yet been fed. She leaned down and scratched him behind the ears.

They both stood in silence for a long time, waiting for the other person to speak.

"What kind of dog is he?" Tibor asked eventually.

"I'm not sure. He's a rescue. The vet thinks golden retriever and German shepherd."

"Yeah, I can see that."

Jess forced herself to smile because she didn't have anything to say. Sometimes she wished she wasn't shit at small talk. It would make human interaction less awkward. She looked down at Stan. Dogs were so much easier than humans.

"Jessie, you okay?" Jamison called from the door.

Relief washed over her when she looked up at him. She always felt safe when he was around. It was an illusion but her body believed it just the same. "Yeah, I'm fine. Officers are upstairs checking it out."

"Why didn't you tell me someone had broken into your apartment before?"

She didn't answer. She opened the fire door and headed for the stairs.

"Where are you going?" Tibor asked.

"I want to see what's going on in my apartment." She took the stairs two at a time.

When they got to top, Tibor was red-faced and breathing heavily but he coughed to cover it up.

The door to her apartment was now wide open and the lights on. "Private Eyes" was still playing, which meant someone had set her Sonos to play the song on repeat. She'd never liked the song but now it made her skin crawl.

"Someone is trying to send you a message," Jamison said.

"Yeah, the real curator."

The first officer Jess had spoken to came out. His face was red. A bead of sweat rolled down his forehead and down his cheek like a tear. He looked everywhere but at her. "The place is clear but... uh..." He bit into his lip as he considered what to say. "There are some... um... unusual decorations in there. I need to know if they're... ah... yours."

"What?" The only pictures in her house were in frames on her bookshelf. "What kind of pictures?"

"Maybe you should have a look," the officer said, clearly feeling uncomfortable.

Stan pulled away from her grip, ran into the apartment, and went straight for the kitchen.

The officer stepped to the side so she could enter her apartment. She gasped when she saw the walls. Her heart stopped mid-beat and then faltered as it tried to start again. Every inch of wall space was covered in black-and-white eight-by-ten photos.

"They appear to be crime scene photos," one of the officers said.

Her gaze darted around the room, taking in each shiny picture. "They're not crime scenes." She tried to say more but her voice came out in a whisper. She couldn't breathe. Her throat constricted, not allowing any air through no matter how hard she gasped.

The officer pointed at the picture of a decapitated boy, his tiny body positioned at the gates of an elementary school. "If this isn't a crime scene, what is it?"

The room flashed bright as someone took a picture to document the scene.

"Turn that music off," Jamison growled.

"I-I d-don't," she stammered. The room spun, whirling faster and faster as all the pictures blurred together into a macabre tribute to evil. Her knees gave way and her legs went slack.

"Jessie." Jamison put his hand on the small of her back, catching her just before she fell. "Are you going to be okay?" His lips brushed against her ear as he spoke.

She tried to speak but her mouth was too dry and the words would not come.

"Dispatch said you're an FBI agent. Are these your cases?"

"No," Jamison answered for her.

Jess closed her eyes. She needed to get her shit together. She squeezed her hand as hard as she could until the scar tissue pulled taut, threatening to tear away from the healthy flesh. Searing pain jolted through her hand and up her wrist, deep into her arm. The excruciating sensation focused her, pushed away the horror, and replaced the emotion with something tangible she could deal with. She pulled away from Jamison's embrace. She wouldn't let herself pretend that she wasn't alone. "That's not one of my cases. That photo is of The Headmaster's ninth victim. The picture was taken near the American military base in Frankfurt, Germany."

"The Headmaster? You mean the serial killer who raped and murdered little boys? Why would someone put that picture on your wall?" The officer's dark brow knitted together in confusion.

A wave of nausea hit her. She was going to be sick. "Because he is my father."

A shocked silence descended on the room.

Jamison tried to reach for her arm but she pulled away. A familiar pressure built behind her eyes but she wouldn't let herself cry, not now, not ever again.

"Wow. I didn't know. I'm sorry. So, did you put them up?" the officer asked awkwardly.

"No. No, I didn't put them up." She wanted to scream but she knew that if she did, she wouldn't be able to stop.

"Well then it appears the break-in wasn't random. I think you might have been targeted. Do you know anyone who would have done this?"

The number of times she'd asked a victim that question and the answer was always no, or the person could name one maybe two people. But she had an almost inexhaustible list of potential suspects. It was most likely this had something to do with the suicide game but it could also be any number of people from her past. Her dad had brutally murdered and decapitated thirteen boys. Any of their families would have motive. There were also the hundreds of people she had put away in her career, and then of course there were the people she managed to piss off on a daily basis just by being her awkward self. Potential suspects were not in short supply but she didn't want to get into all of that right now so she just shrugged and said, "I don't know."

"What about this picture?" the officer asked.

She stared directly at the autopsy photo. It was the only one she didn't mind looking at. "I killed him. He attacked me and I fought back."

The officer's eyes widened in surprise. "Oh," was all he managed to say on the subject. "What about this picture? I thought The Headmaster only killed little boys." The officer pointed to a photo taped to the center of the wall. "It looks like another autopsy photo."

Her chest ached with the sadness she could never fully shake. "That's my best friend Lindsay Dixon. She was murdered last month." She closed her eyes so she didn't have to see Lindsay's body lying naked on a metal slab, or the crudely sewn incisions that fanned out from her sternum. That's not the way she wanted to remember her.

"Did they find the guy who killed her? Maybe he—"

"No. This isn't about her. It's about me. All the pictures have something to do with me. My past."

Another officer rounded the corner from the bedroom. "There are more pictures in here. And the bath has been run and candles are lit. The water is still hot. Did you do that?"

"No, as a matter of fact, I didn't run a bath and light some candles before I decided to call nine-one-one and report the break-in. I called it in as soon as I saw the door was open."

"You don't have to be rude," he snapped.

"You don't have to ask stupid questions either, yet here we are," Jamison said.

The officer didn't challenge Jamison; no one ever did. "The pictures in here are of a more personal nature," he said.

The muscles along her spine tensed at the word "personal." This already felt pretty damn personal. How much more personal could it get?

They followed the officer to the bedroom. The sheets had been pulled off the bed and dozens of condoms had been tossed on the bare mattress. She recognized the black logo on the silver packets. They were the brand she used. They were the safest on the market and she never left the house without a few in her bag.

"The pictures are in the bathroom."

Jess took a deep breath, unsure if she wanted to see any more. This already felt like an intimate invasion but she bit back her feelings. She would deal with the emotion later, the way she always did. She would find a stranger to make a bad life choice with and then she would tell herself it was the last time.

She and Jamison followed him into the bathroom. Like the living room, one entire wall was covered in pictures, but these weren't of crime scenes. They were pictures of her having sex: her back was against an external brick wall, her pants around her ankles.

"Fuck," she whispered. Mortification burned on her cheeks. She closed her eyes tight to block it out.

She sensed another person come into the room. She didn't even know any of their names and they were looking at pictures of her fucking a stranger in public.

She needed to get away. Her skin was on fire and she couldn't breathe. She felt too raw and exposed, like her soul had been ripped from her and laid out for the world to shit on. Every fiber in her body coiled, ready to run.

Light flashed as someone took a picture of the scene. "Don't. Please don't," she whispered.

"Ma'am, we need to document this."

Jamison's hand reached for hers and gave it a gentle squeeze, letting her know he was there, supporting her. She pulled away. He wasn't even shocked or angry by what she had done. He just accepted that was who she was—and that, more than anything, stung. She wasn't sure when she had become this person; it wasn't who she'd set out to be.

He had once told her that they were both too messed up to be together but that was a lie. She was too messed up. She ruined everything.

"Ma'am, did you know these pictures were being taken?"

She couldn't speak, she could barely breathe, so she just shook her head.

"We need to know his name so we can contact him."

"Who?" she managed to ask.

"The man in the picture with you. We need to ask him if he knows who took the pictures. What's his name?"

She shook her head. She didn't know his name. She wasn't sure she would even recognize him if she saw him again on the street. She didn't even know when it was taken. It could have been any night this week. She always told herself that it would be the last time, at least for the week, but it never was. She didn't even believe it but it felt like a promise she should make to herself, something a normal, functioning person would do.

"Ma'am, what's his name?" he asked again.

"I don't know."

Their stares were heavy on her; she could physically feel the scrutiny on every nerve ending.

"What? How do you not know? Not the person who took the picture, the person you were with."

"She's already answered the question. She said she doesn't know." There was a dark warning in Jamison's deep voice, telling them not to press the issue any further.

"I need to get out of here." Jess turned and left. She went to the kitchen to find Stan. She bent down and cuddled him in close to her, petting his rough fur. "Hey, buddy," she whispered against his ear. Somewhere in the back of her mind she registered that she spoke more to her dog than she did to any human, but she didn't care. There was no shame or anger with him. "I forgot to feed you in all this commotion. I'm not even a good dog owner." She stood up and opened the trash can she used to store dog food, scooped him out a bowlful, and then rinsed out his other bowl and gave him fresh water.

She leaned back against the counter; the marble top pressed into her back because she was so short. She just stood and watched her dog eat because she could not bear to face what was happening in her house, or in her life really. At some point, she'd gone from clinging on to completely derailed, and she wasn't even sure what she could do to fix it. She couldn't think about it now because if she did, she wouldn't be able to hold it together.

Stan finished his dinner and then came up to her and pushed her hand up with his snout, asking to be petted.

"Jessie."

She looked up. Jamison was standing in the doorway. He made it seem small. Her apartment felt small with him in it. He had not been here since they'd had sex. It seemed like a lifetime ago.

"They've finished taking pictures and now they're going to dust for prints. It's going to be a mess in here for a few days. Fingerprint powder is a bitch to get off."

She nodded. She didn't care how long it took. She would keep scrubbing until every particle was gone.

"They are going to try to interview your neighbors tonight but it's getting late so it might not be until the morning."

"Okay. But I doubt they saw anything. I don't know any of my neighbors. I never see them. I only know the old guy on the first floor who scowls at people when they park outside because he thinks he owns the street."

"A busybody, just what every investigation needs. Maybe we'll get lucky and he saw something." Jamison gave a small smile. He was trying to be chill for her and ignore the reality of the situation.

"Maybe." She forced herself to try to sound positive and like she wasn't mortified to be in her own apartment with people looking at the most private and painful moments of her life.

"There was no forced entry. Who else has a key?"

"Just Lindsay."

"Did you get it back when she died?"

"No. I got Stan when she died. I didn't think to get my keys back or the umbrella I lent her or the CD I left in her car." Jess shook her head. She wasn't angry at him. Her choices weren't his fault so he didn't deserve her shit. "Sorry."

He held up his hand. "It's all good."

"All of Lindsay's stuff was boxed up and sent to her dad. I doubt he's even gone through it yet. This is about the suicide game. All of this started when I was assigned the case. I've been thinking about it: the pictures in the bathroom were from this week."

"So, you remember?"

She shook her head. "No, the picture looks like the back of the Opal Lounge. I was there last night. I went there after I spoke to Ryan's mom." For a second she felt the need to explain, defend herself, tell him that she was having a bad day and that was the only thing that cleared her mind, but the words sounded pathetic even to her. She made her choices and she wouldn't apologize for them.

"I think you should stay someplace else until this is over. He's been in your apartment twice now. It's not safe here."

She looked away.

"You can stay with me. I've already spoken to Jeanie and she agrees, you shouldn't be here."

Her head snapped back to look at him. "You told Jeanie! How much did you tell her?" Embarrassment pummeled her like a kick to her chest. She wasn't ashamed of the choices she made but they were private. She did her best to ensure that everything in her life was compartmentalized—even if all the ugliness dripped over no matter how hard she tried—but there was one area, one relationship, that was pristine, completely untouched: that was Jeanie.

"Jessie, she needs to know. This is way above our pay grade."

She squeezed her eyes together. "No."

"Jessie. We can't handle this on our own. Some of those pictures need clearance to access. We are dealing with someone on the inside. That's too big to keep to ourselves. This can't be ignored. I know that's what you like to do, just pretend things aren't happening. But this is happening and you're in danger."

"I need to go. I have to get out of here."

She tried to push past him but he grabbed her hand and stopped her. Anger flashed on his dark features. "You can't do that. Someone is watching every move you make. You can't go out and hook up with some guy. You need to handle your shit like an adult this time."

She yanked her hand away. "I meant I need some air. But good to know what you think of me."

CHAPTER TWENTY-FIVE

Jess was startled awake. Cold sweat and tangled sheets clung to her. Her heart hammered against her ribs. She'd been dreaming about her dad again—not the one where she found the body of one of his victims, and not the one where she was screaming while an FBI agent pulled her dad away from her. This dream was worse: it was the one where they were holding hands and the sun was shining and she felt so safe and loved. She hated that dream. She always woke up from it missing her dad. It was perverse to love a killer but he wasn't a monster to her: he was her daddy, the only person who ever looked at her and saw perfection, and the only person who made her feel completely safe.

Her hand banged off something hard when she reached for the lamp on the bedside table. "Shit." She squinted into the inky darkness, suddenly remembering she wasn't in her apartment.

She got out of bed and slowly walked to the door, her feet barely coming off the hardwood floor so she wouldn't trip. She flicked on the light switch and took a hard look at her surroundings. They were why she had had that particular dream about her dad. The walls were a soft, duck-egg blue and the woodwork and muslin curtains were white. They contrasted well with the walnut floors. It was very classic and feminine. Felicia must have designed it.

Against the wall, next to the twin bed, was a white crib with gray striped bedding. She couldn't tear her gaze away. Felicia had been due next month. Jamison was going to be a dad. *Was.* That was also why she had had the dream about her dad.

It was all sorts of fucked up that Jamison made her think about her dad; they were nothing alike except they were the only two men she'd ever loved.

She needed a glass of water. She followed the hall past the closed door of Jamison's bedroom to the kitchen at the back of the house. The light was already on. Jamison was standing at the sink, his naked back to her, his boxers slung low on his narrow hips.

He turned around when he heard her come in. "You couldn't sleep either?"

Her breath caught in her throat when he turned around and she saw his bare chest. The skin under his right clavicle was raised and knotted into a keloid scar. The patch of skin was pale, almost translucent against his dark skin. She looked down at her hand at her own scar from that night and then back at him. Shame settled heavy on her like a weight anchored around her. How could she ever have thought he was a killer? He wasn't her dad, there was no hidden monster lurking in him. She should have trusted him.

"You're a great shot." Jamison's long finger brushed the scar as he spoke. "You missed all the vital organs."

"Was. I was a great shot." She held up her hand to show him her mutilated palm.

His full mouth pulled down into a frown. "Yeah. We both lost a lot that night."

Her throat tightened. "I'm sorry." She'd said it before and she would say it again if he needed it. "I try to pretend that I have my shit together and my past doesn't affect my life, but it does. You saw the proof of that tonight. I'm not trying to make excuses. I just thought maybe… I don't know. I don't know what I'm trying to say… just that one of the biggest mistakes of my life was not trusting you and I'm sorry."

For a long moment he didn't speak, he just looked at her like he was seeing her for the first time. "I know you are and I forgive you. I forgave you a long time ago."

The words should have brought relief but instead they brought the realization that it didn't matter. Things would never be the same and she needed to accept it.

CHAPTER TWENTY-SIX

Jess woke up to the sounds of birds chirping and Stan licking her face. She squinted at the rays of sun that poured through the curtains.

"We need to do something about your breath." She reached out and scratched him behind his ears. "But don't worry, I still love you, buddy, even though you're stinky. We've all got issues, am I right?"

She sat up and stretched her arms above her head. Normally it was still dark when she woke up but last night, after she'd spoken to Jamison, she had fallen into a coma-like sleep. She glanced at her watch to check the time. It was almost eight thirty. "Wow, it's late. You've usually had your run by now. Do you want to go for your run? Are you ready?"

He barked his response. All she needed to do was mention a run and his tail started wagging. Stan could run until his paws bled and he'd still want to go longer.

"Okay, coffee then run."

She paused at the door when she heard a woman's voice in the living room. Jamison had a guest. A twinge of jealousy prickled her. She shook her head. It was the height of hypocrisy for her to be jealous. She'd slept with other people since they were together—several actually.

She scrubbed at her eyes. God, she was crazy. Of course Jamison was going to date, and it was none of her business. Well, technically it was sort of her business right now if she was about to meet her.

"Just like ripping off a Band-Aid," she said to Stan. She took a deep breath and opened the door. She forced a smile wide enough to make her cheeks ache.

As she rounded the corner she remembered she was still wearing sweats. She was sure she looked like death warmed over but she was past the point of caring.

Tina was sitting at the coffee table, her laptop open.

"Oh, thank God, it's just you," Jess said as she let out a sigh of relief.

Tina looked up, her nose crinkled. "As opposed to who?"

"No, I mean… I'm glad to see you, that's all."

Tina smiled but Jamison gave her a dubious look.

Jess shook her head as she realized why Tina was there. "Wait? Why are you here? You should be working the strangler case." She didn't give Tina the chance to answer before she spun on her heel to face Jamison. Anger surged through her, raw and potent. "I don't want to endanger anyone else. You said yourself we don't know what we're dealing with here. It's not fair to put Lindsay in danger. I won't do it."

"Tina," Jamison said gently.

Jess blinked. "What? Yes, Tina. That's what I said."

"You said Lindsay," Tina said.

Jess's cheeks warmed. "Sorry. I-I misspoke. I meant you. Of course I meant you."

"I understand that given everything that has happened you're reticent to involve me, and thank you, but I have the safest job in the office."

Safest job in the office. Jess's heart constricted painfully at the phrase. Lindsay had said the same thing about her job. Her dad hadn't wanted her to join the FBI because he was worried about her getting hurt, but she assured him that hers was the safest job in the office. And it had been, until Jess involved her in an investigation and she was murdered.

"He didn't call Tina. I did," a voice called from the other room.

Jess's head snapped up to see Jeanie standing in the doorway, bifocals perched on her head and hair braided in a neat bun. The red eyes and tear-stained cheeks were gone. She looked like the fearless agent Jess had first met.

"I explained the situation to Tina and the risk involved. She's not coming into this blind."

"I want to help, Jess," Tina assured her. "My other option is sitting in the conference room and listening to Chan trying to impress me but really just creeping me out. Please don't subject me to that."

Tina was trying to make light of the situation with a joke but there was no levity for her. Jess couldn't lose another team member. She couldn't handle it. Life had taught her that she could deal with a lot of shitty things, but being responsible for another person's death was not one of them. "We don't even know if we have the authority to investigate this. I don't even know if we should take it to the Office of Professional Responsibility because I don't know who's involved or how deep this goes."

"Ultimately, we will need to get the Department of Justice involved but not until we know who we are dealing with and who we can trust. Until then, we continue to work this case on our own. The risk is we tell the wrong people and this is buried again, or worse."

"Are you suggesting keeping this from Director Taylor?" Jess asked to be clear she understood. She'd never known Jeanie to deviate from the rules by even a little.

Jeanie took a deep breath as she considered her words. "Taylor is a good man. He was a fine attorney and he is competent in a lot of ways. I don't always know that he puts his trust in the right people. Right now, that skill is paramount so I would suggest keeping the circle as small as possible."

Jess nodded. Without saying much, Jeanie had made her position very clear. She was glad Jeanie was back. Their team was better with her but there was a question she needed to ask before Jeanie made the decision to come back. "Are you sure you want to be here for this part? I have discovered some things… I have some theories that might be difficult for you to hear."

Jeanie took a few seconds to respond. "The simple answer is no, I don't want to be here investigating Levi's death. I don't want him to be gone, but he is, and the only thing I can do for him now is bring his killer to justice. I'm sure I will hear some very painful things but not hearing them won't make them not true."

"Okay, so if we're all in, let's get started." Tina tied her hair in a loose knot on top of her head and stuck a pencil through it. "Where do we start?"

Jess stood for a second as she considered if she should go brush her teeth and change her clothes. Everyone else was wearing appropriate work attire. It felt weird and unprofessional to let Jeanie see her like this. Suddenly, she remembered what else Jeanie must have seen if she was here. Mortification burned through her as she wondered how much Jamison had told her, if he'd told her the exact nature of the pictures that were found at her apartment. Jeanie had to know something about it because she was here.

Jess bit back her embarrassment and ignored the heat in her cheeks. None of that mattered right now. They had a killer to find. "As you know there were photos of Levi and the other Gracemount boys found on Jim Iverson's computer. The theory put forward was that Jim Iverson took videos of the boys because he was a sex offender. It was implied that he abused the boys. To cover it up he invented the suicide game to encourage them to commit suicide, or he murdered them."

Jeanie's lips flattened to a tight white slash but she didn't flinch, she remained focused.

"But I don't buy it," Jess continued. "Iverson's murder was far too convenient. Everything was wrapped up in a nice neat package for us and we all know that never happens."

"So, what do you think happened?" Jamison asked.

She looked over at Jeanie to make sure she was okay before she continued. "I think there could very well be a sexual component to this case but what happened last night in my apartment tells me Jim Iverson is not the guy we're looking for. He's dead so he couldn't have broken into my apartment to scare me off the case."

"Whoever did this knows your history," Tina said.

"Yeah, and as you know, that's not something I advertise."

"You think this is someone you know?" Tina asked.

"Yeah, I do. I think we need to take a hard look at Richard Smart and Calum Scott. They worked the case for almost six months with no breaks, and then as soon as we start to make headway they break it wide open."

"Okay, I'm on it." The keys clicked as Tina began typing.

"Start with Scott," Jess said. "He is the dominant personality and I just get a vibe off him."

"Okay, will do."

"The other person we need to look at is Lynette Hastings. She is somehow involved in this. Levi sent an email that said he was upset by seeing her. I could be wrong but I feel that is connected. It doesn't make sense. And her whole demeanor was off."

"In what way?" Jeanie asked.

Jess shrugged. She couldn't explain exactly, it was more of a feeling than anything concrete. "I get that she is bereaved. She lost a child, that must be the worst pain imaginable, but she wasn't just depressed or angry or any of the other emotions you would expect. She was scared, almost paranoid. She could know who the curator is and be scared of him, but we also need to look at the very real possibility that she is scared of us discovering something about her. We can't rule that out. I know she doesn't fit the profile but I think we've learned that sometimes they just don't."

"Okay, I'll look into her too."

"Thank you. I also need your help identifying an emblem. I tried doing an image search but I don't think the resolution was good enough because I couldn't pull anything up." She turned to Jamison. "Can you pull it up on your computer?"

"Yeah, give me a second."

A minute later he pulled up a still image they had taken from the footage at Pine Ridge. "Here we go." He turned his laptop so Jeanie could see the embroidered chalice emblem. "Do you recognize this? Jessie found the same emblem on Levi's blazer and Chief Hagan was wearing the same thing in a picture hanging in Sturgeon's office."

Jeanie pulled down her glasses to examine the image. "Yes. That is the Founding Father emblem. They are a charity organization at Gracemount Academy. Paul and I have given them a donation every year since Levi started. What does that have to do with this?"

Jess caught Jamison's eye.

"What?" Jeanie demanded. "What is it? What aren't you telling me?"

Jess nodded to Jamison. If Jeanie was going to be here, they couldn't hold anything back from her. "Play the video."

She watched Jeanie as she viewed the video, waiting for some sort of expression, but there was nothing.

"That looks like Pine Ridge," Jeanie said.

"Yeah, it is. And as you can see in the video, he is searching for a disposable camera under the bed. His bag is full of them. We need to look at the possibility that the people who stayed at the lodge were instructed to take pictures of each other." Jess left the rest unsaid as if it were less cruel to let Jeanie connect the dots on her own, but the truth was she didn't want to say it aloud. She was tired of perversion. She could barely remember a time when her life wasn't dominated by monsters and the pain they inflicted.

She watched as Jeanie's expression changed, as the realization set in. "Levi went there in August before school started. He was picked as one of the junior ambassadors for the group."

"For the Founding Fathers?" Jamison clarified.

"Yes. He was honored to be picked. It's a coveted position. All the boys want to be a member but membership is limited to keep it exclusive. He was so excited because some of his best friends were picked. He was excited that they got to do it together." She closed her eyes like she was trying to distance herself from what she was saying.

"Which friends?" Jess asked. "Who all went?"

"There were just the five of them." Jeanie's face drained of color. "And now they're all dead."

CHAPTER TWENTY-SEVEN

Jess took Stan out for a run while Tina worked and Jamison finished getting Jeanie up to date on the case. She felt a twinge of guilt for leaving them for an hour but Stan would not stop whining until he had been out; besides, she needed a break from the bleakness of the situation and running was her one healthy coping mechanism. When the endorphins flowed, it took the edge off. It didn't block everything out the way sex did, but it would have to do for now.

As they rounded the corner back to Jamison's street, Stan stopped to christen yet another fire hydrant. He loved the novelty of the new locale, all the new smells and fresh places to mark as his own. He would happily spend the rest of the day finding new places to cock a leg but they had been gone long enough. He might not be tired from the run, but she was.

Jess's heart faltered when she saw Tina was waiting for her on the front porch when she got back.

She took out her headphones. "Is everything okay?"

"Yeah, fine. I think I might have something."

"Oh good. You scared me." She wiped the sweat off her forehead before it dripped into her eyes.

"Sorry, I just thought you would want to know."

"Yeah, no, please don't apologize." It wasn't Tina's fault that she automatically assumed the worst in every situation; that was just who she was. Jess opened the door to let Stan inside. "So, what did you find?"

"First, I'll tell you what I didn't find: anything exciting on Richard Smart. Raised by a single mom, went to the Naval Academy. Did twenty years in the marines and then began work as a consultant, and started working with the FBI eighteen months ago. He looks squeaky clean."

Jess took the lid off her water bottle and had a swig. "And what about Scott?"

"Also squeaky clean but a few interesting things to note. For example, his mother is a proud member of the Daughters of the American Revolution, and his father's family came over on the Mayflower. They have lots of money, all of the old variety—you know, the way some people have tons of cash but no one really knows how they earned it because the family has been rich for so long? That's his family."

"Interesting, but not sure it's relevant."

"That's what I thought at first but then I got to thinking." Tina broke into a broad smile. "With blood that blue, it would only make sense that he went to a suitably salubrious school. And I was right. Want to guess where he went?"

Jess's heart picked up speed. "Please tell me it was Gracemount Academy?"

"Ding, ding, ding, ding! You got it in one. His father and his grandfather went there as did his great-grandfather and presumably his great-great-grandfather. Those records haven't been made digital yet so I couldn't go back any further, but I think that gives you an idea."

"Tina, I could kiss you." Jess smiled. Jeanie had been right to call Tina. Despite her misgivings about including anyone else, there was no denying that investigations always went so much faster with Tina on the team. She knew her stuff. There was no better analyst in the FBI. "You worked with him the most—did he ever mention to you that he went there?"

Tina shook her head. "No, never."

"That's weird. Scott should have made us aware he went to Gracemount Academy. Even if he didn't think it was a conflict of interest, it would have come up even in an 'oh, by the way' context. Did you find out if he is connected to the Founding Fathers?"

"Only that he makes annual contributions to the charity."

Jess let out a stream of air. "So does Jeanie, so that is hardly the smoking gun we need to take this to the DOJ."

They walked into the living room. Stan had made himself at home at Jamison's feet. Jess took the seat on the couch opposite. Normally as soon as she sat down, Stan was under her, looking to be petted, but he barely acknowledged she'd come into the room. He was too busy staring adoringly at Jamison.

Tina grabbed her computer off the coffee table and pulled it onto her lap. "I'm still looking into the Founding Fathers but so far all I can find are press releases about their charitable contributions. They give a lot to inner-city projects."

"I don't think we're going to find any negative articles. They would bury any bad press." Jeanie looked up at them over her bifocals.

"Yeah, we're not going to find anything online," Jess agreed. "We need someone on the inside. I think we put pressure on Lynette Hastings. She knows something. I feel it. She's holding back."

"Okay, well I've started looking into her and so far there are zero connections between her and the Founding Fathers. She has never donated to their charity and she has no connection to them."

"Other than her son," Jamison reminded them.

"Yeah. Just that."

Jess bit her lip as she thought. "Lynette is a single mom, right?"

Tina nodded. "Yeah, she has two kids. Dad is in California. Doesn't look like he pays any alimony or child support."

"She is an ER nurse. So, she must make what? Eighty thousand a year? Ninety max. That's before tax. Take out rent, utilities, food, all that, and there is no way she had the fifty thousand a year to pay for Ryan's tuition."

"Maybe he was on a scholarship," Jeanie said.

Tina stopped typing to look up. "He would have to have been. Lynette's credit is a mess. She has maxed out two credit cards to the tune of forty thousand dollars."

"Wow. Did she put his tuition on credit cards?" Jamison asked.

"No." Tina pounded the keys as she searched. "Her credit was fine until this past fall, then in late September she paid what looks like a retainer to the law offices of Anderson and Murray for twenty-five thousand dollars."

"What kind of lawyers are they?" Jeanie asked.

"Mostly criminal."

Jess shifted position in her seat so she could fold her leg under her. "Hmm. Why did she need a lawyer? Were any charges filed against her?"

Tina shook her head. "I don't see anything. No convictions or charges, and no arrests."

"Maybe the criminal lawyer wasn't for her?" Jamison offered.

"Who else could it be for? A boyfriend? Whoever it was would have to be pretty important for her to go into debt for. Does she have a significant other?" Jess said.

"I don't know. I'm going to need a little more time to figure that out, but here is something else strange about her finances. Remember I said she was forty thousand in debt? Well, the rest of the money went to a private investigator called Robert Kaplan."

"She hired a private investigator and a criminal attorney?" Jess asked.

"Yep, both within two weeks."

"Wow. That is not the behavior of an innocent woman. I think we need to pay another visit to Lynette Hastings," Jamison said.

"Be my guest. But I don't think you will get on any better than I did. She really does not want to talk to law enforcement.

And since this isn't even an official investigation, we can't compel her to speak to us."

"What about the attorney or the PI? Maybe we will have better luck with one of them," Tina said.

Jess considered for a second. "It would have to be the PI. The attorney isn't going to violate privilege but the PI might. But we still have the problem of authority. We can't compel him to speak to us."

"I'm pretty sure I can compel him to speak to us," Jamison said.

She had no doubt that he could. Jamison could persuade people to do just about anything. Fear was a powerful motivator. "I'd prefer not to resort to witness intimidation."

"Always a good girl, even when breaking the law." Jamison's lips pulled into a half-smile.

"Bending," Jeanie corrected. "We're bending the law until we have enough information to present to the Department of Justice."

Jess nodded. Like Jeanie, she had to tell herself that ultimately, they had the law on their side. Maybe not right now, but ultimately. They were doing the right thing. She had to tell herself that. "Okay, we call the PI. Do you have his number?"

"Yeah, here it is." Tina turned her screen to face them. "Who should call him? Not Jamison," she answered her own question. "No offense. I say that with love but even your voice is intimidating."

"None taken. Jessie should do it."

Jess arched her brow in question. She would have picked Jeanie.

"You think the best on your feet," he said.

"Okay. I'll call." She typed the number into her phone.

The phone rang four times before it cut the call. "Are you sure that's his work number? There should be an answering service."

Tina checked the number Jess had dialed against the one listed on the website. "Yeah, that's him. Maybe he was on another line. Try again."

Jess pushed redial then waited but again there was no answer. "Maybe he changed his number and forgot to update his website. Can you find me a private number for him?"

"Yep, but it's going to take me a minute. Talk amongst yourselves." She winked.

Jess looked from Jamison to Jeanie. Neither one looked like they were up for a chat, which was fine by her because small talk had never been her thing, so they all sat in awkward silence while Tina worked.

"Okay, here we go. He just changed his private number recently too. It's like he doesn't want business."

Jess typed the new number into her phone and waited for it to ring. This time, he answered on the first ring.

"Who's this?" a gruff voice answered.

"Hi, is this Robert Kaplan?"

"How did you get this number?"

He didn't correct her so she would assume it was him. "Mr. Kaplan, I'd like to hire you to investigate—"

"I'm no longer worker as a private investigator."

Click. The phone went dead.

Jess sighed. "Are you all getting the impression that no one wants to speak to us?" she asked as she hit redial to call him again. Without ringing, the call went directly to voicemail. "He's blocked me. Can I have your phone?" she asked Jamison.

Jamison reached into his pocket and pulled out his phone. He typed in his password before he handed it to her. He didn't need to because unless he had changed it recently, she still knew it. She dialed the number and waited. This time it rang four times before it went to voicemail, proving that he had indeed blocked her. She hung up and dialed again. "I can play this game all day." On the fourth call, he got wise and blocked Jamison's number too.

"Can I borrow your phone, Jeanie?"

"Yes, of course."

"Stop calling me!" he screamed down the phone when he answered.

He was about to hang up on her. She needed to keep him on the line because he might not pick up again. *Think.* Suddenly her palms were slick. She gripped the phone harder so she wouldn't drop it. If she said the wrong thing, he would hang up, and next time he might not answer. A million things flooded her mind all at once. She didn't know him so she had no way of knowing if she should threaten or cajole him. She really wished she could see him so she could at least try to get a read off him. But she couldn't, so she was going to have to go in blind. "Founding Fathers," she said and then held her breath, hoping it had been the right thing to say.

The other end of the line went completely silent. At first, she thought he'd hung up on her again, but then she heard his frantic breaths. "Who is this?"

He hadn't hung up. Relief washed over her. She sensed his fear and played on it. "Don't be coy, Robert. You know who this is."

"I don't. Please don't call me again. I did what you told me to do, now leave me alone."

"I'm afraid I can't do that, Robert." She used his name again to reinforce the familiarity, make him think she knew more than she did.

"Please leave me alone. I did everything you asked."

She shot Jamison a questioning look. What had the Founding Fathers asked of him? How was he involved with all this? "We need something else."

"What? You've already taken my job. I work as a fucking barista now. I have nothing." His voice broke. Hushed sobs filled the end of the line. His distress was palpable. He was a broken man.

As a human being, Jess couldn't ignore the ache in the pit of her stomach she felt when she heard his cries, but as an investigator, the state he was in was perfect for her. There was no need to break him. The Founding Fathers had saved her the effort. "We need one more thing, Robert."

"What? What more could you ask of me?"

"I'm not going to speak about it on the phone." Her mind raced as she tried to formulate a plan. If she had her way, she would discuss every step with her team beforehand. They would go over every possible scenario and danger. And then they would look to Jeanie to make the final call, but they didn't have time for all of that. "Meet me this afternoon at Gallery Place. Be there at three o'clock. Come alone and unarmed. And don't try any funny shit," she warned. "We know where you live. Don't ever forget that."

"I have a shift. I'm barely paying my bills as it is."

"Be there or your bills will be the least of your problems." She cut the call before he had a chance to respond. Her hands shook from the surge in adrenaline.

CHAPTER TWENTY-EIGHT

"I still don't think you should be going on your own." The muscle on the side of Jamison's jaw twitched as he clenched his teeth.

"Who else should we send? You?" She slid her gun into her holster, zipped up her hooded sweatshirt to cover it, and then put on her quilted winter jacket.

"Yeah."

"We're trying to be inconspicuous. You're a six-foot-four black man, built like a linebacker. You don't exactly blend in."

Jamison didn't say anything. He just gave her an unimpressed look. He wanted more time to look at all the angles and minimize any risk. But they didn't have that kind of time and they both knew it. They had been dealt a shit hand but she was doing her best to play it.

"I'm fine," she assured him. "We're meeting at a Metro stop. You've taken the Metro before, right? There are always thousands of people around. That's why I picked it. There is a method to my madness."

"Is your wire working?"

"Yeah, it's still working, but if we keep checking it, I'm probably going to break it."

"If you feel scared at any point or think you're being followed, we call it."

Jess noted the worried expression on Jamison's face. Very few things fazed him so it was weird to see him riled. She wouldn't let herself pretend that it meant anything but it was still nice.

"Remember, don't take the red line all the way there. Get off and take the green to Fort Totten and then get back on the red to Gallery Place to make sure no one is following you."

"This is not my first rodeo." She zipped up her coat and pulled on the hood. "I will be fine."

She got out of the car and shut the door then walked down the stairs to the Metro. Jamison would be waiting for her outside the Gallery Place stop to pick her up. They had decided to leave Jeanie and Tina at home, telling them it would be safe for them there, but it was really so they would have plausible deniability.

She fully intended on forcing Robert Kaplan to submit to an interview, no matter what that entailed. What she was about to do was tantamount to kidnapping and forced imprisonment. It was straight-up illegal, and if anyone was going to take the heat for this, it was going to be her.

She had her Metro card in her hand ready to go when she got to the turnstile. She turned and looked over her shoulder, searching the sea of faces and memorizing each the best she could. She would know she was being followed if she saw the same person change stops with her.

The stagnant air underground was stifling. She wished she could take off her jacket. Above ground it was freezing but in the carriage, it felt like ninety degrees.

She stood up as they got closer to her change. It would have been faster and easier to just stay on the red line, but the change was necessary to make sure she wasn't followed.

As the train pulled into the station, there was a group of junior-high students on the platform, being corralled by teachers with clipboards and high-visibility jackets. The city was always teeming with field trips because it was a rite of passage for students to come to the capital.

It was a nice tradition but she was thankful she was getting off so she didn't have to travel beside them. All the screaming and frenetic energy of adolescence would make it difficult for her to concentrate. She stepped to the side to let an elderly passengers off first, but before he had a chance to get off, the group of students had already pushed past them and were making their way on while their teachers screamed, "Be careful!" and, "Stop pushing!" She stepped further to the side to let the entire class on.

Students and teachers continued to push past her as they rushed to get on. Something sharp brushed up against her as she moved forward to get off the train.

A biting pain ripped through her forearm.

She looked down at her arm as she stepped onto the platform. She blinked as her mind tried to make sense of what she was seeing. The polyester material on her coat sleeve had been sliced open. She took off her jacket. The once-white material of her t-shirt was soaked with crimson dots. Her flesh had been sliced clean open. A seven-inch cut ran from below her elbow to above her wrist. With each beat of her heart, the blood sprayed out.

She'd been cut. Someone had cut her.

She looked back up at the carriage, searching the faces to see who had attacked her. In amongst the teachers and students was a man in a black suit, his back to her.

She stepped forward to try to get back on the train but the doors slid shut and the train sped away.

CHAPTER TWENTY-NINE

Jess held her arm tight to her chest, trying to put enough pressure on it to quell the steady torrent of blood.

Her head spun. The cut was deep. She was losing too much blood. She looked down at the small bump along her bra: the microphone in her wire. "Jamison," she whispered. All she had to do was tell him to come find her and he would. She could close her eyes and let the blackness pull her under.

She took a deep breath. She had to be strong. They needed to pick up Robert Kaplan. If Jamison came for her, they would miss a chance to speak to their only lead. Kaplan was scared; he could run at any time. She dropped her coat because she couldn't hold onto them and deal with the cut at the same time. She held her arm against her and used her other hand to take off her belt. She placed it above the elbow of her injured arm and used her teeth to tighten it. She kept pulling until the blood slowed to a trickle, then she wrapped the loose end around her arm and secured it.

She bent down to pick up her coat but her vision went black at the slight movement. She would have to leave it. She had just enough energy to make it to Gallery Place. She didn't have the energy to change lines. She would have to get back on the red. Not that it mattered now. She was only changing lines to make sure no one had followed her, and it was obvious they had.

She waited for the next train and found a seat next to an old woman. She tried to position her body so people wouldn't notice the bloodstains that covered her but there was no hiding it. She looked like a crime scene because she was one. People stared at her open-mouthed but tellingly no one spoke to her or offered any help. A macabre thought came to mind: she wondered what would happen if she bled out on the train. Would anyone step in then or would her dead body be found at the terminus? Some poor shmuck would have to scrub out her blood stains.

That's what her life had come to, stains on the train.

She closed her eyes to dislodge the thought. She leaned down and spoke into her microphone. "Change of plan. Pick Kaplan up. I repeat, pick Kaplan up." Guilt stabbed at her for implicating Jamison any further in this mess but she physically could not do this on her own in this condition. She was barely holding onto consciousness.

She closed her eyes again and concentrated on taking slow, steady breaths until she quelled the wave of nausea. She opened her eyes and focused on the vibration of the train.

Finally, she arrived at her stop. She held onto the seat to balance herself, leaving streaks of blood everywhere she touched. Someone would have to clean that up. She wished she didn't have to make a mess but she couldn't keep upright without leaning on the seats. She lost her footing when someone pushed past her to get off, but she righted herself before she fell.

A bead of sweat dripped down her forehead. Her skin felt like it was on fire. The station was so hot. Slowly she walked to the escalator, never fully lifting her feet off the ground in case she fell because she wasn't sure she could pick herself up.

She squeezed the rubber of the handrail until her fingers drained of color. She stood frozen when she got to the top. For a moment, she couldn't remember the way out. She had been in the station thousands of times but everything seemed different. She blindly followed the crowds past the juice bar and the old man shining shoes.

She breathed a sigh of relief when she saw daylight. A gust of freezing air hit her face. Somewhere in the back of her mind she registered that she should be cold but she wasn't. Her entire body burned.

She spotted Jamison's car parked at the designated spot at Calvary Baptist Church and took a deep breath to give her the strength to keep walking. Her arm was completely numb but her shoulder throbbed with excruciating heat, like hot pokers were being stabbed into it. She had tied the makeshift tourniquet too tight.

"Jessie." Jamison opened the door and ran to her. "Oh, shit. What happened?"

At first her mouth felt too dry to speak. "Kaplan. Where's Kaplan?" None of this was worth it if they hadn't picked him up.

"He's in the car. What the hell happened?"

"We need to get out of here. I don't know if I was followed. I'm sorry. I know I should have doubled back on myself so I wouldn't be followed but I couldn't."

"Jesus, Jessie. We need to get you to the hospital."

"No!" she shouted. "I need to speak to Kaplan."

Jamison opened the passenger door and let her in.

"Shit, what happened to you?" Robert Kaplan asked. In the rear-view mirror, she watched the color fade from his cheeks. His gaze didn't shift from her blood-soaked shirt.

"Are you going to vomit? Open the door if you're going to throw up," she told him. She'd seen other people react this way to blood, and they always either passed out or vomited. She hoped Robert Kaplan was a fainter not a barfer because they didn't need to add vomit to this shitstorm. "Close your eyes and take deep breaths," she told him.

Blood and death were second nature to her, so much so that sometimes she forgot that other people weren't as cavalier. His nostrils flared as he sucked in frantic breaths.

"You're okay. Just relax and concentrate on your breathing. Good. Just like that," she said.

Jamison slid into the driver's seat. "Jessie, we need to get you to the hospital."

"I'm fine."

"You're not fine. You're a lot of things but fine is not one of them."

Jess didn't have the energy to fight with him. She knew she needed medical attention but it had to wait. "Okay fine, take me to the hospital, but drive slow so I can interview Kaplan." Jess tried to reach for her seatbelt but she couldn't.

Jamison reached across her and buckled the belt for her. "You're so… Shit, I don't even have the word for it." Anger and concern creased his brow.

"Who the fuck are you people and what do you want with me?" Kaplan asked.

"I'm asking the questions," Jess said. "Why did Lynette Hastings hire you?"

"You don't know? I thought you worked for the Founding Fathers. Who the fuck are you?" he shrieked as panic set in.

"Answer her question," Jamison growled, his tone harsher than usual.

Kaplan jumped in his seat. "Jesus. I don't want anything to do with this bullshit. I should have never taken the case."

"Well, you did. So, answer the question. Why did Lynette Hastings hire you? I want to know everything you know about the Founding Fathers and The Last Supper. Remember: we found you once. We will find you again. I will keep coming for you. You think the Founding Fathers are scary, you haven't seen anything yet," Jess warned.

"Last supper? I don't know what you're talking about."

Jamison braked hard at the red light, sending Jess lunging forward. The snap of the seatbelt would have hurt if she wasn't already numb.

"That's not good enough. Tell me what you do know. Start at the beginning," Jess shouted. She was running out of time. She felt her tenuous grip on consciousness slipping. Her vision was clouding, going black at the edges.

"Okay, okay. At the end of September, I got this call from Lynette. Her son died at some wilderness camp. The school told her that he had committed suicide but she didn't believe it. She tried getting answers from the school. They completely stonewalled her and then they told her that they would sue her for slander if she told anyone that her kid had committed suicide under their watch. They went after her hard. Threatened her at work. She lost her job, she had to start doing agency work, picking up shifts at any hospital that would take her. And then social services came after her and tried to take her kids. She tried to hire a lawyer. She thought if she sued them she might get some answers. At first the lawyer said she had a case and that he would get her answers, but then he changed his tune. Someone spooked him. He told her to stop asking questions, but it was her kid. She couldn't just stop looking for answers until she knew what had happened."

"So, she called you," Jess guessed.

"Yeah and I wish to hell I would have hung up on her. I would still have a career. And I wouldn't have to look over my shoulder all the fucking time." He scrubbed his face with his hands.

"What did you find out?" Jamison asked.

"That the Founding Fathers will fuck up your life if you mess with them. That's what I found out."

"Who are they?" Jess asked.

"They are a secret society at the school. It's like a fraternity. They say they are a charity group but it's more like the goddamn mafia. Once you're in, you're in for life. At first, I thought it was like some sort of networking cult. They all scratch each other's backs. You know, the usual cronyism. They give each other jobs and write letters of recommendation for other people's kids. All your usual bullshit, but under that is something really dark.

They take care of things. If one of them gets in trouble, the other ones circle the wagons and make sure it goes away, whatever it is: speeding tickets, lawsuits, nasty divorces. Whatever it is, they will fix it for you."

"Why?" Jamison pulled in front of a black SUV. The driver beeped his horn but Jamison didn't even blink. "Why would they do that? People don't just break the law for other people. That's not normal, even for a fraternity."

"They have dirt on each other. All of them. I'm telling you. It's mutually assured destruction. If one of them goes down, they all go down. That's why they are loyal and they are everywhere."

"What kind of secrets?" Jess asked.

"I don't know. That's what I was trying to find out. But then I was contacted by one of the members and told in no uncertain terms to stop investigating or they would make me disappear."

"They threatened to kill you?" Jess asked.

"Yes. Not in those words but it was clear. And even when I agreed to stop investigating them, they kept coming after me. I'm convinced the only reason they didn't kill me is because I told them that I had sent a dossier on them to three lawyers and told them to release it if anything happened to me."

"Good thinking," Jess said. "You're smarter than you look."

"Thanks."

"Do you still have the dossier?" she asked.

He nodded.

"Good. Send it to me," she said and then gave him Lindsay's email. She had no doubt that her own email was now under surveillance but hopefully they wouldn't think to check a dead woman's account.

She waited for him to pull out his phone and forward the email. "Where did you get your information?"

"I promised him I wouldn't tell. He was scared. He only agreed to talk to me if I swore I would never disclose my sources."

"There is no privilege for PIs," Jamison said.

"I know but it's common decency. This could get him killed."

Jamison pulled into the ambulance bay at the hospital. "Yeah, it could, and we're in a far better position than you to protect him. What's his name?"

"Jim Iverson. He works at the school. He said there was some shady shit going down at the school and he wanted nothing to do with it, but he doesn't know what to do. He said that the board of the charity is pulling the strings. Speak to Jim—he will back me up on all of this."

"Jim Iverson is dead. They killed him," Jess said.

"Oh, shit."

"They will kill you too if they get a chance. You need to get out of DC today. You can't wait. Clear your account and go. Pick a city and just go. Take a bus and pay cash so they can't find you."

"Oh, shit," he said again. This time his words were lost to blubbering tears.

Jamison got out of the car, came around to the passenger side, and opened the door for her. He leaned across her and undid the seatbelt.

"Thanks. I'm okay I…" She tried to finish the sentence but the darkness dragged her under. She tried to fight it but she didn't have the energy to keep her eyes open.

Jamison scooped her up off the seat.

She tried again to speak but she couldn't so she just relaxed into Jamison's embrace. Her body felt so light like she was floating, seeing everything from above. She felt warm and safe. Nothing could hurt her. There was no pain where she was.

"Come on, Jessie, stay with me."

CHAPTER THIRTY

"BP is eighty over fifty. She needs another bag of O negative."
A cacophony of frantic noise engulfed her. Machines beeped…
doctors screeched orders… nurses reported stats.

Jess tried to open her eyes but the lids were too heavy. She
wanted to tell them she was okay. They didn't need to waste their
time on her. She was fine. *Go help someone who needs it.* The words
stuck in her throat because she couldn't open her mouth. She was
trapped in darkness. It was like being ensconced in black tar, dark
and hot, but still she shivered.

And then she was flying again… white everywhere… she was
weightless and free… nothing but eternity.

CHAPTER THIRTY-ONE

Something was squeezing her arm. She wished it would stop already. She tried to pull her arm away but she was stuck.

Her eyes fluttered open.

"Hey there. You gave us quite a scare." A nurse looked over at her.

Jamison was sleeping upright in a chair. His head hung to the side in an awkward position that could not be comfortable. His neck would be sore when he woke up.

The nurse nodded to him. "He's been here all night. We don't usually let family back here but he insisted."

Family. She wondered what else he had told them to break the rules. "He's my partner." Her voice cracked.

"Here, let me get you some water." The nurse poured her a glass of ice water from the jug on the bedside table. She put in a straw and then held it to Jess's lips.

"Thank you," Jess said. Her mouth was so dry she could drink forever and still feel thirsty.

"Little sips so you don't make yourself sick."

Jess tried to listen but she kept drinking until all the water was gone. If she could move her arm, she would have fished out an ice cube and sucked on it.

"I'll be back in fifteen minutes to check your vitals again." The nurse put her chart at the end of the bed.

"Hey," Jamison said. Sleep made his voice sound deeper than usual.

"Hey," Jess replied. She glanced down at her bandaged arm.

"You needed surgery to clean it up and close the wound. You were pretty beat up. The cut was really deep."

"Did they find out who did it?"

"We called the transit police to pull the video and they said it's missing for that time and location. They said they think someone might have accidently deleted it."

"Accidently? Huh. That's convenient. Did they just delete the attack? Maybe we can find video of him a few stops back. He was on the carriage with me before. I'd recognize him if I saw him."

"Everything is gone. They managed to find you getting on the Metro but then there is nothing until you come back out."

Jess shook her head. She shouldn't have let herself hope that they would finally have a concrete lead. "Hand me my phone."

"Who do you want to call?"

"Tina and Jeanie. I need to warn them."

"They're in the waiting room. I'll go get them," Jamison said as he stood up.

A few minutes later, he returned with Tina and Jeanie. Again, she wondered how he persuaded the medical staff to break the rules and let them all in.

"Oh, Jessica…" Jeanie stood in the doorway. Sadness clung to her. She didn't finish the sentence, she just shook her head.

"I'm really fine. It looks worse than it is." She didn't want to waste time talking about the stupid cut; she was just glad none of them had been hurt in this. "Did Jamison tell you what Kaplan told us?"

"Yeah, he filled us in," Tina spoke for both of them.

"Good. I told him to leave town. It's not safe for him here."

They both nodded.

"Tina, your brother lives in Hawaii, right?"

"Yeah on Oahu."

"Good. You need to go see him. Take all your holiday time. Stay there until it's safe to come back," Jess said. "I'm sending everything we have to the DOJ anonymously. I think it should be enough for them to act on. Hopefully they will do the right thing but if things don't get resolved, you might need to consider a transfer to the Honolulu office." She tried her best to sound matter-of-fact. She hated mentioning this eventuality but there was every possibility that it would not be safe enough for Tina to return, and she deserved to know the truth. She didn't want her to be blindsided with the information later.

"No, I'm not going to leave you, especially in the middle of an investigation."

"I'm leaving too," Jess lied. "I didn't make it home for Thanksgiving so I'm going to go back to Texas until this blows over. Jeanie, you should go back to Utah. Stay with your family. Take precautions. If these guys stick to their MO, if they come after you, they will try to make it look like a suicide. So, be careful. I don't want to admit defeat but this is too big. I hate saying that but it is, and I want to live to fight another day."

"What about you, Jamison?" Jeanie asked.

Jamison cleared his throat. He looked momentarily back-footed but he quickly recovered. She hadn't discussed the plan with him. "Um… I'm going to go stay with Felicia's family in Alabama for a while."

Tina's eyes welled up. "I don't want it to end this way."

"I know." Jess reached out for her hand and gave it a light squeeze. "It might just be temporary. We have to have faith in the Department of Justice. Things are going to work out. We have to believe that. This isn't goodbye, not forever. I'll see you again."

Jeanie leaned over and hugged her. Her arms felt right around her, like a blanket keeping out the cold. For the first time that she could remember, Jess didn't want to pull away. She wished it could last a little longer so she could remember later what it felt like to have someone touch her and not want anything in return. But too soon Jeanie pulled away so she could whisper in her ear,

"I'm proud of you, Jessica. You're not just a fine agent, you're a fine person. Never forget that."

Jess squeezed her lids together to keep herself from crying. She wouldn't let herself; she'd already cried enough to last a lifetime.

She waited until Tina and Jeanie had gone before she pressed the call button for the nurse.

"What are you doing?" Jamison asked.

"I need to get discharged so I can get out of here. You heard me, it's not safe for any of us to stay here, so I'm going back to Texas to stay with my mom and stepdad." She pressed the buzzer again to make sure it had gone through.

"Bullshit."

Jess's eyes widened.

"They might buy what you're selling but I've known you too long to fall for your shit. You have a plan and you want them gone so they don't get caught up in it."

She didn't insult him by lying to him.

"Dammit, Jessie. When will you start taking care of yourself? You always make sure everyone else is safe. When will you do the same for yourself? I get it, you're brave. But you don't have to be stupid too."

"Just go, Jamison. We don't both need to put ourselves at risk. Go."

"Why? Why do you care so little about yourself? Other people might see this as noble but I'm calling bullshit."

Jess didn't have time to formulate a response before the nurse came in. "Are you ready for me to take your vitals? I didn't want to interrupt you before." She pulled the chart off the end of the bed.

"No, I don't want my vitals taken. I would like to be discharged, please. I know you must be busy but if you could find a doctor to sign off on it, that would be great. Thank you."

The nurse looked up from the chart and then to the IV still connected to her arm. "You're not even done with your antibiotics. You need—"

"Is there any way you can speed them up?"

"No… I mean, you're not ready to be discharged."

"I feel fine."

"Jessie, that is your battle cry." Jamison rolled his eyes. "Just once, I would like to hear you say you need help. Just once."

"You know what?" Jess said, glancing up at the almost empty IV bag. "Never mind. I think you're right. I probably should stay a little longer. I'm kind of tired actually. Can I rest for a while?"

"Yeah, of course." The nurse gave her an understanding smile before she picked up her arm to feel for her pulse on her wrist. "Your partner is right. There is no shame in admitting you need help." She was silent as she counted the beat. "Pulse is fifty-five."

"My resting pulse is always low," Jess assured her. "I run."

The nurse nodded. She took out the thermometer and put a plastic cover on the end before she said, "Open up." She placed it under Jess's tongue. When it beeped she pulled it out and then read the digital number on the machine. "Temp is normal. We'll have you out of here in no time," she assured her. "But for the time being, just relax. You're in good hands."

"Thanks." Jess managed a faint smile.

She waited for a few seconds after the nurse left before she pulled at the adhesive that held her IV in place. The bandage on her other arm made her movements slow and awkward.

"Honestly, what the hell is wrong with you?" Jamison growled. "I can't even deal with your bullshit today. Do you have any idea how seriously you were injured? This wasn't a damn scratch. Your entire arm is covered in stiches." His tone was harsh but under the anger was fear. He was worried about her. She didn't need him to worry about her. She didn't need anyone.

"Kaplan said they have dirt on everyone and the board keeps it in one location. You know who the chairman of the board is? It's Chief Hagan. He has the files on everyone. I know it." She pressed her bandaged arm to the vein on the other side to stem the few drops of blood that appeared when she pulled out her IV. She could really use a Band-Aid but this would have to do. "The Founding Fathers take care of their own. That much we know. All of this is to cover up something that one of their members did. Thirteen people are dead because of it. We owe it to all of them to figure out why."

Jamison scrubbed at his face. "You're suggesting we break into the chief of police's office and steal his files."

"No." Jess swung her legs over the bed. The vinyl floor was cold under her bare feet. "I'm going to break into Hagan's office. You're going to leave town."

"Seriously? You want me to duck and cover and let you take all the heat? What kind of person do you think I am? This is what's wrong with you, Jessie. You always assume the absolute worst of everyone." He shook his head as he reconsidered. "No, that's not true, not everyone, just all men. How many times do I have to tell you I'm not like your dad?"

She didn't answer him. Instead, she leaned on the bed to bend over and open the cubicle that held her clothes. Her underwear, pants, and socks were there but nothing else.

"Where's my bra and my shirt?"

"They cut them off you in the ER."

"Oh." She looked down at her hospital gown. It wasn't ideal but she could tuck it into her pants.

Jamison stood up, stripped off his own sweater, and handed it to her. "Here."

"Thank you." She put on her pants and then turned away from him to take off her hospital gown, which was stupid because he had seen her naked before. She reached up to undo the tie that held the gown closed but her fingers could not manage the tight knot.

His clean, masculine scent surrounded her when she pulled on his sweater.

"There is independent and then there is pig-headed. We both know which side of the line you fall on." He moved closer and undid the knot for her. "You don't always have to fend for yourself."

Jess squeezed her lids together to stop the pressure that was building behind her eyes. "I do, actually." She hated talking about her feelings but this needed saying. "I don't have anyone. I did. I had Lindsay but now she is gone. So please don't tell me I'm not alone because I am. Stop pretending that I'm not."

"I'm here, aren't I?"

Maybe it was the anesthesia or the seriousness of the situation but something made her keep talking. "But for how long? I counted on you once but you left. You were gone for two years." She had been destroyed when he'd left to go undercover in Alabama. She'd tried to ignore it, but she'd felt rejected. He was her best friend and then he was gone, like she'd never meant anything to him.

"Turn around, Jessie. I'm not going to have this conversation with the back of your head."

She didn't want to be having this conversation at all but she took a deep breath and turned around.

He tugged on the collar of his T-shirt, pulling down the white cotton fabric to expose the raised skin of the scar she'd given him. "Grow up, Jessie. I forgave you for this. You can forgive me for leaving."

She bit into her bottom lip to keep it from trembling. It wasn't just the shooting he needed to forgive her for. There was so much more, everything she'd done, and who she was, all the reasons that made him feel like he needed to leave her in the first place. "I need to go."

She shoved her feet into her winter boots. She paused mid-air because the room spun when she tried to bend over and zip them.

"Here, let me." Jamison bent over and zipped her shoes.

"Thank you."

She turned and left the hospital room, Jamison a few steps behind. She walked past the nurse's station, half-expecting someone to stop her from leaving, but she wasn't under arrest; it wasn't like they could keep her there.

She walked to the end of the hall. She glanced at the entrance for the stairs but kept going until she reached the elevator. Jamison gave her a knowing look when he leaned past her to press the button but he didn't say anything, nor did he say anything on the way down when she had to hold onto the railing for support, which she appreciated. She would have liked to tell him she was fine to make her way home alone but he had her stuff and home wasn't safe to go back to anyway.

The sun had not yet begun its ascent, so the sky was pitch-black as they walked outside. And then there was a flash of white and then another as someone took a photo and then someone called her name.

Jess squinted to make out the forms of people that lined the street in front of the hospital. Journalists three-deep, some with microphones and camera crews, stood behind a police cordon shouting her name.

"What?" she whispered, shaking her head. "Why are they taking my picture?" She held up her bandaged arm to hide her face.

One of the journalists broke through the tape and ran toward her. He thrust a microphone at her. "Why did you do it, Jessica? Is this because of your father? Was it just all too much for you? What was it like to be raised by one of the most notorious child-killers in American history? Tell us what it was like to live with The Headmaster. Are you still in contact with him? Is it true you lied for him? Why? Why did you protect a child-killer?"

CHAPTER THIRTY-TWO

Jess stood paralyzed. She couldn't speak or breathe; all the air had been sucked from her lungs. All she could do was stare vacant-eyed as an army of journalists swarmed at her, lights flashing as they took her picture. Live cameras were on her, recording her from every angle.

"Jessica!" one of them screeched.

Jess winced when a microphone smacked against her bandaged arm.

"Back up. Get off her!" Jamison shouted. He wrapped his arm around her and pulled her close to him, sheltering her as he pushed through the crowd to get to his car.

"What's happening? What's going on?" Jess whimpered. This couldn't be happening. All her pain and shame swelled up from inside, consuming her. Her body burned with mortification. "Who?" Her legs went slack. She was going to fall but Jamison wouldn't let her. "Who told them?"

"It's okay, Jessie. I got you." He opened the car door and helped her in, leaning across her to buckle her in.

A reporter tried to lean into the car to get her on tape. "Why did you lie for your father? Did he abuse you? Were you one of his victims too or just his accomplice?"

Jamison spun on his heel. "Back off." He shoved the reporter, who went flying. Water sprayed up as the man tripped over the curb and fell into a puddle.

Jamison went around to the driver's side and slid in, slamming the door behind him.

"What's happening?" Jess asked. She still could not process what was going on around her.

"I don't know. But I'm going to find out."

Reporters swarmed around the car, blocking them in. He put the keys in the ignition and put the car in reverse. They didn't immediately move but Jamison kept driving at them slowly, nudging them out of the way until they did.

The ride back to his house was a blur of motion, Jamison darting in and out of lanes, doubling back on himself to make sure they weren't followed. She knew it didn't matter, though, because they would find her wherever she went. It was only a matter of time.

Jamison pulled into the garage. It was completely black inside once the metal door came down because the single-filament bulb had gone out and not been replaced. They sat in silence for few minutes, neither speaking nor moving, both too shell-shocked to say anything.

The dark was strangely comforting, like they were cocooned in another world, something separate from the ugliness just outside.

Jess was the first to speak. It was obvious that the Founding Fathers were behind this but what wasn't obvious was where they'd gotten their information. The reporters knew things she didn't even like to admit to herself. "No one knows that about me, that I lied for my dad. Just you and Dr. Cameron. I didn't even tell Lindsay, I was too embarrassed."

"Are you asking me if I told anyone? Because I didn't. Never."

She shook her head even though he couldn't see her. "No, I wasn't asking you. I was talking it through out loud. I know it wasn't you so that leaves Dr. Cameron."

"Or your dad," Jamison said. "How can you be sure it wasn't him? They could have reached out to him. He is in prison less than five hundred miles from here. He could have been bribed."

"No," she whispered. "He wouldn't do that to me. There's no way." It had been more than twenty-five years since she'd seen him but she knew with absolute certainty he would never knowingly hurt her because he never had. For all intents and purposes, he was dead to her. That's what she told people, that he was dead, because she couldn't tell them the truth: that her hero, the man she would miss until the day she died, was also a sadistic child-killer. Those words were too shameful to say aloud.

She hated him, what he had done to all those boys and their families, and for teaching her to look for the monster in every man. But she also loved him. She hated herself for it but she did. She loved him and she missed him. And she trusted him. Still. "It wasn't him. It had to be Dr. Cameron."

"Okay," Jamison answered. "I'll call him. I'll deal with it."

"No." She didn't need Jamison to swoop in and clean up the mess that was her life. She could take care of herself. Even if she could depend on him like that, she wouldn't let herself. "I'll do it."

The light in the car went on when he opened the door. He came around to the passenger side, opened the door for her, and then undid her seatbelt.

"Thanks."

"You really hate not being able to do everything for yourself."

"I don't love it." She sighed. The anesthetic that they'd given her was wearing off and everywhere from her shoulder down ached with a burning pain. She reached for her bag but stopped short when she remembered she didn't have painkillers left. "Shit. I don't have any ibuprofen."

"You know where they have a lot of that? In the hospital, where you should be right now."

She followed him up the stairs to the kitchen, where he pulled out a chair at the table. "Here, sit down. I'm going to go close the curtains."

Jess didn't have the energy to argue with him. It was a necessary precaution and she couldn't do it herself. She placed her bag on the table and sat down. Stan ran through from the other room. He nudged her hand up with his nose so she would pet him. "Hey, buddy. Did you miss me? I missed you, my sweet boy." She nuzzled her head against his.

Jamison returned a few minutes later. He got a glass from the cupboard and filled it up from the kitchen sink. He handed it to her with a box of prescription painkillers. "These are all I have. They're from when I got shot. I'll get you some ibuprofen later when I go to the store. I need to get Stan some dog food too."

Her throat tightened. It felt good to be taken care of but she knew not to get used to it because it would only make it hurt more later when he remembered all of the reasons he needed to push her away.

He went to the back door and opened it to let the dog out.

The tamperproof foil made a popping sound when she pressed the white pill against it to break the seal. Without reading the label she swallowed two with a gulp of water. She didn't care what they were as long as they made the pain stop for a while. When she had first injured her hand, she'd refused to take any prescription painkillers in case she became addicted. She didn't care anymore. She'd rather be addicted than live with this pain.

She took out her phone. There were thirteen unanswered messages that she would have to make her way through at some point. But not today. She couldn't face doing that right now. She scrolled through her numbers before she got to Dr. Cameron's.

On the second ring, he answered. "Jess? I've just seen the news. I was going to call you and see how you're doing."

His voice sounded so kind, full of genuine concern. He was good. She could imagine his face, the way he tilted his head slightly and nodded while she spoke. And his kind eyes. It was a lie, all of it was a lie, but she had believed it. She'd picked him to confess her darkest secrets to because she thought he could help her, but he had fucked her over. That would teach her to trust someone.

"Are you one of the Founding Fathers? Or do they just have shit on you?" she asked.

"What? I don't know what that is. How are you? Do you want to come in and speak to me? Or I can come to you. I have a few appointments this morning but I'll clear my schedule."

She gripped the phone until her hand shook. He was still pretending to be a nice guy. "No, I don't want to fucking see you. I want to know what they have on you. What possible dirt could they have to make you violate doctor–patient privilege? What you did is illegal and I'll make sure you lose your license."

He was silent for a beat. "Jess… um… I don't know what you're talking about. Is this a case you're investigating?"

"Stop it!" she screamed. "Cut the shit. Just tell me why you did this to me."

"Jess—"

"Stop using my name. You forget I know all your tricks. They don't work on me."

"Okay, I apologize. I don't want you to feel tricked, that's not what I'm trying to do. Are you alone right now? Is there anyone there? I don't think you should be alone right now."

"What?" She shook her head. What was he talking about?

"I have to ask you this: are you still considering trying to hurt yourself?"

"What in the hell are you talking about?" She shook her head again. He was trying to confuse her, make her seem crazy. It was sick but she couldn't put it past him now. "You're the only person who knows I lied for my father when I was a little girl. You must have been the person who told them."

"Them? Who is 'them,' Jess? Are you hearing voices?" He managed to sound genuinely confused but she would not be fooled again.

"I said stop using my name!" Pain shot through her arm as she slammed her hand down on the kitchen table.

"Jess… sorry. I think we're talking at cross purposes here."

She took a deep breath. "I was just accosted by several journalists asking me questions about my father. You are the only person who could have given them that information."

"Oh God, no. I haven't seen anything. I'm sorry. Oh, shit."

"Oh, shit? That's your answer? You violated privilege in the cruelest possible way and all you have to say is 'oh shit'? What kind of fucking monster are you?"

His breathing quickened, coming in frantic bursts. "Okay, this is all starting to make more sense now. Shit, I knew I should have reported it."

"What?" she demanded. She was tired of playing games. She wouldn't let him gaslight her.

"Two days ago, someone broke into my office. Files were taken out of my desk—your files with all the notes from our sessions."

"What?"

"I didn't report it because I thought you'd done it."

Jess squeezed her lids together. She didn't believe him. She couldn't. She couldn't trust anyone. Her head was fuzzy because the painkillers had started to kick in.

"Are you okay? Are you still there?"

"Yeah," her voice cracked.

"I need you to be honest with me: are you still considering suicide?"

Jess's eyes flew open. "No! What? Why would you say something like that?"

"I've seen the video. It's all over the news. That's why I was going to call you. I need to know you're not going to hurt yourself again. I have a duty of care to you."

"Video! What video?" She bolted upright and ran through to the living room where Jamison was sitting.

"Turn on the television." She didn't wait for him. She grabbed the remote control but it slipped through her fingers and smashed on the ground. The plastic snapped off the back and one of the batteries flew out, landing beside Stan, who looked up at her, confused.

"What's wrong?"

"Just turn on the TV. Please."

Jamison bent over, grabbed all the component pieces of the remote control, put them back together, and then turned on the TV. ESPN flashed on the screen.

"No, the news." Her heart hammered against her ribs.

Jamison turned the channel. The words "breaking news" flashed across the screen.

Jess stood paralyzed as she saw her name in the update that scrolled across the screen followed by familiar photos, the ones that had been plastered over her apartment walls. The top news story was that she had created the Last Supper game before trying to kill herself. That was why she had been attacked. They hadn't tried to kill her. It was worse than that.

"Oh my God. They don't just want to stop me. They want to destroy me."

CHAPTER THIRTY-THREE

Jess's hands shook as she threw her clothes into her suitcase, dirty ones mixed in with clean. She wasn't sure anymore which were which but she could sort that out later, when she got wherever she was going. She just needed to get out of here, to run.

She needed to buy a ticket… to somewhere. Where? Where could she go where the population had not seen her face and secrets splashed across the television and newspapers? She couldn't go anywhere in the continental USA, she knew that much for sure because news outlets from both coasts had been calling her all morning.

Her number wasn't listed so Hagan or one of the other board members would have had to have tipped them off. This was a well-thought-out attack. The Founding Fathers had released the information about The Last Supper. The world knew about it and thought she was behind it.

She jumped when her phone vibrated as another call came through. "Stop calling me!" she screamed. She was about to send the call to voicemail and turn off the phone all together when she saw Jeanie's name.

She froze. There was a moment when Jeanie had been proud of her. Despite everything that was happening, she'd managed to make her proud, and now it had all gone to shit because Jess managed to ruin every good thing in her life. She didn't want to face her now but she would because she owed her that much. She took a deep breath and hit the answer button.

"Hello."

"Have you seen the news?" Jeanie asked. She did not bother with pleasantries.

"Yeah," she whispered. She closed her lids tight together as if not seeing what was happening around her would mean it wasn't real. "I'm sorry."

"For what? Why are you sorry?"

She bit hard into her lip, even after she tasted blood. There was no denying that Jeanie knew all her secrets now. There was nothing for her to say. She couldn't pretend anymore.

"Jessica? Are you still there?"

She nodded. "Yeah, I'm here."

"Are you okay?"

"Um… yeah. My arm is going to be fine. It's not what they said…" She stopped because she was too embarrassed to continue. Images from the photos in her apartment flashed in her mind. By now everyone with a television had seen them and heard all of the allegations that had been made against her. "I didn't stage the break-in at my place. I have nothing to do with any of this."

"I know."

She could hear the saccharine voices of the news anchors listing all of her alleged crimes as they reported with faux sympathy about the daughter of a serial killer, so messed up by the perversion of her father that she'd grown up to be a monster herself.

"It wasn't me who set up The Last Supper. Please know that it wasn't me. Please know that. I did not do this. It wasn't me. I didn't hurt anyone," she begged Jeanie to believe her.

"Of course, I know it wasn't you. You're being set up but we will fight this. The Department of Justice—"

"No." Jess shook her head. Her fight was gone. There was nothing left to fight for anymore. There was nothing left. She didn't have a career to salvage and she needed to face it. People knew about her past now and what she did to deal with it. "It wasn't all lies," she whispered. "Some of it… some of it was true."

Jeanie was quiet for so long, Jess thought the call might have dropped, but eventually she said, "Did you know I didn't always want to be an FBI agent?"

"No," Jess said, unsure why she was telling her this now.

"I was an English major when Paul and I met. I loved poetry. I could happily read it all day. My plan was to be a high-school English teacher so I could get my fill of poetry and still have time to spend with all the children we were going to have. We wanted four at least."

Even through the phone Jess could feel her sadness. Jeanie's life hadn't turned out the way she had planned either.

Jeanie sighed. "But then of course we found out we couldn't have children and I no longer needed the summers off because there was no one for me to take care of, so I stopped reading poetry and I started thinking about how my life could have meaning again. I found the FBI and it healed me in ways I never imagined, so I threw myself into my career."

Jess stared down at her bloodstained bandage, not sure what to say, or why Jeanie was telling her this.

"When I got my first big promotion, Paul gave me the sweetest gift. It was a framed copy of my favorite poem. I still have it in my office at work. It's called 'We Are Many' by Pablo Neruda. Have you ever read it?"

"No."

"You should. It's beautiful, everyone should read it. It's about how we aren't one thing or another but different people at different times, and none of them are more valid than any other. We are all lots of people over the course of our lives, even throughout the course of the day. We are strong and courageous and weak and cowardly and kind and vindictive. They are all the real us. We need all the parts to make us whole.

What I'm trying to say in perhaps a very clumsy manner is… well… I've see the photos—all of them—and they aren't you, not all of you. You are so much more than your mistakes. Do not let anyone ever tell you that that is all you are because you are so much more."

Jess tried to speak but she couldn't.

"I've known you a long time and I have never regretted advocating for your appointment. I saw something in you the first time I met you. You were so young and so timid then but I knew you had fight in you and I was right. No one fights harder for victims than you. You gave me back Levi's memory. The Founding Fathers stole him from me and then they stole his memory but you gave it back."

"I'm sorry I couldn't bring them to justice."

"Justice will happen. I believe that the same way I believe I will see Levi again," Jeanie said with absolute certainty.

Not for the first time, Jess wished she had something to believe in, something bigger than herself to hold onto, because right now she didn't feel like anywhere near enough. But she didn't believe. Justice was not something that was given by a magnanimous creator, it was something that had to be fought for. "Are you still in DC? You need to get out of here. Go to Utah."

"We're on our way. I wanted to make sure you're leaving too. It's not safe for you here either, Jessica."

"Yeah, I know."

There was nothing more to say so Jess said goodbye, hung up the phone, and switched it off completely. She bent her knees and pulled her legs tight against her chest, folding in on herself. She wanted to be small, to disappear.

Jamison knocked on the bedroom door. She looked up when he came in. He stood in the doorway with Stan by his side. The dog followed him around everywhere. If she left, Stan wouldn't mind or even notice as long as he had Jamison.

He came in and handed her a glass of water and a bottle of ibuprofen. "I got stuff to change your bandage."

"Thank you."

"We need to keep an eye on it. You don't want to get an infection."

She nodded. "The news is saying this was a suicide attempt. Some shitty network psychologist was speculating that I created the suicide game because I want to die but I'm too much of a coward to do it. And he said I targeted boys because I was secretly jealous of my father's victims because they got all of his attention." She tried to open the childproof bottle but she couldn't with her bandaged arm.

Jamison took the bottle from her and opened it, pressing his thumb through the foil to break the final seal. "Shit, Jessie. Why are you watching that?"

"How could I not? You would too if people were saying you were a homicidal pervert with daddy issues. He actually used those words."

"When this is over, you can sue the network. You'll never have to work again, but right now, you need to get out of DC. I know there is no way in hell you would go to your mom's but you need to go somewhere."

She took four tablets and swallowed them with a swig of water. He didn't get it; no one did. This wasn't just a job for her. It was her life, her absolution, and her punishment, all rolled into one. She couldn't not be an FBI agent. It was all she had. "There is talk of bringing federal charges against me for the suicide game."

"We can deal with that later. If you don't want to go to Texas—" he paused for a second like he wasn't sure how to finish the sentence "—come with me."

Her mouth dropped open. She couldn't keep the surprise off her face. He was only offering because he thought it was the only way to keep her alive, but still he was offering, which probably shocked him as much as it did her. "I don't want to go to Alabama." There were a million reasons for her to say no but that was all she could think to say.

"No, neither do I. We can go to California, stay there until this blows over... and then see what happens."

She sucked in a sharp breath. Why did he have to be such a thoroughly decent person? She hadn't done anything to deserve it but he was willing to look past the hurt and regret between them because he thought it was the right thing to do. She'd nearly killed him and yet he was still here offering to help her. Part of her wanted to say yes, to depend on someone else to get her through this, but she couldn't. They couldn't outrun this, and even if they could, she couldn't outrun herself. She'd caused this, the choices she'd made. "This won't blow over. It will always be hanging above my head. I won't ever be able to exonerate myself: they won't ever bring charges because if they did, there would be another investigation and it would give me a chance to tell the real story. They're too smart for that."

"Come away with me, Jessie. We can get away from all this. We both need a fresh start."

She looked away. He had to see he would never have a fresh start with her. He deserved more, something better than anything she could offer. "I can't."

"Why? Why can't you? What's keeping you here?"

"I can't leave it like this. I've lost everything—"

"No, you haven't. Stop being such a goddamn fatalist. You're always saying things are going to turn to shit, and when they do, you use it as proof that you're right. But you know what, your life is shit because you want it to be. You don't want to be happy, do you?"

She didn't even know what happy felt like anymore. She just wanted the chance to keep going. Happy didn't enter the equation.

"No, answer me. Are you scared to be happy because you think you don't deserve it?"

"I don't want to have this conversation right now."

"You never want to have this conversation or any meaningful conversation ever. You know why you don't want to talk? Because you might just resolve some shit and you don't want to do that. That's why I left. I left because I didn't want to be in love with someone so self-destructive. That's right, I said it. I love you. But I still left because you don't have a monopoly on shit decisions."

She blinked several times. For a moment, she couldn't think or speak. *I love you.* They were the words she'd wanted to hear for a long time but now she wanted him to take them back. She didn't know what or how to feel so she stood stunned as the words washed over her in a continuous loop. Slowly, something in her shifted, the fear and shame faded, replaced with an emotion she couldn't identify. All she knew was that she wasn't scared anymore and she was ready to fight. "I need to go back to my apartment."

Jamison threw up his hands in exasperation. "Are you fucking kidding me right now? I just told you I love you and that's what you say? Unbelievable. Do you see now why I left?"

"I need to get the blond wig I used when I was undercover in Florida while we were investigating that serial rapist."

He scrubbed his face with his hands. "Have you lost your mind?"

"Probably, but I can't run away. I need to fight. The case isn't over. The Founding Fathers think they've won but they haven't. I can't let them. I don't want to be looking over my shoulder for the rest of my life. I can't do that and I can't ask you or Jeanie or Tina to live like that. I need to finish this."

"Finish this? What are you talking about?"

"I have to expose what's happening at Gracemount. To do that I need to find Hagan's files but I can't very well go into police headquarters. Thanks to those assholes, everyone knows what I look like."

"Are you kidding me right now? You still want to break into Hagan's office?"

"Unless you have a better way of getting the files. I have to do this. I need to finish this."

"Jesus, Jessie. We can still just leave. You don't have to take every bad situation and make it worse." He shook his head. "I swear to God you will be the death of me. You really are a mess. You know that, right?" He let out a long stream of air. "But you're brave. I'll give you that. So, what's the plan?"

"You're going to take Stan and leave. I don't care where you go, just someplace safe."

"Jessie, stop talking. You're not doing this alone."

CHAPTER THIRTY-FOUR

"Did you get it?" Jamison asked.

"Yeah." She got in the back of his car and shut the door. She winced as she lowered herself down on the floor so the journalists could not see her when he drove out of the underground garage beneath her apartment complex. With any luck, they might think she was still in her apartment, and it would buy them a little more time.

She tried to be gentle with her battered body but there was no way she could maneuver herself without putting pressure on her arm, so she just held her breath and did what she needed to do.

"You good to go?"

She took small, panting breaths and waited for the throbbing pain to fade into a dull ache. A red splotch seeped through the bottom of her bandage. She must have ripped one of the stitches. *Shit.* She would add that to the list of things she would deal with later. "Yeah. Drop me off at the National Gallery of Art. Journalists know your car so you can't take me all the way. I'll get changed in the bathroom and walk to police headquarters. You get a taxi to Hagan's." She went over the plan they'd made, looking for any loose ends. That's how she and Jamison worked: they went over things again and again, looking at every angle. They had decided that Jess would check Hagan's work office while Jamison broke into his house and searched there. It was divide and conquer and hope that one of them found something, and that neither of them got caught.

"I got to say, Jessie, I don't love this plan. It doesn't feel right. We need more time."

"Yeah, well we don't have any." She pushed up on her good arm to try to reposition herself but Jamison hit a pothole and she lost her grip and ended up with her head slammed against the back of his seat. She bit into her lip to keep from swearing out loud and letting Jamison know she was hurt.

"Change of plan. I'm going to check both places. You're still hurt." Under his confident exterior there was a thread of doubt. He was nervous. Most people wouldn't have noticed but she did, and she liked it better when he was cool and cavalier. She did not need him doubting her ability to get it done right now. She wasn't her best physically or emotionally but she would sure as hell pull her own weight. She would never ask Jamison to put himself in danger if she wasn't willing to do the same.

"Can you physically be in two places at once?"

"That's not—"

"No. No, you can't. We've already been through this. We need to work fast. You're better with house locks. You just are. And I can't exactly sneak through a window or climb a trellis at this point, so it just makes more sense for you to check his house. Besides, if this goes to shit—"

"There you go again, assuming everything will go to shit."

"That's not me being a pessimist; things do have a nasty habit of turning to shit with me."

Jamison didn't answer. He was too busy maneuvering in and out of traffic. "I don't think anyone followed us," he said when he pulled over near the National Mall.

She held her breath as she pushed herself up onto the seat. The drops of blood that had bled through her bandage had now saturated her sweater, leaving it sticky and wet. Fortunately, it was black so only she knew it was blood.

"I'll see you back at your house by six, seven at the latest. If I don't come back, please raise Stan as your own." She was only half-kidding.

"Don't say that kind of shit. If you're not back at my house at six, I'm coming to get you."

She shut the door without answering. She didn't want to talk about not making it back on time because they had no real plan for that eventuality. They didn't have a choice, they needed to be successful. There was no plan B.

She kept her head down as she walked through the crowds of tourists that lined the pathways beside the National Mall. A group of foreign students all dressed in matching neon-orange sweatshirts were standing in a cluster trying to make sense of a map. "Sorry," she murmured when she ran into a man taking a selfie with the Lincoln Memorial in the background.

She pulled her hood up and kept walking until she reached the National Gallery. She stood at the bottom and looked up the stairs at the looming Doric columns. She glanced over her shoulder to check one last time that she hadn't been followed before she walked up to the entrance. There was no line because the museum would be closing in less than forty minutes.

"Excuse me." A guard stopped her when she got inside.

The hairs on her arms stood taut. She looked up just enough for him to show she was listening, without fully showing her face. Most of her life had been consumed by the irrational fear that someone would recognize her, terrified that people would know her secrets, but now it wasn't irrational; it was inevitable and she was going to have to deal with it.

"The museum is going to close in less than an hour."

"I know. I'm just here to see the..." Her mind went blank. She couldn't think of a single painter's name. Freshman year in college she'd taken Art History as one of her general studies classes. She'd only picked it because it fit in her schedule but she'd still taken it seriously, making flashcards and memorizing everything on the syllabus, but currently she remembered none of it. "Um... the Botticelli," she said eventually, praying that they had a Botticelli in the collection because that was the only name she could remember.

He nodded. "Portrait of a Youth is over there." He pointed down a long hallway. "Would you like me to show you?"

"No, thank you." She looked up just enough to smile.

She started walking in the direction he'd pointed her until he looked away, then she doubled back on herself and went to the women's restroom. An elderly woman was already in there washing her hands.

Jess walked past her into a stall. With her good arm she closed the door and then pulled out the wig from under her sweater. She pushed down her hood, twisted her ponytail into a bun at the base of her neck, and then pulled the wig on, tugging it forward to adjust it. She waited until she heard the spray of water stop and the bathroom door open before she left the stall.

She glanced at her reflection. The hair of the blond synthetic wig fell just below her chin in an asymmetrical bob cut. She looked so much different now than when she'd first worn it, so much older, more tired. The first time round she was posing as a teenager to lure a serial rapist targeting high-school girls. It was only four years ago but her face looked many more years older. Her cheeks were sunken in now and she had dark circles under her eyes. There was no way she would pass for a teenager now, but at least the wig completely transformed the way she looked. No one should recognize her now.

The cold air hit her lungs as she left the museum. She shoved her hands in her pocket to keep warm because she hadn't had a chance to replace her coat yet. That too could go on her list of things she needed to deal with at some point.

The streets were full because people had already started to leave their offices to try to beat rush-hour traffic. It was impossible to walk down the street without bumping into someone but the sea of people made her feel safer, almost anonymous.

Jess walked up the stairs and straight to the information desk. A middle-aged man was manning the desk. She hadn't prepared what to say to talk her way into the building in advance because every circumstance demanded a different dynamic. She stood for a second, taking in as much information as possible to get a read on the situation. Based on the way he kept glancing up at the clock, his shift was about to end. His wedding ring was tight: the skin rose up around it, burying the scratched gold in flesh. He'd been married a long time, long enough for him to get fat. That showed commitment and traditional values. She could use that.

She took out her credentials and flashed it at him, intentionally shielding the part with her picture. "I have a meeting upstairs. Sorry I'm late. I know I've held everyone up and I apologize. Traffic really is a beast out there today. There's another protest at the White House. These people have too much time on their hands to complain. I mean, do any of them have jobs?" She hadn't given him any information about who she was or why she was there, but she hoped it was enough, that she'd conveyed that she was conscientious, considerate, and most importantly that she belonged in the building. If he thought they shared common values, he would be more likely to like her, and if he liked her he would be less likely to question her further. She maintained eye contact the entire time. She couldn't afford to come across as cagey.

He opened his mouth to speak but before he could ask a follow-up question, she said, "I need two minutes to get cleaned up. I'm just going to head to the ladies' for a second."

"Sure. It's that way." He pointed down the hall to his right. "Do you want me to call anyone to let them know you're here?"

"No, that's okay. I know where I'm going. Thank you. Have a great night. I hope you don't get caught up in the traffic. It's brutal out there." She walked away as fast as she could, but instead of going straight to the bathroom she kept walking, down the hall, searching for the stairs. She needed to know exactly where she was going and how to get there, and more importantly how to get out. Confident that she knew the layout, she walked to the bathroom.

She checked the stalls to make sure they were empty and then she grabbed the trash can and put it in the first stall, the one farthest from the sprinklers. It was already full of damp paper towels. She dumped them on the floor. She needed dry towels. She crumbled them up loosely, leaving plenty of room for airflow. She opened her bag and pulled out the bottle of rubbing alcohol she'd taken from her medicine cabinet. Jamison had no idea this was her real plan. If she'd told him, he would've stopped her, and this was their best chance of gaining access to Hagan's office.

She opened the bottle and poured out the entire contents on the paper towels.

She took a deep breath. This was not how she saw her career going, or her life for that matter. If someone would have told her six months ago that she was going to commit arson, she would have laughed in their face.

She struck a match and threw it in. Orange flames exploded, licking the sides of the trash can, changing color and direction as more paper towels ignited.

A loud shriek broke the silence as the fire alarm went off and then the sprinklers came on, spraying water everywhere. She checked again to make sure the can was still burning before she glanced down at the time on her phone. The average response time for the fire department was down from last year to six minutes and thirty-five seconds. She had less than seven minutes to get into Hagan's office and find the files.

The stairs above her rattled as people started running down. Hagan's office was on the second floor. It would look suspicious if she ran upstairs. She needed to be patient even though every muscle in her body coiled, ready to go, because she knew she was running out of time with every second. She went into the farthest stall. She bolted the door and sat on the toilet. She pulled her legs up to her chest so no one could see her feet under the stall. If they adhered to protocol, someone would be sent to check every bathroom to make sure no one was stuck in the fire.

She held her breath and waited. Water sprayed everywhere, soaking her. Drops rolled down her face like tears. Commotion of frantic voices screaming over the alarm and the thunder of feet rushed past the door. Jess closed her eyes and listened, waiting for the cacophony to dwindle until it was just the piercing chirp of the fire alarm.

She checked her phone. It had been almost three minutes and no one had done a room check. It was too long, she couldn't waste any more time. She had to go now.

Her fingers trembled as she unbolted the lock. Blood smeared across the metal door. The surge of adrenaline made her heart beat faster and her blood pump harder, which meant her arm was now dripping. She swore out loud as she stopped to grab a piece of toilet paper to wipe it off. She was leaving biological evidence everywhere.

She opened the bathroom door and looked up and down the hall. The lights flashed on and off to the same pulsing beating of the alarm. It was a visual signal for deaf people that the alarm had been triggered, in case the monsoon flooding the office wasn't a big enough clue.

She looked again to make sure no one was coming before she ran for the stairs. She slipped on the wet tiles. She held onto the wooden banister to steady herself. According to the map she'd found online, Hagan's office was the last office at the end of the hall. She prayed to a god she didn't believe in that he had left his office unlocked in all the commotion; her plan depended on it.

She hesitated when she reached the door because she knew it wouldn't open. This was where everything was going to turn to shit. The plan was pathetic and desperate. They were better than this shit. A pimply teenager in his mother's basement could've come up with something better. They simply hadn't had the time or resources to do this properly.

She heard Jamison's voice inside her head telling her to cut her shit and not to be such a pessimist. Even as a delusion produced from her own mind, Jamison calmed her down. She held her breath as she turned the handle.

A metal click sounded as the bolt retracted and the door opened. Her heart slammed against her ribs as what she assumed was joy surged through her. She wasn't used to the emotion but that's what it felt like: unbridled happiness.

She went in and closed the door. Now-soggy paperwork fanned out over his desk. His computer was still on. There was also a half-eaten chocolate muffin and a cup of coffee, all signs that he had left in a hurry but planned on coming back. She didn't bother looking at the time on her phone because she didn't need the added pressure.

She assumed she was looking for a USB. *Where would it be?* She glanced at his desktop and considered the possibility that he might have transferred it to his computer. No, that didn't make sense. The IT department would have access to his computer, and any internal investigation could mandate a search of his files. Plus, computers were easily hacked. If she was right, she was looking for child pornography. There was no way in hell he would keep that on his work computer.

She opened up the top drawer in the metal filing cabinet. Manila folders bulged with paperwork. She pulled out the first one and fanned through it, waiting for something to pop out at her, a picture or something, but all she saw was page after page of paperwork.

She went through the next file and then the next until she reached the bottom. She glanced at the clock on the wall. She was running out of time. Where could it be?

She pulled open the top drawer of his desk. There was nothing but paperclips and candy bar wrappers. Sirens blared outside. The fire trucks were pulling up. "Fuck." She slammed the drawer. Metal clanged as it thumped shut. A small box dropped to the floor, dislodged from the bottom of the desk by the force.

She picked it up. One side had a magnet, the other a slide top. She held it in her good hand and used her thumb to open it. She stared down at the contents: a single tarnished key. Her eyes narrowed on the inscription: *Alere flammam veritatis.* That was Gracemount Academy's motto.

Realization struck her. A traditional safety deposit box at a bank would require people to sign in. That would leave a paper trail. Given his status in the community, maybe the safest place to hide the pictures would actually be in plain sight. The information was hidden at the school.

She turned the key over to examine it further. Inscribed on the back was the date 1793. She shook her head. That didn't make sense. The school had been founded before the American Revolution but the date on the key was from nearly twenty years later.

She would have to figure it out later. She slid the key into her pocket and ran for the stairs.

CHAPTER THIRTY-FIVE

A frozen, sloshy rain had begun to fall, big chunks that stayed on your clothes to melt later so even after you were warm inside, they could continue their stealth attack by soaking you slowly. A crowd of people stood huddled together on the sidewalk in front of police headquarters, trying to stay warm while they waited for the fire department to clear the scene. Only a few of them had managed to grab their coats when they vacated the building, and fewer still had umbrellas.

From the corner of her eye she spotted Hagan's corpulent figure.

Her pulse pounded forcefully in her neck as she pushed through everyone to get to the street. She pulled out her phone and dialed Jamison's number but it went to voicemail. She hung up and called again. "Come on, answer," she whispered but he didn't so she left a message. "There's a change of plans. I found a key."

A taxi pulled up to the curb. Before she could finish the message, she had to shove her phone back in her pocket so she could hold out her hand to wave it down. A woman stepped forward to get in the car.

"I'm sorry. I need this." Jess pushed past her and got in. The woman shouted something but Jess slammed the door.

"Gracemount Academy please."

She pulled out her phone again to look up Gracemount. The official website was just a montage of shameless self-promotion. Picture after picture of smiling boys with captions about how well the school was supporting their development. From the pictures, it looked like they were doing an excellent job, right up until the point they murdered them.

She went to the Wikipedia page instead. She scrolled past the section with the official history to the list of important dates in the school's history. The third date listed was 1793: the death of the founder, James Montrose.

"That's it. Of course," she whispered to herself. She knew what the key was for. She clicked on another page to read further. She looked up at the driver. "Okay, slight change of plan."

The seatbelt bit into her when she leaned forward to give the driver instructions.

She closed her eyes and leaned back in her seat, taking a deep breath to try to calm the frantic pace of her heart, but it didn't work.

"Which way do you want me to take?"

She shrugged. There was too much adrenaline surging through her to think clearly enough to make a simple decision. "I don't care. Just get me there fast. Please."

She stared out the window, watching drops of rain trace a path down the glass, observing as they stagnated and engorged until their weight pushed them further. It kept her from looking over her shoulder to see if they were being followed. There was nothing she could do now if they were, so she had to believe they weren't.

Eventually the driver glanced at her in the rear-view mirror. "I had no idea any of this was here."

Jess jumped when he spoke. "Yeah," she croaked. "I don't think very many people do."

Fir trees and a soft incline of grass-covered slopes. There were patches of white, snow that the rain had not melted, but otherwise it was green as far as the eye could see. A slice of nature, cut out from the surrounding urban sprawl. It felt like a different world, a different time. She imagined this was how it looked when James Montrose had founded the school. In her mind, she could see him sitting next to the stream, planning the future of the school, the legacy he was going to leave.

"Is this like a park?" he asked.

"No, it's part of the Gracemount Academy grounds."

He stopped the car. "I can't get any closer—there is a fence. Do you want to see if there is a gate? I can take you around to the front."

"No, thank you." She pulled out a wad of cash from her pocket. "Here, I have a hundred and ninety dollars. I'll give you thirty now and the other one hundred and sixty when I get back. Wait for me. It should only take me five minutes. If you wait and take me home, I'll give you the rest of the money. Do we have a deal?"

"Yeah, sure." He put the car into park and turned off the engine.

Jess got out and walked over to the fence. She glanced back at the taxi. If she was prosecuted for this, the district attorney's office would have a circle jerk to the slam dunk of a case she'd handed them. They had her on video and she'd left biological evidence at the scene of the crime, and now she had given them a witness wrapped up in a bow.

This had to be worth it. She needed to find something to bring them down.

She reached her hand up and grabbed the fence, fanning out her fingers to get a good grip. The wire mesh was slick with rain. She wedged the toe of her boot into the link of the fence and pulled herself up.

As fences went, it was surprisingly easy to scale, even with her injured arm. Most likely it was just for keeping animals out. She put her leg over the other side and then dropped the ten feet to the ground.

A dull ache pounded up her shins at the impact. She gave it a few seconds for the sensation to wear off and then she stood up and walked down toward the stream, following the winding path. Pebbles crunched under her boots, the only sound other than the gentle babble of the current. At the end of the path stood a small octagonal building. Its domed roof was propped up with marble columns.

Above the door, the school motto was inscribed along with the year 1793. This was where James Montrose was buried, here in this mausoleum. She squeezed the key until her hand ached.

Please let it be here. Silently, she begged the universe to give her another break. Just one more.

Jess slid the key into the lock. It clicked when she turned it and the door creaked as it opened. A musky smell wafted out. She walked in and looked around. Her heart sank when she saw nothing but the marble tomb of James Montrose. She looked around again but there was nothing, not a single box or scrap of paper. Nothing.

A scream formed in the pit of her belly. She really thought it would be here. Where else would it be? Why would Hagan go to the bother of hiding a key to a dead man's grave?

"Fuck." The frustration and disappointment ripped her from the inside. It felt like someone had reached into her chest and torn out her heart. Angry tears threatened in her eyes but she wouldn't let herself cry, not for these bastards. She wanted to scream until she ripped her larynx. This wasn't how it was supposed to turn out.

She collapsed down on the stone casket. The marble was cold on her thighs; even through her pants it felt like ice. She shivered when she realized she was sitting on a dead man.

She bolted up.

A slow realization crept over her. What else could she be sitting on? She looked through the glass panels of the domed roof. "Please." She didn't know if she was talking to God or Lindsay but she was asking for help, begging for it.

She lowered herself to the ground beside the coffin. She placed her hands on the cold lid. "Please," she whispered again, and then she took a deep breath and pushed with all her might. The marble croaked as the stone cover ground against the base. Slowly, the lid slid open.

She wiped her brow and then stood up to look into the casket. There was no smell, just bones, stripped bare hundreds of years before, and seven USB sticks, each on a chain with the name of the committee member it belonged to.

Exhilaration shot through her. This was it. She'd found it. She reached into the casket, scooped up all the sticks, and shoved them into her pocket. She looked down at the lid. For a second she considered trying to move it back into place, but it was too heavy and it would waste time she didn't have.

"Sorry," she murmured to the skeleton. The remains had been a person once, with hopes and dreams and people that loved him, and she wanted to honor that.

She closed and locked the door behind her before she ran up the path and climbed the fence. It was more difficult going over this time because of the slight pitch of the ground but she made it.

She dropped to the ground on the other side and ran back to the taxi. Thankfully, he had waited for her because it would be a long hike back into the city. She got in the car and slammed the door. She pulled out her phone and called Jamison but after four rings it went to voicemail. "Come on, Jamison. Where are you? Call me. I found the USBs. I have them. We have the proof. Call me."

She looked at the time on her phone. Hagan would know by now that she had found his key. They would be looking for her. It wasn't safe to go home or to Jamison's. She needed to find a computer, upload the contents of the USB, and send it to the Department of Justice, but she couldn't even go to her office to use her computer. Nowhere was safe.

She swore under her breath, trying to figure out where to go from there. A few seconds later it dawned on her. "Can you please take me to the nearest Apple Store? I think the one in

Georgetown is closer than Pentagon City. Last stop. I promise and then I'll pay you." She opened the browser on her phone to look for an address.

"Yeah, that one is closer." He glanced at her in the rear-view mirror. His expression told her he wanted to ask her something but he didn't.

She dialed Jamison's number again but still no answer. She pushed down her unease. He was fine. He had to be fine. His phone was on silent or his battery had run down. Whatever the reason, he was fine. She had the USBs. Things weren't going to turn to shit, not this time.

She sat back in the seat, closed her eyes, and took a deep breath to try to slow her frantic pulse. The nightmare was almost over but her body was still on high alert. Her endocrine glands kept pumping adrenaline through her to prepare her for battle because it refused to believe she was safe.

She focused on the pattern of her breath, slowly filling her lungs and holding it, doing her best to override the natural fight or flight instinct. Eventually the vibrating sensation of her heart rate was replaced by a steady beat.

She opened her eyes and watched the sea of taillights blinking off and on in rush-hour traffic. She rubbed the memory sticks in her pocket and willed the driver to drive faster. She was almost done. The nightmare was almost over.

Finally, they arrived in Georgetown. "The light is red. Just let me out here." She pulled out the wad of money and slipped it through the partition. "Thank you. And thank for waiting. I really appreciate it."

"No problem." He reached for the money and put it in his shirt pocket without counting it. "I hope you found whatever you're looking for."

"I hope so too. Thanks again for the ride." She slammed the door just as the lights turned green.

She ran into the Apple Store and glanced around at the minimalist décor. The walls and the floor were white. The only color came from the yellow-stained oak tables. She looked at the computer models on display—any of them would do. She just needed a free computer. All but one had a millennial perusing or typing away. She walked up to the iMac. She reached into her pocket, pulled out the USB sticks, and laid them all on the table. In theory, they would all have the same information on them, but it made sense to start with Hagan's first.

She slid the memory stick into place then went to Finder and opened up the folder poetically called "*Veritas.*" *Truth.* That was exactly what she was looking for: the truth. A list of files appeared, each named after a Founding Fathers' member. She glanced over her shoulder before she clicked on the first one. If it was indeed child pornography like she suspected, she didn't want to subject anyone else to it. She wasn't immune to ugliness and depravity but she was used to it in a way no one should be. She looked around. No one was remotely interested in what she was doing; they were all too busy dealing with their own shit.

The first file looked like evidence of fraudulent tax records for a sitting senator. There were also pictures of him kissing a young woman who looked barely legal. She closed the file and kept looking. For every member, there was a file with incriminating information. All of it would be illuminating for a prosecutor but none of it explained why Levi and the other boys had been murdered.

She kept scrolling, taking in every name, every man they had dirt on. Their network was vast. They had members from virtually every walk of life. No wonder they'd been able to organize something so complex.

An electric current bolted up her spine. They had infiltrated the police and judiciary; there was even a name she recognized from the Department of Justice. That's why she couldn't get her warrants. "Shit," she murmured. It would take some digging to figure out who was safe to choose to move this investigation forward.

Later she would go through each with a fine-toothed comb, but right now she needed to find out what happened to Levi. She scrolled through file after file of evidence until she reached the bottom. The last file didn't have a name, just a date: "August 27."

Her pulse picked up speed. This was what she was looking for. Her fingers trembled as she clicked on the icon. A grainy video loaded. She immediately recognized the dormitory-style room at Pine Ridge and watched as Ryan Hastings walked into shot. He was wearing loose-fitting basketball shorts with no shirt. His hair was wet like he had just been for a shower or gone swimming. Fresh bruises covered his back.

She watched as the other boys came into the room. This was the last time all of the murdered boys had been together. She held her breath as she watched the scene unfold.

She gasped. She could not even move to blink. She stood frozen; all the energy in her body was needed to try to make sense of what she'd just seen. "Oh, fuck," she whispered. Suddenly she didn't know what to do, who to show. She needed to think. She swore again. She needed time she didn't have. She opened Lindsay's email account and uploaded everything to a draft. Her own email had been compromised but hopefully they wouldn't think to check a dead woman's.

She needed to speak to Jamison about what they should do next, who they could trust to move this forward. Where in the hell was he?

She reached into her pocket to pull out her phone, but before she had a chance, a hand clamped hard around her wrist.

CHAPTER THIRTY-SIX

Jess winced from the pressure on her stiches. Her head snapped up. Two uniformed officers stood behind her.

"Jessica Bishop, you're under arrest for the murder of Jim Iverson."

"No." She shook her head. She tried to pull her hand away but the officer slapped handcuffs on her, pulling her arms behind her as he snapped them into place. This was damage control. They were trying to pin it all on her. But she wouldn't let them, not without a fight.

"You have the right to remain silent. Anything you say can and will be used against you in a court of law."

"No!" she screamed louder. "I'm not going to remain silent. This is about the Founding Fathers. I know what you did."

Everyone stopped what they were doing to watch. Some had taken out their phones and pointed them at her to record her arrest. One of the officers yanked her back. She lost her footing and stumbled backward. The small of her back collided with the hard edge of the table before she crashed against the tiles. She winced at the impact. Because her hands were pinned behind her back, she couldn't shield herself from the fall.

"Don't make a scene," the officer whispered. The hiss of his voice was menacing, but not as much as the way he smiled when he said it. It was a silent challenge, telling her he would make things very difficult for her if she didn't cooperate.

"You have the right to an attorney present. If you can't afford an attorney, one will be appointed to you." He continued as he yanked her up by her cuffed arms. Her shoulder screamed out at the jerking movements. He snatched off her wig and threw it to the ground so everyone could get a good view of her while she was being arrested. He wanted to humiliate her. Someone whispered her name and another one pointed as she whispered behind her hand.

The familiar weight of shame pummeled her from every direction. There was nowhere to hide. All the ugliness of her life was laid bare for everyone to see. Her throat constricted, she couldn't breathe. The corners of her vision went black. She thought she might pass out but she didn't. She clung to enough consciousness to realize that her life would never be the same again. People would always know who she was. She wanted to run. She always wanted to run but she couldn't. She realized that now. Suddenly the shame turned to anger.

Her instinct was to lower her head to try to prevent people from seeing her, but it was too late now so she lifted her chin and forced herself to make eye contact with everyone she passed. Let them judge her. She was done running from her past. She wasn't ashamed anymore, certainly not for things she hadn't even done.

She was the daughter of a serial killer but she was also the woman who was going to bring these killers down.

The officer marched her to the front of the store. As they walked, he pressed his fingers into her stiches. He wanted her to scream out in pain but she didn't. She wouldn't give him the satisfaction of letting him know she was hurt.

"Chief Hagan and Greg Sturgeon are behind the Last Supper suicide game. Levi Smith did not kill himself, he was murdered. I have proof," Jess shouted. When this footage was picked up by news outlets, she wanted that to be the sound bite.

They led her outside to a patrol car and one of them pushed her head down so she would not bang it on the car when he pushed her in. She landed face first on the vinyl seat and grimaced when her cheek rubbed against something sticky. She hoped it was food but she knew it was more likely to be a bodily fluid.

They got in and slammed the doors.

"Where are you taking me? Which precinct?"

Neither of them answered.

She was still lying face down on the backseat so there was no way to get her bearings. They had done that on purpose to discombobulate her. "I'm a federal agent. I demand you call Jeanie Gilbert or Director Taylor immediately to inform them of my arrest."

Still neither of them said anything.

"Which judge signed off on my arrest?" She was making a mental list of people she was going to bring down when this was all over. She was not going down without a fight.

Jess realized they were not going to speak. She flopped onto her side so she could try to see the street names as they passed. The car stopped and started in the rush-hour traffic. The sun had started to set and the streetlights had gone on. It looked like they were driving west out of DC.

Anxiety scraped every nerve ending when the tall buildings became spaced farther and farther apart. They were definitely leaving the city. She pulled on her handcuffs to try to allow her the space to sit up, but she couldn't. Her training had taught her that assailants only move victims to kill them. She tried to tell herself that this was an arrest not a murder attempt, but her body didn't believe a word of it. This wasn't a normal arrest. She would have been taken to a precinct in DC if it were.

Finally, the car pulled over. One of the officers came around and opened the door. "Sit up."

Jess didn't move because she couldn't. If she had been able to sit up, she would have before then.

"I said sit up."

"And I said call my boss. I get one phone call. I want it before I speak to you."

Instead of answering, he yanked her up by her arm. She bit hard into her lip to keep from screaming out.

He pulled her to her feet.

"Why didn't the Metropolitan Police Department arrest me?" She already knew the answer. She knew they might not actually have the authority to arrest her but she wanted them to admit it. "I demand to see my arrest warrant."

"Lady, you don't get to make demands." He pushed her forward toward the entrance of the police station. She stumbled but she didn't fall.

She looked around, taking in her surroundings. She relaxed a little when she realized they were at a police station in Virginia. At least they hadn't taken her someplace completely remote.

"What's your name?" she asked. "I want to be very specific with my complaint. I can't very well call you the asshole who wears too much aftershave to cover up the stink of his body odor. If nothing else, that's kind of wordy."

From the corner of her eye she saw the other officer smile. It was gone as quickly as it appeared but she'd seen it.

They took her into the police station. There was no one at the front desk; in fact, there was no desk. It had been removed and the walls had been ripped to the studs. The entire building was a construction site. Wires dangled from the ceilings and plastic sheets covered the floor to protect it from dust… or to make it easier to clean up the blood when they killed her.

They guided her through to an interview room. There was a small horizontal window at the top of one wall, just big enough to let in light but not enough for anyone to use to escape. On the opposite wall, there was a camera perched in the corner pointed down at her, but there was no light to indicate that it was on.

A metal table was pushed against the wall, leaving only enough room for three chairs. She looked around for a two-way mirror but there wasn't one.

"I would like to call my lawyer."

Again, neither officer spoke.

"I have asked to speak to my lawyer three times now. That is my right. I know you both know that because you read me my rights. Don't be dumb enough to violate them now."

One of the officers glanced up at the clock. It was nearly eight.

The other pointed to the metal chair. "Sit down."

"Are you going to take off my handcuffs? I just had surgery on my arm. This is not good for my circulation."

"Just sit down and stop whining."

Jess sat down. "Are you going to fingerprint me?"

Again, there was no answer, just another glance at the clock. They weren't even going to go through with the motions to pretend this was a real arrest. They were waiting for something or someone. Her unease blossomed into an anxious heat at the thought of the unknown. "Please turn on the camera. I want this documented." She knew they wouldn't but she had to try.

Instead of saying anything, they left the room.

Jess waited for a few minutes to see if they would return but they didn't. She tried to move positions to get comfortable but nothing worked. Her arm and hand were in agony. Everything below the shoulder ached. Her only hope was that they would eventually go numb because the pain would drive her crazy. She could tolerate a lot of shit but that would push her over the edge.

She laid her head down on the desk because the position took a bit of pressure off her arm. The minutes dragged on for hours without any sign of the officers coming back. She counted the ticks of the clock rather than turn around to check the time. With every passing second, the pain pounded harder. She hadn't taken anything in hours and her body was rebelling against the withdrawal. She closed her eyes and breathed through it.

Eventually the sun rose and light streamed through the small window. Jess strained to turn around and look at the clock. She'd been sitting in the same position for nearly twelve hours. Neither officer had made any attempt to question her. They were killing time. Whatever their plan was, it didn't involve charging her. They couldn't because then she would get her day in court and all their secrets would be exposed.

They wanted her out of the way. Something bigger than her was at play. She pushed back from the table to try to stand up but both of her legs had fallen asleep. She quietly cursed her body for allowing her lower extremities to go numb but still allowing for every acute sensation in her other limbs.

She wiggled her toes in her boots to get the blood flowing. As the circulation returned, it felt like electric needles being jabbed into her feet. She stood up and walked to the door.

"Hello!" she shouted.

No one responded. She waited for thirty seconds and then shouted again. "Hello! I need the bathroom. I'm going to pee on myself."

Still no response.

"Let me use the toilet or get a mop because I haven't had a piss in fifteen hours."

One of the officers came in.

"I need to pee. You are violating my rights by denying me access to a toilet. I'm going to pee on myself and then you will either have to leave me in my own filth or strip me naked. Neither of those things are going to look good for you," she warned.

His eye twitched. He looked around the room. The cockiness from before was gone; he seemed nervous, like he was in over his head.

"Where's your partner?" she asked.

He didn't answer.

"He's left you, hasn't he? You're the only one here. He realized that holding me in a derelict building without an arrest warrant is kidnapping and false imprisonment, so he left and you're stuck cleaning up the mess. If anything goes wrong, it's all on you."

The muscle in his jaw bulged as he ground his teeth together. "Stop talking."

"Why? That's what happened, isn't it? We both know it. This is illegal. The longer you keep me here, the worse it gets. He knows that too. If he's smart, he's already called his union rep to help him out. He'll cut a deal. He'll turn on you. He already has."

"I said shut up." His voice was frantic now, high-pitched and clipped. The color in his cheeks darkened.

He had already thought about all of this. She was just rubbing salt into the wound.

He opened the door for her. "The bathroom is at the end of the hall."

She stood up and walked to the bathroom door. She waited for him to open it and then turned around to face him. "I need you to unbutton my pants."

His face contorted in a surprised expression. He came a bit closer and extended his arms as far as he could to reach her. He looked away, clearly uncomfortable, as he unfastened the button. "There," he said.

"I need you to pull down my underwear too."

His eyes widened. He gave a small shake of his head, dubious like it was a trick.

"I can't pee unless you take off my underwear."

He pinched the bridge of his nose between his thumb and forefinger.

"I'm also going to need help with the toilet paper. I can't wipe with my hands behind my back. A female officer should be here to help me with this." She didn't spell out that by being alone with her in this position, he had left himself open to a world of allegations. It was better for him to come to that realization on his own.

"Turn around."

Jess complied. Her hands dropped to her sides like dead weight when he freed them. Immediately, the pain increased with the blood flow. She'd thought they hurt before but she'd had no idea.

"Just go do your business. You have two minutes. Leave the door open and don't try anything stupid."

Jess pulled down her underwear and sat down. She hadn't been lying when she said she was going to wet herself. She let out a deep breath. The relief was almost euphoric.

A minute later she got up and washed her hands. Fresh blood trickled down her arm as she pulled back part of her bandage to check her wound. The gauze stuck to the stiches, pulling up the skin as she peeled the fabric back. The skin around the wound was red and puckered but it didn't look infected. At least she had that going for her right now.

The officer was standing around the corner waiting for her when she got out.

"Can you please handcuff my hands in front of me this time? My arm is still healing. It's really sore."

"Um… yeah. I guess." He kept his eyes down. He did not make a move forward to cuff her again, he just continued staring nervously at the floor. He was nothing like the cocky officer who had arrested her yesterday. The bravado was gone. He obviously knew that the situation had gotten out of hand and he had no idea how to rein it back in.

"Thank you."

He looked again at the clock. He was obsessed with the time. He was waiting for something.

He had made no attempt to interrogate her. He didn't care at all about the information she had. This was about containing her for a certain length of time. But why?

The Founding Fathers had shown their hand when they had cut her arm. They wanted people to think she was suicidal. They were trying to paint her as insane. That was how they were going to deal with her. They had publically disgraced her. She had no credibility left. They thought that would be enough to silence her. They didn't see her as a threat anymore. They just wanted her out of the way long enough to contain the situation, which meant neutralizing the players.

She needed to make sure her team was safe.

She glanced around the room, looking for a way out, desperately trying to formulate a plan.

He stepped forward toward her.

"Can I please get a glass of water? I'm really thirsty. I think I'm dehydrated." She tried to make her voice sound as pathetic as she could. The more vulnerable she appeared, the more scared he became because it showed him how wildly the situation had spun out of control.

She wondered what he had been told. Who'd given him the order to pick her up? At what point did he realize he was just a pawn?

"Um, yeah."

He turned to get her a glass of water. As he bent over the water jug, she lunged forward and grabbed his truncheon. She swung it at his head. A cracking sound splintered the silence of the room when the metal connected with the side of his skull.

His eyes widened in horror as he stumbled back, stunned. She squeezed the stick until her palm ached. She could not afford to drop it and lose her advantage. He was a foot taller and at least seventy pounds heavier than her.

She swung again and hit his arm. He held his hands up to shield his face. She pulled the baton back, ready to strike, but instead of hitting him she slid it under his armpit and then grabbed the other end, twisting his arm up above his back. His body spun away from hers, desperately trying to get away from the painful maneuver. She used his own momentum to push him to the ground. She fell heavy on top of him, never letting go of the nightstick. If she lost the upper hand for even a second, he would overpower her.

She pulled up again on the nightstick to be sure she had completely incapacitated him. There was a loud ripping sound as the ligaments in his shoulder tore clean away.

He screamed out in agony.

"Shit." She shook her head. That wasn't an injury he was going to walk away from. He was going to need surgery. She'd known that she was going to break one of the bones in his arm, but she hadn't realized his shoulder would be ripped from the socket.

She pulled the cuffs from under him and fastened them. His arm dangled behind him. There was nothing but skin holding it in place. "Shit," she said again. She hadn't meant to hurt him that much.

She took off her sweater and stuffed it in his mouth, tying the arms behind him to muffle his screams.

She reached beneath him again to search for his car keys. When she found them, she stood up. "I know that hurts like a bitch. I'm sorry. If they offer you morphine, take it. Don't be a hero."

She ran for the door. She stopped before she opened it and turned to look at him. "If you hurt anyone on my team, I will find you and make you pay."

CHAPTER THIRTY-SEVEN

Jess jumped into the police cruiser. She silently calculated how many years she would spend in prison if she were convicted for everything she'd done in the last twenty-four hours. She didn't care because it didn't matter. She would rather spend the rest of her life in prison than let these men get away with what they had done.

She turned on the engine, put her foot down on the gas, and drove until she felt safe enough to pull over.

She reached into her pocket for her phone. The battery icon in the corner was lit up. She only had ten percent left. She needed to work quickly. There was a text message from Tina to say that she had landed in Hawaii and was safe with her brother. Jess breathed a sigh of relief; that was one less person to worry about.

She opened up Lindsay's email. She held her breath as she waited for the page to load and she could see if the draft had been saved. "Hurry, hurry, hurry." She tapped the steering wheel as she waited. "Don't run out on me now."

Finally, it appeared. The draft was still sitting in the inbox. She looked up into the bright-blue sky. "Thank you,' she whispered.

As fast as her thumbs could type, she composed a message explaining the contents. She paused for a second. Jeanie and Lynnette Hastings and all the other families deserved to be told this in person, to deal with their grief in private, but this case needed transparency and there was only one way to guarantee it.

She opened the browser to look up the email addresses she needed. In the recipient bar, she typed in the addresses of every major news network. She stopped before she hit send because there was no going back after this.

This would destroy Jeanie. Her loyalty to her demanded that she bring this information to her first. Jeanie was not just her boss but her mentor and her friend.

Her mind swam in uncertainty but there was no time to try to sort out her thoughts: her battery was about to die. She used to be so sure about right and wrong, good and evil. She wasn't sure of anything anymore except that this secret had hurt too many people.

This needed to be made public. That was the only way she could guarantee that this wasn't buried again. Too many lives had already been destroyed.

The phone shook because her hands trembled so much. She held her breath and hit send.

Immediately relief and regret collided in her. She didn't have time to think about whether or not she'd done the right thing. She still needed to make sure her team was safe.

She dialed Jamison's number again but still no answer.

"Dammit, Jamison." Fear clawed at her. Something was wrong. She had tried to ignore the anxiety that had taken root in the pit of her stomach but she couldn't ignore it any longer. The kernel of dread had blossomed into a full-fledged panic. Something was wrong. She felt it. This was like Lindsay all over again.

"No." She couldn't lose anyone else. She couldn't do it again.

Jess jumped when her phone rang beside her. She looked down at the familiar name.

"Jamison!" she shouted down the phone.

"Is this Jessica Bishop?" an unfamiliar voice asked.

A bolt of terror ran up her spine. "Who is this?" she demanded.

"This is Chief Hagan of the Metropolitan Police."

Jess dropped the phone. Pain shot through her head when she bent forward to pick it up off the floor and banged her head on the steering wheel. "Where is Jamison?" she demanded when she managed to pick up the phone. Her entire body vibrated with rage and fear. If he had hurt Jamison… She couldn't even contemplate what she would do.

"Agent Briggs is being questioned about his involvement in the Last Supper suicide game."

Jess shook her head. "He has no involvement in this." They weren't going to pin any of this on Jamison. She wouldn't let them.

"Why don't you come into headquarters so we can discuss it? I know you know your way here."

"Is that where you're holding him?"

"Yes. I think there has been a serious misunderstanding. If you come in, I think we can get this all squared away. I know you wouldn't want your partner taking the rap for something you did."

Jess sucked in a sharp breath. "Are you saying you will let Jamison go if I…" She could barely get the words out. "If I take responsibility?"

"I'm saying it is such a tremendous injustice when people are wrongfully accused of anything. That destroys lives. You can never really wash the stink of that shit off."

Jess bit into her lip. She knew what he was saying. Hagan was going to make up false allegations against Jamison, frame him for something. They couldn't blame him for The Last Supper because they had already publically named her as their only suspect, but they could accuse him of other things.

"Let me speak to him."

"You can talk to him when you get here."

"No." Jess shook her head. "I need proof that he is alive."

"I don't think I like what you're implying."

"I'm not implying anything. I'm saying we both know you're capable of murder. I won't hand myself in unless I know Jamison is alive."

There was a long silence. Jess thought Hagan had hung up but he said, "You have ten seconds."

"Jessie." Jamison's voice was hoarse.

"Oh, thank God." Her throat tightened from the overwhelming intensity of her relief. He was alive. That was all that mattered. "Are you okay?"

"Yeah. Yeah, I'm fine. I just can't see anything without my glasses."

Jess shook her head in confusion but before she could ask him what he meant, the call was cut. She called back but it immediately went to voicemail.

"Dammit!" she screamed. Jamison didn't wear glasses. He never had. He was trying to tell her something. What? What was he trying to say? That she wasn't seeing something? Her mind went blank. She slammed her hands against the steering wheel. The impact sent an unbearable jolt of pain up her arm, probably damaging herself even further, but she didn't care.

She couldn't do this, not on her own. She needed her team. She wasn't like Jeanie. She wasn't a natural leader. She never had been. She sat back in her seat and thought about Jeanie, about how she would handle this. In her mind, she saw her pull down her bifocals when she was about to get serious and then push them back up when she looked up to speak to someone.

"Jeanie," she whispered. Is that what Jamison was trying to tell her, that they thought Jeanie was involved with the investigation? How? That didn't even make sense. Jess had done everything she could to keep the rest of her team out of this, especially Jeanie.

Jess shivered as a cold chill washed over her. Of course, they had been watching. They knew that Jeanie had come to Jamison's house after her apartment had been broken into. And Levi's phone records: he had called Jeanie just before he died. They thought Levi had confessed and that was why Jeanie had called Jess the night he was murdered, because she had uncovered the secret about that night at Pine Ridge.

"Oh my God." She called Jeanie's number. "Come on. Please be safe in Utah," she said as she waited for Jeanie to answer but she never did. She called again but still no answer so she left a message. "Jeanie, this is Jess. Please call me when you can. I think you are in danger. Please call me."

She hung up the phone and then opened the browser to look for Paul's number, but the screen went black as the battery went dead. "Shit!" she screamed. She threw the phone down.

Jess turned the key over in the ignition. She didn't even know exactly where she was. She looked at all the buttons on the dashboard. One of them might have been satellite navigation but she wasn't going to start messing around with them.

She pulled onto the road, searching the street signs for a clue to her location. The first one came in the form of sign indicating that she was nearing Fairfax. That was good. She knew roughly how to get back to DC from there—she just needed to find I-66.

Once she hit Fairfax, she got her bearings and knew roughly where she was going. It took her a few minutes to realize why the other cars were going so slow, or pulling over to let her pass: they were scared of being pulled over by her.

She merged onto the interstate, pressed down harder on the gas to accelerate past a minivan with a Coexist bumper sticker, and moved into the fast lane.

Several miles later she passed a Virginia State Police cruiser. She glanced at the driver in the rear-view mirror as he pulled into the lane behind her. He was too far away to see his face. She pulled into the middle lane, hoping he would pass her but he didn't. He continued to stay a car's length behind her for another mile.

Her hands went slick on the steering wheel. She told herself not to panic. They were just going in the same direction. At the next on-ramp, two more State Police pulled onto the interstate followed by two unmarked black SUVs.

Shit. They were FBI. Her own people were hunting her. Betrayal stabbed her hard in chest. "Come on, come on, come on." She urged the morning traffic to go faster. She looked up at a police helicopter that was hovering above her.

"Oh, shit." Her mind raced. This wasn't going to end well. She bit back the fear that was rising in her. She needed to find Jeanie. That was all that mattered.

At the next on-ramp two more police cars joined the interstate in front of her. They were trying to block her in but she hit the gas hard and sped past them. Another police cruiser pulled in front of her and she slammed on the brakes to avoid colliding with the back of his car.

"Shit!" she screamed again. Her heart pummeled her ribs as she veered into the middle lane to avoid a collision. She clipped the front of the police car in the next lane. In her rear-view mirror, she saw it lose control and plow into the center divider. What were they doing? The proper protocol was to follow at a safe distance to minimize risk for other drivers.

They didn't care about civilian casualties, they just wanted to stop her, whatever it took.

She squeezed the steering wheel until the blood stagnated in her hands and her knuckles were like white boulders beneath translucent skin.

She put her hand on her blinker to indicate she was about to change lanes before she realized what she was doing and pulled her hand away. She didn't want to tell them where she was going but old habits die hard. Jamison was right: even when she was breaking the law she liked to follow the rules.

She pulled off the freeway and prayed she remembered the way to Jeanie's house. She wished she had paid more attention the last time they were there. A second helicopter was now above her, this one from a local affiliate of a national news station.

She could see the headlines in her mind about a psychotic rogue agent. All her life she'd been motivated about what people thought of her, making sure they knew she was a good person. Nothing like her father. In the space of a week that illusion had been blown to shit and she didn't have the energy to care right now. None of it mattered. She could deal with everything later, once she knew Jeanie was all right.

She rolled through a stop sign. Once she knew she wasn't going to hit anyone, she floored it.

There were now seven police cars behind her and two FBI SUVs. It was like a funeral procession commemorating the demise of her career and freedom.

A screeching sound exploded when her side mirror hit the brick column of the gate as she sped into Jeanie's driveway. She pulled past the garage to the front door. She took off her seatbelt and bolted to the front door. She jabbed her finger into the buzzer. They hadn't yet left for Utah. The lights were still on and suitcases were sitting beside the door along with Jeanie's purse.

"Come on, Jeanie. Please answer the door. Please be okay."

"Jessica Bishop, put your hands above your head and get on the ground," an officer commanded through a megaphone.

She pressed the buzzer again and then thumped frantically on the door before she raised her hands above her head. Slowly she turned around to face them and the reality of the situation.

The police were lined up on the street, guns drawn, pointing at her.

"I'm unarmed!" she shouted at them. She glanced up at the sky, grateful the news helicopter was there to document her downfall because if the police killed her now, the world would know they had murdered an unarmed woman.

"Get on the ground!" he shouted back.

Jess closed her eyes to block it all out, to lessen the blow of her world imploding, but her mind flashed back to the day her father was arrested. Immediately she was transported back. Guns were pointed her direction that day too as she clung to her father's hand and she begged and screamed for them not to take him away.

This wasn't how her life was supposed to go. She wasn't like him. She was one of the good guys. That was all she'd ever wanted, to be part of the light in a dark world.

Everything was silent except for the occasional chirp of birds and distant whoosh of helicopter blades.

She closed her eyes and listened harder. There was another sound… a mechanical purr… like an engine.

Jess's eyes flashed open. Her head snapped back to look at the closed door of the garage. That was where the noise was coming from.

"Get on your knees!" another voice screamed.

Jess ran back to the police car.

"Stop or we will shoot."

Jess turned on the engine and then put the car into reverse. She didn't have a lot of room to maneuver. She had to hope it was enough.

A shot rang out. The left side of her car dipped as the back tire blew out.

She snapped her seatbelt into place and took a deep breath before she put the car into drive and then closed her eyes. She pushed down on the gas pedal with all her weight.

Inertia pushed her back against the seat as she accelerated straight ahead. Her body jolted forward as the car slammed into the garage door. Wood splintered as the panels of the door snapped.

The airbag detonated. The force was like a blow to the chest. For several seconds, she couldn't breathe. She tried to suck in air but it was like trying to get a marble through a straw. Her chest burned from the impact of the airbag and the seatbelt holding her in place.

Another shot fired, shattering the back window. She jumped out and ran to Jeanie's car. The engine was still running. Jeanie was slumped over the wheel.

Jess opened the door and Jeanie's lifeless body flopped out onto the concrete floor.

"Oh God, no!" Jess screamed until her throat burned. Not again. Not Jeanie. She couldn't lose her too. "No," she cried again. She dropped to her knees and gathered Jeanie against her, to shelter her. She couldn't be dead.

A small drop of blood formed along Jeanie's eyebrow, slowly getting bigger. Jess shook her head. She was seeing things. Her mind was playing tricks on her, to make it not real or at least lessen the blow. She had done the same when Lindsay died. She had sworn she could see the rise and fall of her chest even as she lay cold in her casket. Her mind just refused to believe she was gone and now she was doing the same with Jeanie.

Jess blinked to dislodge the tears welled in the corners of her eyes but they wouldn't shift so she wiped her face with the back of her hand.

"I'm sorry. I'm sorry I got you involved. And I'm sorry I couldn't get here in time." Jess gently rubbed the blood off Jeanie's temple, but in an instant it was replaced with a fresh drop.

Jess's eyes widened. Again, she wiped away the blood on Jeanie's forehead and again the drop formed again. Her heart was still beating.

She was still alive!

Jess turned and screamed. "Get a paramedic. She is hurt."

She leaned into the car to turn off the engine and then walked out of the garage with her hands over her head.

"She needs an ambulance!" Jess screamed again before she dropped to her knees from exhaustion and relief.

CHAPTER THIRTY-EIGHT

Jeanie's eyes fluttered open.

Jess stood up and walked closer to her hospital bed. "Hey," she smiled. "Sorry. I didn't mean to wake you. I was just about to leave a note and come back tomorrow. You must be exhausted. Get some sleep."

Jeanie reached out her arm to touch Jess's hand to make her stay.

Jess smiled. "You don't know how glad I am to see you."

It had been six days since Jeanie had been admitted to the hospital. The emergency room doctor that had first treated her said that she was lucky to be alive. A few more minutes and she would have died or been left with permanent brain damage.

Jeanie managed a weak smile.

"I hear they are releasing you today."

"Yes," Jeanie's voice cracked.

"Here, let me get you some water." Jess poured a glass from the plastic jug on the bedside table.

"Thank you." Jeanie took a sip of water. "For this and for saving my life. I'm grateful for the risk you took for me."

Jess shrugged, unsure of what to say. It wasn't a risk to her. It was just what needed to be done. She would have done anything to try to save her.

"Has Paul told you that Sturgeon and Hagan have been arrested?"

She nodded. "He said according to the news, more arrests are imminent."

"The district attorney's office is still making their way through all the material from the USBs. There is a lot to get through. But the good news is that the Founding Father members are turning on each other. They're all trying to cut a deal."

"That is good." She shook her head. "It's true what they say, there really is no honor among thieves."

"No, at least not when they are facing federal death penalty charges."

Jeanie shifted to push herself up on the bed.

"Here. Let me help you," Jess said.

Jeanie moved into position and then smoothed down a lock of her faded red hair. "Thank you."

"You're welcome." The vinyl chair creaked as Jess sat down again.

"Are you going to tell me what happened? I have stopped asking Paul because I don't want him to have to lie again and tell me he doesn't know anything else."

Jess gave a slow nod. That was why she was here. She wanted to be the one to tell Jeanie. Not that she relished the idea of seeing her in pain, but because Jeanie deserved to hear it from her.

Paul and the medical staff had intentionally kept all news away from Jeanie while she was healing but she was being released today. They couldn't keep it from her any longer.

"You know the camp Levi went to, Pine Ridge?"

"Yes."

"You know that it's a camp owned and operated by the Founding Fathers?"

Jeanie nodded.

"The week in August when Levi and his friends went up to the camp was the initiation ceremony for Ryan Hastings." Jess took a deep breath. She didn't want to have to tell Jeanie this but she deserved to know the truth, and if she didn't hear it from her, she would see it on the news. The video had been played on a constant loop. "Part of the induction was hazing."

Jeanie's eyebrows knitted together in confusion.

"All week they made Ryan do things, just stupid kid stuff, but the last night it went too far." Jess looked away because she couldn't bear to see Jeanie's face when she told her the truth. "They put a dog collar on Ryan, left him tied to the bed, and went to dinner. They didn't realize it was too tight. When they got back he was dead. It was an accident."

When Jeanie didn't answer, Jess turned to look at her. Jeanie shook her head. The furrow between her brows deepened to a pronounced crease. "No," she whispered.

"I'm sorry."

"No." Jeanie shook her head. "That's not like Levi. He wouldn't have done that. He was a good boy. He would never hurt anyone."

"It was an accident."

"No." The monitor beeped as Jeanie's pulse crept dangerously high. "He would have told me."

"I'm sorry," Jess said again. "He was scared. Things spun out of control and he didn't know what to do. Greg Sturgeon came in and said he would handle things because it was his neck on the line. He would have been fired and faced possible charges because he sanctioned the initiation and the hazing. It was a school tradition. It's been going on since the school began but this time things went wrong. It was just an accident but Sturgeon asked Hagan for help and the cover-up turned deadly. All the Founding Fathers have dirt on each other so when they started calling in favors, no one could say no. They didn't know what they were covering up, they just knew they didn't want their own secrets exposed."

Jeanie held her head in her hands and wept. Her shoulders went up and down as she sobbed.

Jess wanted to look away. She wanted to run and get numb and pretend this wasn't happening but she stayed frozen in place. She forced herself to be present for her friend, to face the emotion, every uncomfortable sensation, just sit with her as she cried so she knew she wasn't alone. She wouldn't run from this. Not this time.

Eventually the tears stopped. "That's not the boy I knew. I always thought he was a good boy."

Jess reached for her hand. "He was good. He did something stupid but he was a good person. He made a mistake. Remember what you told me? That my mistakes are part of me but they aren't me. If that's true for me, then it's true for Levi. He was a good person. Don't let yourself ever doubt that."

"Thank you." Jeanie's lip trembled. "He was good and I loved him."

EPILOGUE

Jess straightened the collar of her shirt and then buttoned and unbuttoned her suit jacket, trying to decide which looked the most professional. She was nervous, terrified actually. She wanted to run but she couldn't. She had made her choices and now she needed to accept the consequences.

She knocked on Director Taylor's door to let him know she had arrived for the appointment and then opened the door. She stopped when she saw four men in suits seated at the table with Taylor. She didn't recognize any of them.

"Sorry. I thought my appointment was at one. I'll come back later."

Taylor stood up. "No, come on in."

"Um, okay." Jess went in.

"Please have a seat." Taylor indicated to the chair opposite him.

Jess sat down. She glanced around at the other people at the table, wondering why they were there for what should have been a private meeting. She would rather not have an audience when she was told what disciplinary action was going to be taken. Unease rose in her. Maybe Taylor was going to fire her then and there, and he wanted witnesses to ensure it was done by the book. None of them were smiling, which was never a good sign.

"Thank you for joining us." Taylor turned to the men at the table. "This is Special Agent Jessica Bishop." He turned back to her and introduced the other people at the table but Jess was too agitated to take any of it in. She didn't care who they were, she just wanted to know the extent of legal and disciplinary action she would be facing. She couldn't live with the uncertainty hanging over her. She'd committed arson, destroyed police property, and hospitalized two police officers during an unauthorized investigation. She wouldn't walk away from this unscathed.

"Hagan accepted a plea agreement this morning. He'll serve twenty-five years," Taylor said.

"Did he turn on Sturgeon?" Jess asked.

"Among others." Taylor nodded. "He also signed a sworn affidavit stating that he started the fire at police headquarters to frame you."

"What? Why would he do that?"

"He also has admitted to Photoshopping the pictures of you in a compromising position."

Jess stared down at the scar on her hand as she took in the new information.

One of the men looked up. Light reflected off the gold band of his Rolex as he shut his laptop. "Tomorrow there will be an expert on *Good Morning* explaining how easy it is to manipulate pictures. He will do a live demo with pictures of the anchors. The audience will love it. We've also booked Dr. Abrams from the University of Toronto on *The Today Show* to discuss the cultural and psychological implications of shaming women for their sexuality and why Hagan chose that as the route to try to discredit you. That will play really well given the current climate. We're still in talks with *60 Minutes*. A sit-down interview would be ideal so we can really get ahead of this, lean into your backstory, paint it as more phoenix rising from the ashes and less chip off the psychotic block."

Jess's back stiffened. There was so much wrong with what he had said. She didn't know where to start. "Sorry, who are you?"

"Duncan, Shapiro, and Schwartz are the lawyers working on this, and Larry Knox—" Taylor pointed to the guy with the

Rolex "—is in charge of public relations. He's our go-to clean-up man. He knows his stuff. By the time he gets done, you will be the most admired woman in America."

Jess gave him a hard look. "Clean-up? You mean cover-up."

"I'd prefer not to call it that. This is damage control. You handed me a pile of lemons, and I'm going to present the world with the best damn lemon meringue pie they've ever tasted. Seriously, they will be begging for more. The bureau has had a bit of a PR beating recently but we can turn it all around with this. People will eat it up. That reminds me, I still need to speak to the warden and see if he will allow us to film an interview with your father. That would make amazing television." He picked up his phone.

"No!" Jess didn't mean to shout but the idea of seeing her father again after all these years sent a bolt of terror straight through her chest. He was dead to her. That was the only way she could cope with the shitstorm he'd left behind. "Giving air-time to serial killers is never the answer."

His thin lips pulled into a condescending smile. "With all due respect, this is my job. I know what I'm doing."

"I'm sure you do. But what are you doing? Covering things up? With all due respect to you, I just worked a case where thirteen innocent people died because of a cover-up. I just don't see…" Her voice trailed off. He was trying to help her. He was giving her an out, a way to walk away from this, but the irony of the situation wasn't lost on her. They were conspiring to cover up the fallout from unearthing a conspiracy.

She should just be grateful that she wasn't going to face charges, and she was, but she couldn't shake the feeling that they were doing the same thing as the Founding Fathers. What made it right for them to lie? Because they were the good guys? Didn't everyone think they were the good guy? She took a deep breath. She couldn't pretend she had any of the answers anymore.

She wasn't facing jail time and no one on her team had died. That was the good news, she would focus on that. Later she would deal with the shitty feeling that had settled in the pit of her stomach.

She listened silently as the five men outlined how they were going to cover up the fallout from the case.

When they were done, Taylor looked at her and said, "You happy with all of this?"

She nodded. The answer was she didn't know how she felt but that was nothing new for her.

"Okay great. Then I think we're done here." Taylor stood up and thanked the men for their help.

Jess stood up to leave too.

"Do you have a second?" he asked.

"Yeah, sure."

He waited for everyone to leave before he turned back to her. "I just spoke to Jeanie."

Jess nodded, waiting for him to continue.

"She has had a good career. She's a great agent."

"Yes, she is."

"But she's tired. She said so herself. She's ready to retire and move on to the next stage of her life. She and her husband are going to move back to Utah. They have like eighty-five nieces and nephews there."

"Oh," was all she could manage to say. She knew this day was coming, that Jeanie would retire at some point, but it still felt too soon. Selfishly, Jess wanted her to stay forever; she depended on her for guidance and knowledge. She didn't want to work under anyone else. She was a great leader, and no one could fill that position.

"We had a long talk. She is adamant that you are the person that should take over the team."

Jess's mouth dropped open, stunned.

"As you know I was never a fan of your appointment. I've made no secret of that, but saying that, your dedication to your team and to uncovering the truth is admirable. That is exactly the quality we want."

"I-uh-I don't know what to say."

"I'm not done yet. What you did was stupid and irresponsible, and if you ever disobey orders again, you will be fired immediately."

Jess nodded. "Yes, sir."

"All right, then. I think we're done here unless you have any questions. Your team has not made any progress on their current case without you. Fix that."

"Yes, sir."

"I've told them to meet you in the conference room this afternoon so you can get started."

Jess managed a smile. This was real. She was officially coming back to work as team leader. It was never a job she wanted but it felt right. She felt excited and scared in equal measure. She had no doubt that she would mistakes but she also knew she would never stop fighting for victims.

"One more thing. Jeanie asked me to give you this." He handed her a package wrapped in brown paper. "There is no card. She said you would know what it meant."

"Thank you." She took the package and walked back to her office.

She sat down at her desk and unwrapped the package. Her heart caught in her throat when she saw the contents. It was the framed Pablo Neruda poem Paul had given Jeanie, the one she'd told her about. She'd seen it countless times on the wall behind Jeanie's desk and now it was hers.

Jess closed her eyes and let an unfamiliar feeling wash over her. She didn't know what it was but she wasn't going to fight it because it felt good.

"Jessie," Jamison called from her doorway.

She looked up at him and smiled.

His eye was swollen shut and his lip was busted from his time with Hagan.

"Taylor called and said there is a team meeting at two."

Jess glanced up at the clock. She was already five minutes late for her first official team meeting as leader.

"Yeah, here I come." She pushed herself back from her desk and stood up.

She walked side by side with Jamison to the conference room. She turned to him just before they got to the door. "Hey, when Hagan was holding you and I got to speak to you on the phone, I was cut off before I could finish saying what I needed to say." She took a deep breath. "Thank you, Jamison." There was so much more to say but there were no words. Maybe there never would be but that was okay.

Jamison's full lips hitched in a lazy smile. He opened his mouth to speak but before he could say anything she opened the door to the conference room.

Tina, Chan, and Milligan were all seated. Milligan, like always, had a stain of undetermined origin on his suit. Tina looked tan and beautiful from her time in Hawaii and Chan was busy trying to impress her in the hope of getting her into bed. These were her people, her team.

Jess went in and put her stuff on the table. "All right, guys, let's get started. We still have a strangler to catch."

A LETTER FROM KIERNEY

Thank you for joining Jess on her latest case. If you enjoyed this book and would like to keep up with all my releases, just click on the link below. Your email address will never be shared and you can unsubscribe at any time.

www.bookouture.com/kierney-scott

It has been a pleasure to tell Jess's story and I'm eternally grateful that you have chosen to join me on this adventure. If you enjoyed the book, I would appreciate if you left a review. Reviews are the lifeblood of writing: they are how new readers find a book, so even a short review would be tremendously helpful.

Thanks,
Kierney Scott

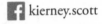 kierney.scott

ACKNOWLEDGEMENTS

Thank you to all the readers, reviewers, and bloggers. I am tremendously grateful for all of your support. Thank you for every review and message. They are greatly appreciated.

Thank you to everyone at Bookouture. Each one of you is more talented than the last. I'm so fortunate to work with such a dynamic and hardworking team.

And last but never least, thank you to all the members of That Secret Author Group. I love watching your success and I love pointing to your books on the shelf and saying, "That's my friend." Thank you for all your help and support over the years. This writing thing is so much more fun because of all of you.

CPSIA information can be obtained
at www.ICGtesting.com
Printed in the USA
BVHW031826010821
613369BV00002B/20